HIGHE
HOM

We at Jove Books are thrilled by the enthusiastic critical
acclaim that the Homespun Romances are receiving. We
would like to thank you, the readers and fans of this
wonderful series, for making it the success that it is. It is our
pleasure to bring you the highest quality of romance writing
in these breathtaking tales of love and family in the
heartland of America.

And now, sit back and enjoy this delightful new Homespun Romance . . .

FOR PETE'S SAKE
by Debra Cowan

FOR PETE'S SAKE

DEBRA COWAN

J

JOVE BOOKS, NEW YORK

FOR PETE'S SAKE

A Jove Book / published by arrangement with
the author

PRINTING HISTORY

PRINTING HISTORY
Jove edition / April 1996

All rights reserved.
Copyright © 1996 by Debra Cowan.
This book may not be reproduced in whole
or in part, by mimeograph or any other means,
without permission. For information address:
The Berkley Publishing Group, 200 Madison Avenue,
New York, New York 10016.

The Putnam Berkley World Wide Web site address is
http://www.berkley.com

ISBN: 0-515-11863-X

A JOVE BOOK®
Jove Books are published by The Berkley Publishing Group,
200 Madison Avenue, New York, New York 10016.
JOVE and the "J" design are trademarks
belonging to Jove Publications, Inc.

PRINTED IN THE UNITED STATES OF AMERICA

10 9 8 7 6 5 4 3 2 1

To Jim, Robin, and Scott.
Happy Trails! This one's for you
(and remember, it's fiction).

ACKNOWLEDGMENTS

My deepest gratitude to Patsy Klingstedt, who
encouraged, goaded, and cheered while standing at the ready with a net.

And to my husband, Roy, who made me laugh and
kept me sane.
I absolutely could not have done it without you,
honey.

FOR PETE'S SAKE

PROLOGUE

Spinner, Missouri
May 1875

Julia Touchstone heard a smattering of gunfire, then an explosion of sound. *Not from my house. Please don't let those shots be from my house.* Dread pounded through her, cold and numbing. Sweat slicked her hands and under her arms.

After only a heartbeat of silence, a horse screamed shrilly. Deep-throated masculine shouts were followed by a single agonized cry, then the harsh keening of a wounded animal. Or was it a child?

Fear clawed through her and she laid the whip to the bay pulling the wagon. A damning quietness shrouded the peaceful homestead that was situated a couple of miles from town.

Julia couldn't look at her mother, couldn't bear to see on India's face the same fear she felt. The modest frame house of her childhood, which she now shared with her mother and son and oft-absent husband, came into view.

Spring sunshine glittered off the polished windows, gilded the bright cleanness of the whitewashed house and fence. The wagon bolted past the corral and careened to a stop in a cloud of dust at the back of the house.

Shouts echoed from the woods beyond, then the air reverberated with the sharp crack of another gunshot. The unmistakable sound of Pete's screaming voice ripped through the afternoon.

Her heart thudded to a painful stop. Julia scrambled off the wagon, heedless of the reins and the brake, tripping over her skirts and tearing her hem in her hurry to get to her son.

"Pete? Pete, honey! Where are you?" Her voice was shrill with fear.

The sudden thunder of retreating hoofbeats rumbled through the air and vibrated the ground. She wheeled around the corner of the house and tore blindly through the knee-high grass, running toward a grove of poplar trees.

John would never let anything happen to Pete.

She repeated the thought fiercely. Her husband was a Pinkerton agent. No one was better able to protect his family.

Two gray horses disappeared into the trees, and a chill stroked her spine. After months away, posing as an outlaw with the Thompson gang, John had returned home the previous night for a short stay. He had always been scrupulously careful to avoid being followed, but had his destination somehow been discovered?

Had Scotty Thompson and his gang learned that the man they knew as a card cheat and a thief was in reality one of the best detectives Allan Pinkerton had?

The scent of gunpowder burned the air and the bitter smell nudged at the fear uncoiling deep within her. "Pete? Johnny?"

She dodged an oak tree and came within sight of the grove. Pale streaks of gunsmoke spiraled through the air and a dark sticky substance coated the grass. Blood!

Julia's heartbeat stuttered. "Peter! Peter!"

He lay motionless on the ground, his fair hair bright against the green velvet grass. She ran faster, her heart pumping painfully as she dropped to the ground beside him. "Oh, Pete. Oh, please, no!"

The plea wrenched out of her; her chest squeezed with a breath-cutting pressure. She blinked, unable to register the thought of blood on her seven-year-old son. Gently, she lifted his head and cradled it in her lap, her eyes scanning over him in horror as her mind raced to take stock of him.

Blood spotted his shirt-sleeves and suspenders and saturated the right leg of his breeches. She laid her head on his tiny chest and heard the faint but steady thrum of his heart. Tears stung her throat. "Oh, Petey, stay with me, son."

"Ma?" he croaked, struggling to open his eyes.

Tears spilled down her cheeks. "Yes, honey. I'm here."

"What . . . about . . . Pa?" He labored to breathe.

She rocked him gently, her own breathing ragged as she scanned the area for her husband. She couldn't see him, and a frisson of fear snaked up her spine.

"Julia, I'll look after Pete." Her mother touched Julia's shoulder. "Go see to John."

As though through a screaming wind, Julia heard her mother's voice, but couldn't make herself respond. Several yards away, she saw her husband, limp and lifeless and partially hidden by the grass.

"Johnny." Her voice sounded as weak as a mewling kitten. Fear and rage and nausea churned through her. "Johnny?"

Somehow she made her way through the bloodstained and trampled grass to her husband's side. His eyes were closed. His face was pale and waxy, but the rest of his body was covered with blood. Four bullet holes gaped in his chest and legs.

She sank down to him, clutching his hand and feeling for a pulse. "Oh, John, not like this."

He didn't move and she leaned closer in sudden panic. His breath brushed faintly against her cheek.

"Johnny," she whispered. His hand lay cold and heavy in hers. Her tears mingled with the blood on his face as she gently traced his features.

His eyes fluttered once, then slitted open.

"Johnny?" She cupped his cheek in her palm, wanting to hold him close, to protect him.

"Petey?" He mouthed his son's name, but no sound came from his throat. Agony and guilt creased his features, and Julia knew what he was thinking. He hadn't been able to protect his son.

His eyes drifted shut; his pulse faded.

Panic choked her. "John? John?"

She placed two fingers against his thready pulse and willed him to open his eyes. Instead, he grew still and lifeless beneath her hands. Tears burned her eyes, her throat, her chest, but she couldn't release them.

A blanket suddenly appeared and was draped gently over him. Julia looked up, feeling lost and disoriented and confused.

Her mother knelt, tears streaming down her lovely face, pain sharp in her green eyes. She pulled the blanket over John's face and reached for Julia's hand, squeezing hard. "I'm so sorry, Julia."

She nodded, mute with pain and shock. *What had happened? What would they do? Pete needed his father—*

"Honey, Pete needs a doctor. He can't wait much longer."

She stared at her mother, trying to make sense of what India said. Pete! Julia shot to her feet, then hesitated, staring down at her husband. She couldn't leave John like this.

Her mother gripped her hands. "I'll stay with him. Unless you need my help with Pete?"

"N-no, you take care of Johnny." A chill twisted through her, reaching deep. "Take care of him."

She turned, unable to see through the tears blinding her, but finding her son with the unerring instinct of a dowser. He lay where she had found him, now covered with a quilt.

"Ma, where's Pa?" Pete's voice was thin and high with fear.

"Hush, now. Mama's going to take care of you. You'll be fine."

"But . . . Pa . . ." His lashes fluttered shut and his head lolled to one side.

Gently Julia lifted her son, nestling him to her breast as

she had when he was a babe. She carried him to the wagon and placed him carefully on the worn wooden seat. Climbing in, she gathered him to rest on her lap and drove into town without letting go of him.

CHAPTER ONE

Crowley, Missouri
Mid-August 1876

"We're robbin' the bank. Open the safe!" The words were punctuated by the click of a revolver.

Standing in place behind the counter, Marsh Granger stiffened. Five men wearing bandannas over the lower half of their faces took up positions inside the Crowley Bank and Trust, their weapons drawn.

Marsh's gaze shot to the German shepherd crouched behind the door. The dog kept his dark gaze glued to his master, his body tight as he waited for Marsh's command.

A sixth man stood watch outside, and Marsh knew Gyp could handle the man easily. The thieves didn't notice the dog, and Marsh lowered his hand slowly in a signal to stay. Gyp maintained his position, his sleek muscles bunched in tension.

Marsh's nerves hummed. In the week since the Thompson gang had been spotted in the area, he'd been waiting there for them. He'd been looking for the outlaws since John Touchstone's death a year earlier.

Scotty Thompson, the smallest of the six, shoved a revolver into Marsh's face. "You hard of hearin', boy?"

He shook his head, biding his time. The edge of danger sent a thrill rushing through him. *Come on, you bastards. Let's dance.*

He cut a warning glance at Mr. Wilhite and Mr. Ross, relieved to see that the teller and the cashier stood quietly, as he had instructed. Despite the absence of their sheriff, they had agreed to help.

Come get me, Scotty. Come on. Tension coiled through Marsh's shoulders, tautened his muscles. He kept his place behind the counter, still assuming the mien of a timid man. He wore a nicely fitted houndstooth suit and a pair of spectacles perched on the bridge of his nose. His dark, neatly trimmed hair was parted down the middle and slicked with hair oil, giving him a dandified appearance.

He relaxed his body so that his normally proud shoulders appeared stooped and bony. His quick glance around the bank gave the impression of fear, but in reality he stored details in his mind.

All five men leveled their pistols. Marsh scanned the dirt-streaked, hard features partially hidden by bandannas. Thompson's eyes glowed a cloudy green, cold as a dormant winter pond. The other men had various-colored eyes, but they were all the same shade of mean. A tuft of red hair poked out from one hat, a tuft of blond from another.

Besides the Peacemaker, Thompson carried an army issue repeater Winchester. The other four held their pistols with the ease of long practice. Except for the man outside, Marsh knew them all by name.

The red-haired man to Marsh's left was Bill Eckland and the blond to his right was Jasper, Thompson's cousin. Lawson and Cary stood behind Thompson, their faces obscured. After tracking them for the last year, Marsh had finally outmaneuvered them.

Come on, boys. Make a move. He licked his lips, hoping they would believe he was nervous. Excitement steepled inside him, begging for release.

He had deliberately placed himself next to the vault, and as he waited with wide eyes, Scotty Thompson stepped forward.

"You there, open the vault."

He adjusted his phony spectacles, veiling a surreptitious glance at Charles Wilhite. At the signal, the teller covertly reached for the gun hidden beneath the counter. Marsh smiled at Thompson. "No."

The outlaw blinked.

Jasper and Eckland gaped in unison, then Jasper gave a snort of laughter. "What did he say, Bill?"

"He said no." Eckland blinked in disbelief. "I think."

Thompson jiggled his rifle at Marsh. "Perhaps you didn't notice my hardware."

"So happens I did." He drummed his fingers on top of the marble counter, his palms itching to reach for his Colt. "I'm not opening the safe, and neither are these other two gentlemen. You can either lay down your guns real peaceable like, or I can take them." He smiled. "Being as how this is America, it's your choice."

Outrage slowly swept the faces of the others, but Thompson roared and charged over the counter. "You're a dead man!"

Marsh lunged straight for the outlaw. He hoped Ross and Wilhite had the balls to shoot or the sense to duck.

Slamming the top of his head into Thompson's face, he reached at the same time for the man's revolver and wrested it free. The outlaw jabbed him in the stomach with the butt of his rifle. Gunfire exploded, reverberating in the small space like cannon fire.

"Down, Gyp!" Marsh yelled as he slid behind Ross's desk, firing twice. A body crashed to the floor with a sickening thud. He turned in time to see Wilhite fall, blood soaking the sleeve of his right arm. A bullet burned past Marsh's ear and drilled into the wall behind him. Smoke singed the air.

Ross huddled on the floor, fumbling to load the gun Wilhite had dropped. Eckland peered over the counter and fired at Marsh. The sound roared in his ears, but he sighted the man and squeezed the trigger. Eckland fell, his head cracking against the counter.

A shot zinged past Marsh's knee and he rolled, facing the opposite end of the counter. Ross fired and Jasper slammed into the wall, trailing blood as he slid to the floor.

The bank door slammed open and a spray of gunfire peppered the wall behind the desk. Marsh tossed the Peacemaker and grabbed his Colt, leaping out from behind the desk to fire at the new man. Thompson had disappeared.

Cary edged around the counter and advanced from the opposite end, moving in like a rattler on a rat.

Marsh stared into the man's cold, empty eyes, wondering if he had become as hard as these men. "Attack, Gyp!"

The dog launched himself through the air and hit the outlaw's chest with his full weight.

Cary fired and Marsh's finger jerked on the trigger. The outlaw took the bullet and dropped to the floor, causing the dog to leap off and scramble for balance. Marsh whirled, poised to shoot, but the sound of thundering hooves stopped him.

He rushed to the door of the bank in time to see Thompson, Lawson, and the third man disappear over the hill.

Rage pumped through him and obliterated his reason, as it usually did. He hated vermin like this, hated the way they bullied and intimidated and maimed and killed. And now they had escaped to do more of the same.

Damn! Marsh turned back to survey the bank.

The sudden silence was startling and caused a ringing in his ears. For a moment no one moved. Gunsmoke clouded the air, and in the stillness a piece of glass fell from the window to tinkle hollowly against the wooden floor. Slowly the smoke cleared.

He leaned over and braced his hands on his knees, sucking in air. "Good boy, Gyp," he panted.

"Is it over?" Henry Ross peered out from behind a desk.

"Looks that way." Marsh scanned the room, taking in the broken glass, the shattered wood and bullet holes in the bank's plaster molding. He glanced over at Mr. Wilhite, who struggled to his feet. "How are you, Charles?"

"Fine," the teller croaked, gripping his left arm. "It's just a nick."

Ross moved out from behind the counter and walked over to Wilhite. Both men looked dazed as they stared at the three dead men.

"Good Lord," Ross said.

Gyp plopped down on his haunches and huffed out a loud breath.

Glass and wood crunching beneath his feet, Marsh walked over and looked down at Cary. Anger sliced through him. He thought of the people in Jones and Kansas City and Marietta who hadn't survived this gang's visits, the old woman who'd been murdered for a pair of silver earbobs and a horse.

His cheek stung and he took off the phony spectacles, thumbing blood from a fresh graze on his left cheekbone. The sound of voices and footsteps rumbled into the bank.

"What the hell!" A tall, lean man wearing a badge appeared in the door. "What happened here?"

Mr. Ross rushed over, explaining to the sheriff how Agent Granger of the Pinkerton detective agency had been waiting for the Thompson gang since receiving a tip about the robbery.

"I'm gone for a week and this is what happens," the sheriff lamented. He grinned at the cashier. "You're a regular hero, Henry. Didn't know you had it in you."

"I don't." Henry Ross wiped his forehead with a handkerchief and stared dazedly at the devastation of bodies and blood and glass and wood. "I didn't do any of it. In fact, neither did Charles. Mr. Granger did it all."

"I've never seen anything like it. There were six of them, all told." Charles Wilhite leaned against the counter, holding tight to his arm to stanch the blood. He shook his head and a grin spread across his face. "They told Marsh to open the safe and he didn't even blink. Just said no, polite as you please."

The sheriff cocked one brow at Marsh. "Leave anyone alive?"

He jerked his head toward the street. "The three who rode out."

Several men crowded into the doorway. A gray-haired man carrying a black bag pushed through the throng. "Charles, let me look at that arm."

Wilhite stood unmoving, grimacing as the doctor tore away his shirt-sleeve.

Gyp waited patiently next to Cary's body, and the sheriff glanced at Marsh, incredulous. "I'll be damned. That dog took him down?"

Marsh nodded, snapping his fingers for Gyp to come.

The sheriff's gaze again scanned the bank lobby. "You threw down on all six of them?"

"It was either that or let them all throw down on me."

The sheriff thumbed his hat back. "Well, I'll be."

"Suicide," the doctor muttered, stitching Wilhite's arm.

The teller nodded. "It was almost as if he didn't care whether or not he died."

The lot of them stared anxiously at the frustrated Marsh as if he might take them on as well. He itched for a cigarette, but settled for a match between his teeth. More people trickled through the door, coming to gawk at the dead outlaws. Impatient to get away now that the place was filling up, he quickly relayed the entire story to the sheriff.

After a final thank-you, he and Gyp headed to the stable for his horse, Sarge. Tired and battered, Marsh considered getting good and drunk for about a week.

But he needed to see Pinkerton before Thompson's trail got cold. Besides, if he sat still that long, he'd think. And the guilt would catch up to him.

"Gordon's dead. Strangled."

That evening, Marsh stood in Allan Pinkerton's secret Kansas City headquarters and stared intently at his boss. Hamp Gordon was one of Pinkerton's youngest agents and the latest to go undercover on the Thompson case. Marsh tossed his cigarette to the floor and ground it out. "Hell."

"My thoughts exactly." Fatigue drew deep lines around Pinkerton's long face; his deep-set eyes were weary and sad. The Thompson gang had so far managed to cause as much destruction as the Jameses, and Pinkerton was determined to get them. "This makes the fifth agent they've gotten."

"In the last fifteen months." Anger gathered to volatile iciness inside Marsh.

"I want you to go."

"I'll be there in two days."

"You need to see this." Allan handed him a piece of paper.

In the flickering candlelight he read a telegram from Gordon. "Have discovered Thompson informant."

"Gordon started to send more, but was interrupted during transmission. He was found dead a few days later."

Marsh's jaw clenched. First Touchstone, then Paulson, Perkins, McBain. Now Gordon. Like John Touchstone, it appeared that Hamp Gordon had finally learned who in Spinner was responsible for passing information to Scotty Thompson. How were they doing it? And when was it going to end?

Pinkerton slammed his fist against his desk and his eyes burned with rabid intensity. "I want Scotty Thompson."

Never having seen Allan this upset, Marsh checked his own anger. "What do you want me to do?"

Spinner, Missouri
Two days later

He arrived in Spinner well after dark on Saturday night. Before leaving Kansas City, he and Allan had argued vehemently about this assignment.

Allan wanted Marsh to tell John Touchstone's widow why he had come. Besides being certain that the woman would help, Allan believed the family's excellent reputation would permit Marsh's acceptance into Spinner without suspicion. Marsh flatly refused.

He had no intention of telling Mrs. Touchstone anything except that he needed a job. Hiring on as her hand would give him easy access to the town while allowing him to move around without arousing suspicion. That part of Allan's plan was acceptable, since it posed a threat to no one, but Marsh wanted no more involvement than that, no more responsibility.

Located between Kansas City and Springfield, the town was bigger than he'd expected. Spinner was situated in a lush valley of the western Ozarks cut with streams and hills and mountains. The beauty of this part of the state was nearly as impressive as his native Tennessee.

He approached the town and reined Sarge to a stop. Golden spots of light danced through the main street like fireflies, giving an aura of tranquility to the twilight setting.

A small white frame church sat on Marsh's right and in front of him a wooden footbridge led into town. He urged his horse across and Gyp trotted alongside.

Voices rose and fell, punctuated by the smooth chords of a piano. A small breeze kicked up and stroked the nape of his neck. He rubbed at the itch on his chin, brought on by the two days' growth of beard. After being buttoned up in a prissy suit and perfumed like a damn fancy shop, it felt good to wear his faded denims and well-worn boots.

And he refused to shave until he was forced. Keeping his beard scraped off for the job at the bank had damn near chafed his skin to bleeding.

The main street of Spinner was wide enough for three wagons to travel abreast. The livery stable, a general store, a doctor's office, a law office, and the jail lined the east side of the street. All were dark and quiet except the livery.

On the west side of the street was the Spinner Hotel, Lil's House of Boarding and Fine Dining, a barbershop, the telegraph office, and a saloon proclaiming TULLY'S in tall white letters across the wooden awning. A blacksmith occupied the lone building across the alley from the saloon.

Behind the businesses on each side of the street was a row of houses. Lights flickered in several of them and in the doctor's office. Lil's restaurant looked busy and Marsh figured he could stay the night at her boardinghouse until he hooked up with Touchstone's widow.

Light spilled over the swinging double doors of the saloon, and the soothing sound of a waltz drifted out, accompanied by rhythmed tapping and muted voices. He frowned. He had never known a saloon to play a waltz. Or host a dance.

A piece of paper fluttered on a post outside the saloon and Marsh glanced at it. LADIES NIGHT. Ladies in a saloon?

He peered over the doors, and a slow smile stretched across his face. Sure enough, there were real ladies inside in addition to the soiled doves he spotted in a far corner.

Gyp stuck his head under the doors, his tail thumping against Marsh's leg. An extravagant gaslight chandelier hung from the ceiling in the center of the room. Light bounced from the crystal swags, reflecting pale rainbow-colored prisms that shimmered like sun on water.

This was the nicest saloon Marsh had ever seen. With the card tables crowded against one wall to make room for chairs, the small jar of flowers on the piano, and the spotless though scarred floor, Tully's looked more like a recital hall.

The absence of smoke allowed Marsh to see the gleaming wood of the long bar, the painstakingly carved design in the mirror that stretched several feet along the wall behind the counter. Glasses and bottles winked in the light.

Scents of soap and toilet water and warm bodies mixed with the hint of smoke and cheap perfume, a testimony that the establishment was indeed a saloon and not a piano hall.

Still there was no card playing, no raucous laughter, no saloon girls strutting through the crowd. In fact, this crowd more resembled one at a church social than a saloon.

The piano sat in the middle of the room and faced the

doors, so he was unable to see who played it. The slow poignant strains of "When You and I Were Young, Maggie" floated to him.

Men and women filled the chairs that were arranged in five rows in front of the piano. Several men sat at the bar, and among them Marsh spied the shiny silver of the sheriff's badge. As always, his first stop included plans to gather information and a sizing up of the local law.

A tall blond man behind the bar waved Marsh inside. He commanded Gyp to wait and pushed through the doors.

The man who had invited him in looked to be about the same age as Marsh's own thirty-six years. He raised his voice to be heard above the music. "What'll you have?"

Marsh glanced pointedly at the female customers. "You servin' tonight?"

"Yep. Brandy for the men and lemonade for the ladies."

"I'll have brandy." He placed two bits on the smooth wood counter.

The sheriff glanced at Marsh but didn't speak.

The bartender placed a shot of brandy in front of him. "That'll be another quarter."

Marsh raised his eyebrows, digging into his britches again.

The bartender grinned. "Come back on a regular night. You can have anything you want and it's cheaper."

He nodded and savored his first sip. Smooth, with just the right smoky burn. "Never seen a saloon that allows women."

The barkeep dropped his voice. "I figure if the women come here and have a good time, there'll be less squawking when their men come here to do the same."

"Tully's always trying new things." The sheriff turned toward Marsh. "Anything to make money."

"Seems to be working so far." Tully moved down the bar to refill another glass.

The piano player broke into "Pop Goes the Weasel." Men rose from their chairs and escorted the women to a small patch of floor that had been cleared for dancing. Over the piano, Marsh caught a glimpse of a blond head and a delicate profile.

"Got business in Spinner?" The sheriff angled one hip into the bar and sipped at his brandy. "Or just passin' through?"

Direct, but not abrasive. Marsh took in the shrewd hazel eyes, the intelligent face, and wondered if the lawman knew anything about Scotty Thompson's gang. Or the Pinkerton agents who kept turning up dead. He deliberately let his gaze rest on the badge pinned to the man's sturdy chest. "Lookin' for work, actually."

"What kind?" Curiosity edged the amiable words.

"Anything. I'm good with livestock and crops, pretty handy with a hammer."

"You from around here?"

Marsh took another sip of brandy. "Just came from Crowley."

"What'd you do up there?"

"Worked in a bank."

"A bank?" Suspicion narrowed the sheriff's eyes. "Pretty good with numbers too, huh?"

"Yeah." He gave a short laugh. "But I didn't really cotton to an indoor job."

The sheriff nodded, looking out over the crowd. "You didn't happen to be up there when the Thompson gang tried to rob the bank? Heard some man took 'em down single-handedly a couple of days ago."

"I guess that was after I left."

The sheriff's gaze moved to him, probing. "I see."

The music changed to "Oh, Dem Golden Slippers," and the dancers clapped in time.

A tall, pleasant-looking man walked up and Tully refilled his empty glass with lemonade. "There you go, Reverend."

The reverend nodded and resumed his seat in the back row, his gaze trained on the piano player.

Tully refilled Marsh's brandy. "Did I hear you say you're lookin' for work?"

He nodded, scanning the room. Three saloon girls sat in a corner away from the piano and the crowd. One of them, dressed in purple, kept tugging at the skimpy shoulders of her dress. A lanky cowboy sat next to her, fidgeting awkwardly as he watched the dancers. The pair sat primly, as if they were courting.

"Tub Gibson might need a cowhand. One of his boys busted a tailbone last week trying to break a horse. And Chuck Madill needs help harvesting wheat."

"Thanks, I appreciate that." He looked out over the crowd. "Would they happen to be here tonight?"

"Nope, but I can tell you how to find them."

"Thanks." He had no intention of asking either of these men for a job, but when he hired on with Touchstone's widow, the sheriff and bartender would remember that Marsh had asked about work, which would help his cover.

"Oh, hey." The bartender snapped his fingers. "You could check with Julia Touchstone. She and her mother might need some help."

Surprised to hear the name of the woman he'd come to see, Marsh's gaze sliced to the man. "How can I find her?"

Tully gestured toward the piano player. "That's her."

He turned, seeking a glimpse, but could see only a flash of blond hair. "Not very big, is she?"

"Nope," the sheriff drawled, watching Marsh. "But pure iron. Her husband was killed last year, and she's been taking care of her son and mother ever since. I think she could probably use the help."

The music ended and the crowd burst into applause. As it faded, people shuffled out the doors. Marsh watched Julia Touchstone.

He didn't know what he'd expected to find in John Touchstone's widow, but it hadn't been the beguiling golden vision rising from the piano. While Touchstone hadn't been the homeliest man Marsh had ever seen, he'd been damn close. Marsh had assumed that Touchstone's wife—

Well, he'd been dead wrong. While Julia Touchstone wasn't beautiful in the heart-stopping way Beth had been, she was definitely pretty. Very pretty indeed.

She was no taller than five foot two, and Gyp probably weighed more than she did. She was slender, her breasts and hips gently rounded.

Thick flaxen hair was piled atop her head, and tendrils escaped to frame her face and neck, shimmering in the light like spun honey. Creamy skin gleamed like alabaster. Her dark shirtwaist emphasized her slightness and made her appear frail. No, delicate was a better description.

"Hey, Julia," Tully called over the noise of chairs scraping the floor and the swinging *thunk* of the saloon doors. "Got someone here who wants to talk to you about a job."

Marsh remained in the same easy, spread-legged stance, but a low-throbbing tension coiled through him. "She works here *and* has a farm?"

"That ain't all." Tully laughed. "She plays the piano once a month for ladies night, then cleans the place during the day."

The petite blonde walked toward them, smiling at a woman who patted her shoulder. The smile warmed her features in a way that made Marsh want to know her.

As she neared, he could see that her eyes were the pure deep green of new grass. In the paleness of her face, they glowed like heated emeralds, and despite the smile she wore, there was a maturity there brought on by sadness.

Intriguing. He didn't lose his train of thought, didn't forget why he'd come, but suddenly the case seemed less important. Which was insane.

She stopped a few feet away and a light flowery scent wafted around him. Her lips were a deep rose color, still parted in a half-smile. The muscles in his belly clenched and the blood surged in his veins.

"Julia, this is—sorry." Tully turned to Marsh. "Didn't get your name."

"Marsh Tipton," he said hoarsely. As a precaution, he

used his mother's maiden name. Realizing he was staring like a besotted schoolboy, he cleared his throat and removed his hat. She blushed, but gave him a warm smile.

"Marsh is passing through and looking for work." The bartender gathered up several empty glasses and put them behind the bar. "I told him you might need a hand."

Her smile dimmed and her green eyes became guarded. "Have you ever cleared land before, Mr. Tipton?"

"Yes, ma'am." When she didn't accept his extended hand in greeting, he settled his hat back on his head. He grinned, hoping to charm the wariness out of eyes. "I've done a little of everything."

"Even used to work at the bank in Crowley," the sheriff put in quietly.

Julia glanced at the sheriff and a small frown puckered her brow. The reverend, who had come up to the bar earlier, walked over to stand between her and the sheriff.

"It's backbreaking work, Mr. Tipton," she said. "If you're not used to that kind of labor—"

"I'd have no trouble doing it, ma'am. And I really need the job."

"Learned anything new about Gordon?" the minister, Riley, asked the sheriff in an aside.

Despite the men's lowered tones, Marsh heard them, and he could tell Julia Touchstone had too.

Worry clouded her features, and her gaze shifted from Marsh to the two men beside him.

"No, not yet," the sheriff answered.

Tully moved down the bar toward the two men and shook his head, glancing at Julia. "Not in front of the lady, please."

Marsh covertly studied the saloon owner. So, Julia Touchstone had a protector.

The reverend nodded and leaned closer to the sheriff. "Where'd you say Bundy found him, Rob?"

"Just outside of town about a mile, where the road forks east and west."

Riley shook his head, his voice deep with compassion. "Such a tragedy. He was so young."

Julia's gaze returned to Marsh, her features now a mixture of caution and suspicion. "Do you have family around here, Mr. Tipton?"

"No, ma'am, just passin' through." Unease snaked along his spine. Was she concerned because of the talk about Gordon? Or was she suspicious of Marsh?

She gave him an apologetic smile. "I don't think I'll be able to hire you, but I imagine you'll easily find something else."

"Are you sure? I can do just about anything." *And probably would, for you.*

She studied him as though trying to peer inside his skull. "I'm sorry. I don't think so."

Surprise rocked him. He had never considered that she might reject the idea, had never really considered her as anything other than a detail to be dealt with. He certainly hadn't considered that she might intrigue him.

Marsh wanted to protest, to reassure her that she didn't need to be cautious of him, but he could feel the sheriff's shrewd hazel gaze boring into him. "Yes, ma'am. Thank you."

He drained the last of his brandy, thanked Tully, and walked out into the night. *You're not quite rid of me yet, Mrs. Touchstone.*

He *would* be her new hired hand.

CHAPTER TWO

Had she met Marsh Tipton before? He looked so familiar. Julia looked away, but she was all too aware when the man walked out of the saloon. With his absence, the room grew smaller, dimmer. She felt a vague sense of loss, as if she would later regret her decision not to hire him.

Perhaps she should have. There was nothing inherently wrong with a man who wandered, and Tipton had seemed decent enough. He had accepted her decision with gentlemanly grace, though she had sensed that he wanted to try to change her mind. Odd that her refusal hadn't seemed to disappoint him, but rather surprised him.

His reaction had provoked the wariness that had been such a part of her since John's death. And though she felt a little silly about the degree of her unease, she wouldn't take chances with Pete's safety. Not after the tragedy last year.

She couldn't shake the unsettling feeling that she somehow knew Marsh Tipton. What bothered her about the man? She wasn't likely to forget meeting someone like him. He was a man who commanded attention, and it wasn't strictly due to his size. Though he stood only about six feet tall, he looked to have the cunning eyes of a wildcat and the unshakable strength of a mountain.

Goodness, but he was big. His loose, light-colored shirt couldn't disguise the brawn of his chest; the sturdy column of his neck hinted at thick ropy muscles in shoulders that were nearly as wide as a wagon brace.

His short hair was walnut-dark and neatly trimmed. Silver threads glinted at his temples. A few days' growth of beard shadowed his square jaw and chin, defining wide, firm lips that looked as though they could also be cruel. A raw scrape, almost a burn, marked the crest of his left cheekbone.

He exuded power and energy, a leashed wildness that was reflected in his unusual silver eyes. He didn't look to be more than forty, if that old. His face was the color of weathered copper, and small lines fanned out from his light-colored eyes.

Deeper grooves bracketed his mouth, hinting at a ready laugh, but his eyes were flinty, branding him as someone who had seen too much violence and harshness. The eyes triggered that nagging sense of familiarity again.

His request for work had seemed sincere, yet something about him disturbed her. His gaze had moved slowly over her, not thorough enough to insult, but enough to cause an unsettling flash of heat to lick through her. She thought that was reason enough to refuse his request for a job.

Sheriff Kisling poked a matchstick in the corner of his mouth. "Seemed like a decent fella."

"I'm sure he was." Julia took her shawl from Riley.

"I'll ask around at church," he said. "Someone might need an extra farmhand with the fall coming on."

"Sorry if I was out of line, Julia." Tully gave the gleaming counter a last swipe. "I thought you or India mentioned clearing another twenty acres."

"We did, but I'd rather use someone we know." Suspicion now seemed an integral part of her, and she couldn't dismiss it no matter how much she wished. Marsh Tipton probably did need a job, but she didn't like the idea of a drifter working near her son.

"You okay, Julia?" Riley touched her elbow.

"Of course."

"If it would make you feel better, I can ask around about Tipton," Sheriff Kisling said. "Check up in Crowley for you."

"Thanks, Rob, but that's not necessary." She smiled warmly at the man who'd been her and John's friend for years. "I'll be able to find someone to help me."

Tully walked over to extinguish the gaslight chandelier he'd ordered all the way from St. Louis. He pampered it more than he would a baby. "Julia, this was our best night yet!"

She willingly pulled her thoughts from Marsh Tipton. Tully's dark blue eyes lit with pleasure. He was an avowed bachelor, notorious for dallying with the girls who worked in his place, though he had never made advances toward Julia.

The women at church and in her mother's sewing circle were appalled that she worked in the saloon, but Tully had been the only one in town to give her a job, and she was grateful. Thanks to him, a few months earlier she had paid the last of the doctor's bill they had incurred after Pete's injury and now she was saving up to buy livestock.

Tully had helped her in more ways than one since John's death. Besides checking in on her frequently, the saloon owner had insisted on paying for John's burial and flatly refused repayment, saying he wanted to do whatever he could to ease Julia's burden.

"We sold more drinks tonight than ever before." Tully dipped into the cigar box that served as his safe and slapped a five-dollar gold piece in her hand. "Good work."

"Tully! I can't take this."

"You're the one who brought this crowd here."

"Nonsense." Julia thrust the money at him, but he ignored her.

"You did. None of the women who came tonight would've darkened my door if you weren't here."

"That's ridiculous." She dropped the coin back into the box, then gestured to the young saloon girl wearing a purple dress. "You play beautifully, and so does Hazel, if you'd let her."

"No woman in this town would come to hear me or a

whore play the piano." Tully unwrapped a long cigar and stuck it in his mouth. "And you know it."

Julia flinched at his description of Hazel. Even though it was true, it sounded cruel. Filene and Millie, the other two girls, kept to themselves, but Julia and Hazel had become friends.

The girl didn't appear to have heard. She stood in the corner deep in conversation with Bill Young, a cowboy from a nearby ranch who gazed at her with rapt attention. He kissed her hand and turned, walking out with an expression of total adoration.

"Hazel, where you going?" Tully barked, scowling.

"I don't feel so good, Tully," the girl said.

Julia turned to see Hazel halfway up the stairs. Alone. She smiled encouragingly.

Hazel grimaced and rubbed at her stomach. "I'm just gonna rest a minute."

Tully snorted and turned away. "She never feels good."

"Maybe it's woman trouble." The sheriff colored as he shot an uneasy glance at Julia.

Tully sighed. "Ain't it always? Julia's the only woman working for me who's never sick." He pressed the coin firmly into her hand. "Here, you earned this."

"It seems like a lot for just one night." Her hand itched to close over the warm gold and claim it, but she refrained.

"Are you saying you can't use it?"

"Noooo."

"All right, then. Put it in your livestock fund."

She smiled, feeling a new burst of hope. Her dream of owning cattle was really going to happen. "Thank you."

She had worked hard at forgetting the past, focusing on the future for her and Pete. Now they could concentrate on the farm, which actually belonged to her mother. While John was alive, they had lived in town until Pete was born, then, due to her husband's frequent and long absences, she and Pete had moved back into Julia's childhood home.

In the last year, she and India had decided to clear more

land for alfalfa and to raise cattle. The original twenty acres of alfalfa crop had been sold to pay for John's burial and medical expenses. Needing the extra money to purchase more seed and livestock, Julia had begun working for Tully.

The bartender replaced his cigar-box-cum-safe under the counter. "How much do you have?"

"Almost enough to buy a bull and a few cows."

"Is that right?" Admiration gleamed in his eyes. "Pete will make a fine cowboy."

"It's thanks to you, Tully." Julia smiled warmly. "You're the only reason I have a job. Our first calf is yours."

"Good." Walking over to the bottom of the stairs to join his two saloon girls, he pulled them close with a wicked smile. "Guess I'll see you tomorrow."

"Ready?" Riley said from beside her.

"Yes." She looked at the minister, knowing he didn't approve of Tully's actions either, but he said nothing.

She was suddenly grateful that he would see her home. Julia wasn't a skittish person, but since John's death she had come to appreciate having company on the two-mile ride. Especially tonight, after being reminded of young Gordon's death and meeting that disturbing Marsh Tipton.

She and Riley moved toward the door.

"Julia?" Tully called from the top of the stairs. "Tomorrow, could you wash those glasses behind the bar?"

"All right."

"Oh, and I bought some new sheets," he hollered. "They're for the two front rooms."

Her face burned at the reference to the place where the girls "entertained," but she nodded.

"And the banister needs beeswax and honey—"

"Every other week," she finished with a smile. "I know, Tully."

Riley chuckled.

The saloon owner grinned. "I'm not used to someone who can keep up with me."

She waved, stepping outside.

"Oh, and, Julia!"

"Don't disturb your office," she chanted in a singsong voice. "I remember, Tully. I remember."

She had cleaned it once, about eight months ago, when she had first begun working for him. Upon finding her there, he had panicked and ushered her out, sheepishly explaining that he liked things just so. Their agreement for her to clean the rooms and the main floor didn't extend to his office.

Julia supposed most men weren't sticklers for neatness, but Tully seemed to have an unusually strong aversion to organization.

Papers and receipts and notices were strewn in shameless disarray across his desk. She didn't understand how he could find a thing that way, but he always located what he needed with the instinct of a bird dog on point.

"All right," Tully said with a laugh. "Hey, Julia!"

"What now?" She turned in mock exasperation.

His smile dimmed to concern. "You gonna be okay?"

"Yes." She smiled at the man who'd quickly befriended her after arriving in Spinner. "Riley will see me home."

"Good night, then."

She smiled at Riley as they walked toward her wagon at the corner of the saloon.

He stood just over six feet tall, taller than the man who'd asked for a job tonight, but, Julia realized with surprise, Riley never made her feel dwarfed, whereas Marsh Tipton had. The realization renewed the niggling certainty that she somehow knew the man, but how?

After helping her into the wagon, Riley mounted his gray mare and they started for Julia's house. The wind blew gently, mixing the odors of dirt and the hint of rain with a faint spicy scent from Riley. Stars winked in a clear sky.

"Your playing was lovely tonight." His horse plodded alongside the wagon.

Another thing she liked about Riley was his love of

music, and she smiled. "I hit a wrong note during the Minuet in G Minor."

"The key was a trifle flat. I'll have Tully tune up the piano before next month. I don't think you could hit a wrong note if you tried."

"Of course I could."

"I don't believe it," he dismissed with a flirty smile.

She wagged a finger at him. "You know, Riley, I believe you enjoy providing fodder for the gossips as much as you like the recital at Tully's."

"What do you mean?" His eyes twinkled mischievously.

"How many ministers do you know who actually spend time in a saloon?"

"Maybe more of them should." He smiled. "Besides, there's not a woman in town who can say anything improper happens at Tully's on ladies night. We certainly can't say that any other time."

Riley was prudent, but not a hypocrite, and he lived as he preached. Jesus hadn't separated himself from sinners, and neither did Riley. She liked that about him too.

"I think you just like to stir things up in your congregation, set people to talking."

"It does seem to improve church attendance," he said with a grin.

"That's because of you."

"Because of the Lord."

Julia smiled. She believed in giving the Lord his due, but Riley was the one who had met the men of Spinner on their own terms. They respected him for it, and that respect showed in the increased numbers of men who attended church recently.

Riley was a good man, as John had been. She liked his sense of humor and compassion and his ability not to be preachy, but mostly Julia liked that he wasn't involved in anything dangerous.

As a detective, John had often pretended to be someone

other than who he was. His jobs had included everything from a tanner to a railroad scout to an outlaw. Riley was what he claimed to be, a preacher. Period.

They turned off the main road and he said, "I was hoping Robin might have learned something about Hamp's death."

"Yes, I was too." Her gaze roamed over the darkened landscape, seeing shadows where there were none, wondering if perhaps John might have mentioned Marsh Tipton. But her husband had never discussed cases.

They reined up in front of the house where Julia had lived practically her entire life. Set off from the surrounding pasture and barn by a white rail fence, the modest frame house was tucked cozily into the lush side of a foothill.

Though old and worn and needing paint, she saw it with the biased eyes of love. She had been born here, married here, and widowed here. The swing on the east end of the porch had seen thousands of tears, withstood tantrums and whispered promises, cradled her in times of fear as well as times of joy.

After John's death she had come often to the swing, sometimes better able to find comfort here than with her mother.

Recalling John's death triggered a flash of memory, another thought of Marsh Tipton. Before she could grasp it, the image disappeared. Why had she assumed that she knew Tipton through John, when it could have been through India or even someone in town?

"Thank you for seeing me home."

"It's entirely my pleasure. I like to know that you're safe, Julia."

At the warmth in his voice, she snapped to attention. He had made it clear that he wanted to court her, and when she was ready, she would allow it. But tonight she smiled and bade him good-bye.

She drove the wagon into the barn and hopped down to unhitch her chestnut mare, Noonan. Thoughts of Hamp

Gordon badgered her, and despite the heat of the night, Julia shivered.

When Riley had told her earlier that evening about the young man's death, she had wondered if the Thompson gang was involved, but they weren't the type to kill quietly. They struck boldly and brutally and took vicious glee in their destruction. She had witnessed that firsthand.

Meeting that drifter had unsettled her enough to consider the possibility again of Thompson's involvement, but it was not the outlaw who invaded her thoughts. Marsh Tipton's quicksilver eyes held secrets, although she had been able to read no emotion until his surprise when she had refused him a job.

Moving automatically, she hung the harness on the wall. The man had certainly looked as if he needed a job, although he hadn't worn that aimless, indifferent look she had seen on other drifters. And he wasn't unkempt, simply unshaven, which served to give his chiseled features a dangerous allure.

Julia sighed, exasperated at her constant suspicion of everyone. Perhaps she should have hired him, but just the thought caused a nervous flutter in her stomach. It wasn't fear, but caution. There was something about him she didn't trust, something disquieting.

"Oh!" she muttered in frustration. *Why* was she thinking about him at all? If he didn't find a job in Spinner, he'd move on and she would never see him again.

It was the news about Gordon that made her so nervous, and again she tried to reassure herself that everything was fine.

After Pinkerton and his men had failed to apprehend the Thompsons for John's death, they had all but given up, and Julia was glad. Oh, there was a part of her that still yearned for justice, even revenge, but more than that she wanted security for her boy.

She and Pete had put the past behind them. They had a good future ahead and she wouldn't allow it to be threatened, certainly not by silly thoughts of a no-account drifter she had met in town.

"Ma'am?"

At the deep voice behind her, Julia's heart knocked painfully against her ribs. She spun and fumbled in her skirt pocket for her derringer, peering blindly into the barn's dim shadows. "Who is it? What do you want?"

A broad shadow separated itself from the darkness, and the man moved into the amber light.

"You!" Julia recoiled in shock, and fear knifed through her. Holding the gun steady with both hands, she leveled it at Marsh Tipton. "What are you doing here? How did you find me?"

With his hands spread wide at his sides, he moved slowly toward her. He nodded toward the gun. "You don't need that."

She kept the gun leveled at his gut. He wore a large revolver strapped to his thigh. Fearful visions that she'd carried since John's death returned and alarm knocked at her. "What do you want?"

"I'm not going to harm you, Mrs. Touchstone." He kept his hands in the air, his eyes searching hers. "But I do intend to talk to you."

"About what?" The man hadn't reached for his gun. Was he perhaps really looking for a job? Her earlier alarm mixed with irritation. "I told you I can't give you a job."

"It's okay, Mrs. Touchstone." Marsh Tipton stepped closer, his sharp silver eyes now gentle and reassuring. Hazy light played over his dark features, giving him a hard, ruthless look—a look she recognized. That nagging sense of familiarity crashed back and she felt light-headed.

A fuzzy memory, shoved away until now, rippled into focus. A photograph of five men, given to John by Allan Pinkerton. Though the picture was grainy, the men were easily distinguishable.

"You don't need to be afraid of me."

Panic buzzed in Julia's ears. The photograph flashed full-blown into her mind. To the undiscerning eye the picture depicted five friends posing in front of a St. Louis beer garden, but Julia knew differently. Her chest ached and she struggled to breathe. "You're one of them."

Shocked surprise flared in his eyes, and she knew she was right. "What are you talking about?"

"You're a Pinkerton." In fact, he was one of the men who had been handpicked to help establish the secret headquarters in Kansas City. Fear and pain and anger crowded through her. "Why are you here? Why?"

He hesitated briefly. "I'm here to get the Thompson gang."

"They're not here!" she shrieked. "Why are you?"

"They killed your husband as well as some other damn fine agents. I'm going to get them, ma'am. You and your son will never need to worry—"

"Did Allan send you?" A cold knot wedged in her chest. This man was more trouble than she'd suspected, and she wanted to run away, pretend she'd never met him. "Is he feeling guilty about John's death? Why now?"

"We've had word Thompson is in and out of the area."

"He's been wreaking havoc all over the state for a year," she said coldly. "None of you seemed too concerned after my husband was killed."

"Of course we were." He frowned suddenly, his gaze narrowing. "Ma'am, we've never closed this case."

"But . . ." She shook her head. "That's not true. Allan hasn't been looking for them. No one has."

"*We have,* ma'am, and we're going to keep looking until we get the bastards."

"Not here. You can't look for them here." Her gaze darted around the barn, searching for a place to hide, wishing she could wake up and escape this nightmare.

He stepped closer. A clean, soapy scent floated to her, mixed with warm male and the faint odor of horseflesh. Concern stamped his shadowed features, and his voice

stroked over her like dark velvet, slow and whiskey-hot with
the lazy drawl of the South. "Are you all right?"

Fear sliced through her. She felt unsteady, unbalanced, as
though clawing her way up the sheer face of a cliff. She
couldn't let Pete be involved in this again. *She couldn't.* Ter-
ror tightened her throat. "Get out."

He blinked. "What?"

A tremor ripped through her body, leaving her weak and
frightened. Desperate. Sweat slicked her hands and they
trembled uncontrollably, causing the gun to wobble. Still,
she managed to thumb down the hammer and aim the gun at
him. "I said get out."

"Hold on, lady." Intensity darkened his eyes, and he studied her as if trying to determine whether she would really
shoot. "If I get killed while I'm on this case, it won't be by
you."

"I'm counting to three." Her voice was hoarse and the
trembling in her body grew more violent, working down her
legs. She wouldn't allow him to risk Pete. "If you're not
gone, I'll shoot."

"I'm here to help you." Thick muscles bunched beneath
his shirt; his legs were braced like iron tree trunks. "I'm only
asking for a place to stay," he said calmly.

"One." The rational part of her mind told her to turn and
walk away, but reason was drowned by the desperate desire
to protect her son, to elude the past that bore down upon her.
Her hands tightened on the gun, almost as if she drew reason from it.

"Are you telling me you don't want to get those bastards?" Anger edged his lazy drawl. "After what they did to
your husband?"

Of course she wanted them to pay for John's death, but
not at the risk of danger to Pete. Her legs wobbled. "Two."

"Dammit." A muscle flexed in his cheek and he stared at
her as if she were unhinged. "What about the harm they did
to your son?"

He never should have mentioned Pete. Fear exploded like loose shrapnel. "Three."

"Hell's bells!" He pinned her with a look of utter frustration. "What is the matter with you? If you'll help me, we can finally get the bastards!"

Panic turned to hysteria. Desperation erased every thought except that of survival, escape, and she squeezed the trigger.

In the confines of the barn, the shot reverberated with a sharp *crack!* and she flinched at the gun's kick.

Marsh threw himself on the ground, shock creasing his features. As the sound ebbed, he pushed himself to his knees and looked over his shoulder.

The bitter smell of gunpowder tinged the air, and a thin wisp of smoke curled from her derringer. Dazed, Julia stared at the place where moonlight now trickled through a penny-sized hole in the wall.

CHAPTER THREE

Astonished, Marsh's gaze swung back to her. She stared at him, her eyes bright with tears. He hadn't counted on Julia Touchstone. He had definitely not counted on this.

At first sight of her at the saloon, he'd been struck by her petite size. He'd thought she looked delicate, almost fragile. Right now she seemed about as fragile as an anvil.

He released a loud breath, nursing his stinging ear with one hand. "I guess you can shoot that thing after all."

Bleak green eyes stayed locked on him.

He rubbed his chin, compelled to assure her that he intended no harm, hoping to convince her to change her mind about allowing him to stay. "I understand why you don't want anything to do with this."

"How could you?" she asked bitterly, the fear slowly leaving her eyes.

"Because . . ." *I lost someone too.* But he couldn't say the words. After Beth's death, he'd vowed never to risk anyone because of his job again, and now Julia Touchstone had recognized him. How?

"Ma! Ma!" shouted a boy's voice. "We heard a shot!"

"What on earth is going on?"

An older woman rushed into the barn, followed by a young boy who limped. Upon seeing Marsh, both of them jerked to a halt. They looked from Julia to Marsh and back again.

Astonishment rounded the boy's eyes. "Ma, did you shoot that man?"

Marsh's gaze darted to Julia's. She stared at the gun in her hand as if seeing it for the first time. Horror crossed her features. At another time he might have found the instantaneous change funny; instead, it brought an ache to his heart.

Her gaze moved to her son, and her features softened with vulnerability. Watching her, Marsh's chest ached, and he wondered if Beth had ever felt such devotion for him, if anyone besides his mother would ever feel that for him.

"Julia Ann, are you all right?" The older woman frowned and moved closer to Julia.

The boy followed, favoring his right foot. Though his eyes were bright with excitement, his voice was subdued. "Ma?"

Julia looked bereft.

Marsh stepped up, feeling an alien twinge of regret about his job. "I'm afraid it's my fault. I startled her."

The boy moved next to Julia and put an arm around her waist. The older woman did the same on the other side, watching warily. "I'm Julia's mother," she said. "Perhaps I can help you?"

Even from where he stood, Marsh could see that tremors still tripped through Julia's body. Was she afraid of *him?*

"No!" She suddenly snapped out of her dazed state. "No, Mother, don't!"

The other woman drew back, alarmed.

"I mean—" Julia pulled the boy close and hugged him tight. "I'll take Pete inside and you direct this man to town." Her voice shook as she said pointedly, "Perhaps someone there can help him."

The boy pressed closer to his mother but eyed Marsh curiously. "But, Ma—"

"Everything's fine, Pete. Your gran can handle it."

The boy balked, obviously wanting to stay and see what the commotion had been about. But finally he went with her.

Julia stopped beside her mother and whispered something. The older woman's eyes widened, her gaze shifting to Marsh. So Julia had told her mother who he was.

Mother and son walked out the door, her steps matching her son's uneven ones. Pete cast a last look over his shoulder before disappearing.

"What exactly is going on here?" Julia's mother folded her arms and regarded Marsh with determined authority.

Though never easily intimidated, he decided it wouldn't be prudent to alienate the mother as he had done the daughter. Julia's mother looked to be in her fifties, about his own mother's age.

Though the hair was a darker gold than her daughter's, the eyes were the same vibrant green. Dressed in a fawn-colored shirt and split skirt, she could have been Julia's sister.

But where her daughter's eyes were wide and serious, the older woman's eyes sparkled with an impishness, an ever-present squint of laughter that he had also noticed in her grandson. Pete seemed also to have inherited her height and long legs, while Julia was petite.

"So?" She tapped her foot impatiently. "You're from the Pinkerton agency?"

Out of habit, Marsh glanced warily over his shoulder. Gyp waited in the darkness, invisible except for the intelligent gleam of his eyes. The dog was a damn sight smarter than he was, he thought wryly. At least Gyp had stayed out of sight. "Yes, ma'am."

"I see." She nodded as if she had solved a riddle, angling the lantern so she could study his features. Cautiously, she extended her hand. "I'm India Blackwell."

He shook her hand. "Marsh Tipton, ma'am."

"I don't suppose that's your real name?" She laughed. "Of course not. How safe would you be if you gave your real name?"

He smiled, bemused. She seemed much easier to deal with than her daughter. He reached inside his vest pocket for the letter he usually carried in his boot sole. "I have a letter from Mr. Pinkerton, if you'd like to see it."

"Fiddle! As if you couldn't write that yourself. What I'd like to know is if you're wearing any other weapons."

"Ma'am?" She couldn't know about the knife in his boot.

"Come now, Mr. Tipton. I *have* read adventure novels, and the dashing hero always conceals a weapon. Perhaps a knife hidden in your sleeve, or a small pistol tucked in your waistband just so?"

"Is that right?" He grinned before he realized it. "Sorry to disappoint you, ma'am. I guess you wouldn't find me in any book."

"Hmmm." She cocked her head. "Was Julia really going to shoot you?"

"I'm not sure." He rubbed his neck, massaging the tight muscles. "She looked serious about it."

"Why didn't you defend yourself?"

"I couldn't pull a gun on her!"

"She pulled one on you."

"True enough," he conceded with a shrug.

"Were you a friend of John's?"

"I met him only once, but admired his work greatly."

"Yes, he was quite something else." She studied Marsh with openness and friendly curiosity. "Why did Pinkerton send you?"

Marsh hesitated, unwilling to chance the same kind of reaction he'd gotten from Julia Touchstone.

"You certainly don't have to tell me, but I may be able to help you." She smiled kindly. "My daughter doesn't appreciate men in your line of work."

"I got that impression," he said dryly, reluctant to reveal more details about his job. On the other hand, two women already knew the one thing that could get him killed—that he was an agent. "It's about the Thompson gang."

"Have you captured them?" Her eyes lit with hope.

"Not yet, but I'm trying." He quickly explained about his

request for a job and Julia's refusal. "So I followed her here, planning to convince her to hire me."

"Telling her who you work for would hardly do that," India Blackwell said quietly.

His mouth twisted. "I didn't tell her. She knew somehow. I never figured . . ." He shrugged, still amazed that she had recognized him.

India's frown cleared as realization stole across her features. "Ah, yes. The photograph." At Marsh's perplexed look, she explained. "Allan gave John a photograph of the men who helped establish the Kansas City office."

"Oh." Her explanation kindled a surge of frustration. Marsh preferred complete anonymity, but he'd make this situation work to his advantage. "It's best if no one else knows."

"So you're staying?"

He had seen the color drain from Julia's face and recognized her fear. How many times had he seen that same fear in Beth's eyes and done nothing? His gut had wrenched with a sudden responsibility to comfort Julia, reassure her. Leaving was probably the only way to do that, but he couldn't.

"Too many men have died because of Scotty Thompson and his gang," he said. "I can't ignore the information I've gotten or be swayed from the case just because your daughter doesn't want to cooperate, ma'am."

"No, I don't suppose you can." She eyed him speculatively, as if she suspected that he had other reasons. "Are you saying that men besides John have died trying to catch this outlaw and his gang?"

"Yes, ma'am." Disquiet inched through him. How much of a problem would Julia Touchstone cause? "Every time we get closer to discovering their whereabouts, they discover our man and kill him."

"More than one?"

"Five, in fact."

India gasped. "Oh, my goodness."

He sensed that she might be convinced to help him, but how much did he tell her? Only what was necessary to make her understand, he decided. "Thanks to John, we know they have a contact in Spinner. I need a legitimate job, a way to stay in close contact with the people here."

"And that's why you approached Julia about the job." She tapped her foot, frowning a bit. "So you would live here, work on the farm, and gather information?"

He hesitated. He didn't want any trouble here, certainly not with two women. "Your daughter made it very clear that she's not interested."

"Yes, I'm sure she did, but this is *my* place, Marsh. If I choose to hire someone, then I will. Perhaps you should've been talking to me all along."

He studied her, contemplating the odds of Julia Touchstone throwing him out. Or, worse, revealing his true motives for being in Spinner.

India's eyes glinted. "We do need someone around the place. Another twenty acres should be cleared for alfalfa, and there are several repairs that need to be made. I trust you can handle a saw and a hammer?"

"Mrs. Blackwell, we could all be in danger if your daughter decides to reveal my real identity."

"Just consider Julia another risk of your job. Come now, Marsh. I'm offering you what you want."

He still felt uncomfortable about Julia's vehement objections, but he'd been sent to do a job. He grinned. "You'll hardly know I'm here. I'll stay in the barn and—"

"Mother, what are you doing?" Julia sailed through the doorway, a look of alarm and betrayal on her features.

India said gently, "I'm doing the right thing. I'm trying to help."

Julia's gaze, accusing and angry, shot to Marsh. "Why can't you just leave?" She turned to India. "Don't do this, Mother."

He kept his gaze glued on Julia, his heart twinging as he remembered the earlier emptiness in her lovely eyes. He recognized that void too—he had felt it since Beth's death.

"I think we should give him a chance," India said.

"No!" Julia's gaze raked over him.

His body, long dormant, tingled with awareness, and his gaze slid over her in return.

She stiffened, and resentment hardened her green eyes. "No."

"Julia, honey, I don't think—"

"Mother, you can't seriously consider this."

"Mrs. Touchstone," Marsh tried. "Please just hear me out."

"I don't care how you explain it," she said hotly. "You're still putting my son at risk."

"It wouldn't be like that." He struggled to keep a rein on his temper.

Her eyes blazed with green fire. "You can put the notion out of your head. And tell Allan Pinkerton the same."

Marsh noted the desperation beneath her anger and gentled his voice. "I need a cover, and you're my best chance for one."

"Did you see my boy?" Rage and pain darkened her features. "*Did* you? He will walk that way the rest of his life. Do you know why? Because of my husband's precious job. I won't let him be involved in anything like this."

"He won't be. I give you my word."

"And what is that worth in the middle of a gunfight?"

Marsh reined in his frustration. "I'd think you would want to apprehend the men who hurt him."

"Don't patronize me. You can't guarantee he won't be hurt."

"No, I can't." He heaved a sigh and turned to India. "I didn't come here to cause problems, Mrs. Blackwell."

"Then go," Julia urged. "Please."

He studied her. Not for the first time, he was unwelcome, but there was too much at stake here to leave. How much had he taken on with the Touchstone widow? "I'm sorry, but I can't. You'll be safe, you and your son."

"You can't promise something like that," she said sadly, and walked out.

He watched her go, fighting anger and frustration and a crazy urge to follow her. She needed him and she didn't even know it.

India turned to face him. "I'm sorry. She'll soon understand that this is the only way she and Pete can move on with their lives."

Marsh didn't know what she meant and didn't want to know. "Do you think she's angry enough to ruin my cover?"

"And tell people what you're really doing here?"

He nodded.

"No. Absolutely not."

"Good." Marsh didn't believe her one whit. "I won't let your grandson get involved, Mrs. Blackwell."

"I believe you won't."

She bade him good night and Marsh followed her to the barn door, watching until she disappeared inside the house. Gyp nudged his leg, and he reached down to rub the dog's head. "I should've followed your lead and stayed out of sight."

The shepherd thumped his tail as though agreeing.

Marsh released a breath born of frustration and started down the road to get Sarge. Gyp followed. About a half mile away in a stand of hickory trees, Marsh collected the big gray gelding and the three of them returned to the Touchstone place.

He halted next to the oak where he'd hidden earlier and stared at the house. Regret and curiosity mingled. He had followed Julia from town in order to persuade her to hire him, never imagining that she would fathom who he was.

He didn't appreciate her obvious resentment toward Pinkerton's agency, but he understood it. He had hated the job for causing Beth's death, while holding on to the connection with quiet desperation. In the end, the job was all he had left, and it was the one thing that had enabled him to survive this long.

The moon hung heavy and full in a clear black sky and light flowed over the surrounding landscape. A sprawling oak tree stood in the center of the yard. Knee-high grass, deep green despite summer's end, rippled in a slight breeze.

The house faced south, a modest white frame that wasn't large, but still almost more than three people needed and clearly visible from the road.

Moonlight flowed onto the porch, sketching a large window on his left and another slightly smaller one on his right. Perhaps a parlor or a bedroom? The door, too, had a paned glass window that was covered with a curtain.

A porch ran the length of the house, set off by a waist-high rail. A swing hung on the east end. Behind the house, he could see a grove of trees, and farther up a small hill was a heavily wooded area.

Despite Julia's refusal to hire him, Marsh was her new farmhand. Irritation rose. The more people who knew about his cover, the greater the risk.

On the other hand, her full knowledge could work to his advantage. He was in a prime place to gather information, and that was more important than her knowledge of his real identity.

Scotty Thompson and his gang had to be stopped. Whatever he had to do, Marsh wouldn't let anything happen to Julia Touchstone or her boy. He'd sworn to that with his life.

Julia stood in the doorway of Pete's bedroom and watched him. He sat at the small desk next to his bed, hunched over the open middle drawer. A stubby candle flickered beside him and cast shadows through the room.

On the wall hung the tintype of John, Julia, and a month-old Pete. Since John's death, Pete had kept a discarded nail box full of his father's things.

Inside the box were a lock of John's hair and a wooden duck call that he had given Pete for his last birthday. John's gold watch, a gift from the Pinkerton family, was inscribed with the firm's symbol, an all-seeing eye, and underneath, the words WE NEVER SLEEP.

Pete's hand closed over the watch, and her heart clenched.

"Ma?"

"Yes, sweetie?"

He turned to look at her. "Are you okay?"

"Of course I am." She walked into the room, stopping beside the chair to ruffle his hair. "You should douse that candle and go to sleep. It's past time, you know."

"I was worried about you." He carefully replaced the items and closed his wooden box. "You looked pretty scared out there in the barn."

"I suppose I was." She'd never shot at anyone before. Sinking down onto the edge of his bed, she met her son's eyes, which looked older than any eight-year-old's should.

He stared solemnly at her. "Was it because of that man?"

"Yes. He startled me." It was more than that. Marsh Tipton, or whoever he was, had unleashed an icy fear that Julia had managed to blanket with activity and denial for the past year.

Pete rose and stepped toward her, draping an arm around her neck. "I won't let anything happen to you, Ma."

Her throat closed up and she hugged him tight. "I know that, honey," she choked out.

He plopped down beside her on the bed. "He seemed nice."

Julia could read the loneliness beneath the words. Pete wanted a new friend, a *male* friend. As much as he loved his mother and grandmother, she knew he missed a masculine presence in his life.

Despite his tender years, or perhaps because of what had happened during them, Pete saw himself as the man of the house. She knew he was lonely, knew he carried burdens no child should have to carry. He worried about her as much as she worried about him, and she hated that, hated the injury that had caused him to.

She stroked his head and her heart squeezed. *Why, Lord? Why Pete?*

Countless times since her son had been injured last year, she had asked the question, until it seemed as much a part of her as breathing. There was no answer. There never would be.

And living in the past, dwelling on the trouble that John had left behind, wouldn't change that.

CHAPTER FOUR

The past closed in on Julia like the steel-tipped jaws of a trap.

India had been wrong to allow Marsh Tipton to stay on in the guise of a hired hand, and the next day her actions still stung. She knew that Julia had vowed to never involve Pete in anything even marginally dangerous.

That Sunday afternoon, Julia stood in the open, airy bedroom beside the heirloom bed that was too big and lonely for one person. Because of John's prolonged absences, they hadn't shared this bed often, but the memories were there along with John's things.

Pete was outside, and her mother was lunching in town with a group of widows from church. Marsh Tipton was nowhere to be seen. Julia wished he were gone for good, but knew he wasn't. She had told Pete that Gran had hired the man and warned her son to be careful around him.

After she had cleaned the saloon that morning, she had met Pete and India at church. Riley had joined Julia and Pete for lunch at the house and left about an hour before. He hadn't asked about Marsh Tipton and she hadn't mentioned their new hand. All day India had given Julia a wide berth, letting her temper die down.

Late August heat, suffocating and thick, crowded into the bedroom. Even the window, opened so she could hear Pete outside, didn't admit cooler air.

She didn't care what Marsh Tipton promised. After all this time, it was unlikely he would be able to capture the Thompson gang. All he had done was stir up vicious memories.

He and her mother could do as they wished, but she refused to dwell on the past anymore. In this bedroom were the last visible reminders of John. Julia had put it off for fifteen months, but today she would pack away his clothes and belongings.

She licked her suddenly dry lips, willing away the sense that she shouldn't disturb his things, the feeling she still had sometimes that John would walk through the door. He would never walk through their door again.

Quaaaack. The simulated sound of a duck call came through the window. Pete passed and flashed her a smile. Her heart twinged, as it always did when she saw her son's uneven gait.

He walked carefully, but still more briskly than she liked. Setting down a crate in front of the wardrobe, she smiled and moved to the window. "Slow down. You'll wear yourself out."

"Oh, Ma," he groaned, slowing his awkward gait a fraction. For her benefit only, she knew.

He limped to the west end of the porch and eased down to sit, again taking care only because she was looking. If alone, he would plop down just as any normal child, whether it hurt his leg or not.

She watched her eight-year-old son, his fair hair burnished to platinum by the sun. He had John's blond coloring and a gold-flecked combination of her green and John's brown eyes.

Despite Pete's injury, his eyes still sparkled with the excitement and energy of a typical young boy. He'd handled his lameness much better than she. His attitude had remained the same exuberant, mischievous one he'd been born with. Only his pace had changed.

The stillness of the day was broken by the sound of galloping hoofbeats. India, on a dainty roan mare, flew across the thick grass toward the house.

"Gran!" Pete struggled to his feet, steadying himself with a hand wrapped on the porch post. "Go, Gran!"

India urged the horse into a flat-out run, then reined to a skidding stop in front of the boy.

"Voilà!" She removed her flat-brimmed hat with a flourish and bowed at the waist, holding her seat with the practiced ease of a lifelong rider. A passion for horses flowed in the veins of all Blackwell women, including Julia, but her mother seemed to share some secret language with the animals.

Pete clapped and laughed. "More, Gran. More."

India pulled up the mare's head and the horse danced on her hind legs, as much a showoff as Julia's mother. Horse and rider spun in a pirouette, then the mare dropped her two front legs gracefully to the ground and bent, dipping her head in a mock bow.

Julia smiled despite the lingering hurt of her mother's disregard for her feelings about Marsh Tipton's presence.

Pete grinned. "Someday I'm gonna have me a horse like Ginger, Gran. 'Cept he'll be a boy. One that can do tricks, and when I whistle, he'll come."

"I know you will." India dismounted and reached for the saddle bag draped across the front of the saddle. "Would you like to practice on Ginger?"

"Mother," Julia warned, leaning farther out the window.

India shot her a disapproving look over Pete's head, but her voice was ebullient. "Go on, Pete. Just remember to be careful. Ginger won't do anything you don't tell her to do."

He stepped toward the horse, then turned with a pleading look. "It's okay, isn't it, Ma?"

"Of course," she said lightly, curbing the urge to follow, to watch, to help. She was unable to deny her son this small pleasure, but neither could she squash the anxiety she constantly carried. "I know you'll do as Gran says."

India hoisted Pete into the saddle and he leaned over to

stroke the mare's neck, speaking softly to her. He clucked to her and waved as he rode toward the barn.

"Come straight back." Julia chided herself even as she said the words. He was a good boy, and even though he might want to go exploring, he knew how she worried, so he wouldn't.

India stepped onto the porch and shot her an exasperated look. She turned away. Her mother believed Julia was too protective of Pete, but she couldn't help herself. When she had found him and John last year, she had feared Pete dead.

As it was, he had been left a cripple, stripped of feats that other eight-year-old boys took for granted. To go to the creek without their mother tagging along. To run and skip and climb trees. Besides his father, things such as that had been taken from him as well.

The front door clicked shut as India came inside. Julia opened the wardrobe door, and the earthy masculine scent of her husband floated out, tinged with a hint of sandalwood from his shaving lotion. Regret and longing and sadness rippled through her.

Her mother stepped into the bedroom, pulling off her riding gloves. "May I come in?"

"Yes."

"Oh." India's voice was subdued. "You're going through John's things?"

"I decided to pack them up," she said with forced brightness.

"I see." India's tone said that she knew Julia was closing the door on the past, refusing to believe that Marsh Tipton could be the key to keeping it closed.

Julia stared into the wardrobe, at the sack coats and trousers hanging neatly on pegs where John had left them. Her chest tightened and she murmured, "I shouldn't have waited so long to do this."

India tossed her gloves on the bed and walked over to stand beside her daughter. "I could go through his clothes if you'd like."

"Yes, thank you." She met India's gaze, biting back her frustration at their differences. "I'll gather his shaving things and undergarments. And his books."

Her mother nodded, and Julia turned toward the broad three-drawer bureau on the far wall. John's shaving mug, brush, and razor sat on one corner of the age-dimpled oak piece.

Though she and her mother kept the room dusted, a thin film covered the articles. John's beloved tintype of him with Allan Pinkerton and the other agents was stashed in the bottom drawer. She reached inside for it first, her jaw clenching as she recognized Marsh Tipton. Quickly she stuffed it into the crate.

"You're still angry at me," India said quietly.

She reached for the shaving mug and cradled it in her hands. "You know I don't want Pete exposed to any danger."

"I don't believe Marsh will put him in danger."

Julia turned, trying to keep her voice low even though panic clawed at her. "How can you say that? Just the fact that he's here puts Pete, all of us, in danger. I don't understand, Mother."

India was silent for a moment, folding a sack coat and placing it in the bottom of the crate. "Julia, I never criticized you for the way you dealt with your grief over John."

"What does that have to do with Marsh Tipton?"

"I loved John too," India said. "And I want those outlaws to pay for what they did to him and to Pete."

"I'm thinking of Pete," Julia said hotly. "Having that man here won't be good for him!"

"Oh, Julia." Pain glittered in India's eyes. "What happened to him last year was terrible and tragic, but you can't shelter the boy from everything."

"Yes, I can. At least things like this." Sadness and loss and bitterness bubbled up inside her. She didn't want to feel those things, had felt them for far too long.

India draped a pair of trousers over her arm. "When I thought Pinkerton's had given up the search, I was willing to live with the fact that the Thompsons might never be brought to justice. I didn't want to cause you further pain."

"Then why allow him to stay? Why welcome him?"

"When I met Marsh last night, I realized he can catch the Thompson gang."

Feeling a new stab of anger and pain, Julia took a shuddery breath. "John was the best agent Pinkerton ever had, and he couldn't get them. It's been over a year since Pinkerton has even looked, and he comes here! Why? The Thompsons haven't been back."

"They have, Julia." India placed the trousers into the box, then reached into the wardrobe for another pair. "Or at least around here."

She shot her mother an exasperated look. "I think I would've heard if the Thompsons had been around here."

"Evidently, other men worked on this case after John did." Disquiet clouded India's eyes. "They were found out and killed."

"What are you talking about?" Alarm thumped at her. "I've heard nothing like that."

"Marsh told me."

"Marsh." Julia's lips twisted. "I don't really want to hear what *Marsh* said."

India looked about to argue, then nodded. "All right."

They worked in silence for several minutes. The vague scent of spice floated to her, and Julia stared down at the undergarments clutched in her hands.

The smell unleashed a flurry of memories—of their courting days, of the first commendation John had received from the governor for capturing a renowned criminal, of that day late spring when she had seen him lifeless and covered in blood.

Don't think about it. She shoved the clothes into the crate and turned to pick up his shaving things.

"There's something in here." Concern deepened India's voice.

Julia turned to find her mother holding a pair of John's

trousers and examining the seat. Several dark stains marred the wheat-colored material, and she stared, startled by the sight of the trousers John had been wearing when he died.

Her heart tripled its beat and she suddenly felt light-headed. "Mother, what are you doing?"

"Look at this." India turned the trousers inside out and spread the material across her hand, pointing to an attachment at the waist. "This lining is like a big pocket, and there's something in there. Don't you hear that crinkling noise?"

"He had those made for all of his trousers." She turned back to the bureau and reached for the shaving mug.

Her mother reached around her to grab the razor. "I think there's paper in here." She sliced at the waist seam, her voice rising excitedly. "Yes, I see it."

"Paper?" Julia glanced over her shoulder. "Why would there be—Mother?"

India's face had turned ashen and her eyes were bleak with pain and uncertainty.

"What is it?" Alarm tripped through her and Julia moved closer.

Her mother held out three sheets of paper. "These are in John's handwriting."

"What?" She took the papers and stared at them. Brown smears—blood—smudged the edges of the top page. A chill raked across her back and she turned away. "It's probably nothing, most likely scribbles he made when he was bored."

"They're not scribbles. John never wrote down anything," India protested, her voice pitched queerly. "Never."

Julia's fingers tightened on the paper. It was true. John had never written down a thing in all the time she'd known him because he'd never had a need. He could look at a page in a book or a sign or a map and recall every detail with uncanny clarity. His amazing memory was one of the qualities that had made him such a great detective.

She glanced at the top page. Underneath the bloodstains

was a message written in her husband's neat hand. *Thompson contact suspected in Spinner. Not yet sure who.*

Dread clotted her throat and foreboding swept over her. Julia sank down onto the soft mattress. *No, no, no!*

"What does it say, honey?"

She shot up from the bed and thrust the entire sheaf of papers into the crate. She didn't want to know, didn't want to be reminded. She wanted only to live with her mother and her son in peace.

India plucked the papers from the box. "Oh, my goodness."

Julia squeezed her eyes shut. She hated it when her mother got that awed tone of doom in her voice.

"Oh, my goodness."

"Mother—"

"I think you'd better look at this, Julia."

"John is gone and that stuff doesn't matter anymore."

"I—" India paused, reading more. In spite of herself, Julia looked over at her mother.

India's eyes clouded with grim realization. "These pieces of paper might be able to help us find those murdering Thompsons."

"Stop it!" Panic sharpened her voice. "Sheriff Kisling couldn't find them. The federal marshal couldn't find them. Nor, for that matter, could Mr. Allan Pinkerton and all his *special* detectives. What makes you think you can figure it out?"

"Because I think John left us some evidence."

Julia exhaled and turned back to the bureau, yanking out socks and suspenders and handkerchiefs, throwing them all into the crate. She fought to keep her voice even. "Stop."

"Listen to me, Julia Ann. This has to mean something."

"It means that those papers were in his—" Her voice broke, but she forged on, trying to sound calm. "In his hidden pocket whenever he was killed. Those smudges are blood, Mother."

"There's a map here."

She pressed her fingers against her throbbing temples. "A map of what?"

"I don't know. It doesn't say."

"That doesn't seem very useful as evidence, then, does it?" She reached into the bottom drawer and her fingers brushed something smooth. She pulled out another tintype, this one of Allan Pinkerton with John and Pete when Pete was just a year old.

"It looks like a creek and some kind of cave."

Oh, how Julia resented his job! And the Pinkerton detective agency. She shoved the tintype into the crate.

Her resentment had grown over the last few years of John's life as he had stayed away for longer periods of time, coming home only when he could free himself without suspicion from the outlaw gang into which he had managed to insinuate himself.

"And this last piece is a wire. It says, 'Send to St. Louis.' It's an announcement of a bank robbery and—oh, my goodness."

Julia's nerves coiled with tension. "Mother, please!"

"Here's the date of the robbery—oh, my goodness," she whispered.

"Throw it in the fireplace or pack it with John's things. Can't you understand how much I hate talking about this?"

India's voice rose. "Julia, this bank robbery was one of the most brazen heists ever staged, and they took more money than anyone ever had before. Even the James boys. And it was right here in Spinner."

"In Spinner?" Dread uncurled in her belly and she turned slowly to stare at her mother. "But . . . that robbery was three weeks after John died."

India nodded, worry creasing her features.

"Then how could he write a notice to the newspaper about it? And why would he do such a thing?"

"I don't know. Obviously he knew it was going to happen."

"Well, he was right." Julia stood up, her throat burning. "So what does that prove? Nothing!"

"You might be right," India said slowly, looking up. "There could be nothing to it, but we can't take that chance."

"What do you mean?"

"We should show these things to Marsh, let him decide."

"No!" Julia cried, astounded at the vehemence of her protest. "Absolutely not."

"Marsh said that Pinkerton's has been working on this case since John's death. He told me that four other men have been killed, and all of them were close to getting Scotty Thompson."

Shock rocked through Julia. "That's horrible."

"That means Allan never stopped looking, never stopped trying to get the Thompsons."

"And now he's just sent another man to his death, although Marsh Tipton seems willing enough to me," Julia said darkly.

India studied her for a moment, then seemed to reach a decision. "I can't refuse to help him, Julia. Not when it might bring those horrible men to justice. I can't believe you can refuse him either."

"Well, I *can*." The past crept through the room like an insidious shadow, grasping with invisible fingers that strangled her air, her freedom. Her peace. "Doesn't it tell you anything that all these men have died? This . . . this renowned detective agency—with who knows how many men at its disposal—can't even catch these outlaws."

She tried desperately to push away the fear churning inside her. "In fact, they're responsible for getting John killed. And you want to show them these papers and open the way for more men to die? John never would've carried around anything that might jeopardize his case. Those papers *can't* mean anything."

"Maybe he didn't mean to be carrying them around. Maybe he was planning to give them to someone. To Allan. And he was killed before he could."

"Mother," Julia begged in a broken voice. "Please."

"You can't ignore this just because you're afraid."

"I'm afraid for Pete! Look what happened to him."

India hesitated a moment. "Maybe it's only because I want to believe it, but I think Marsh can catch those bastards who murdered John. He looks like a man who never gives up."

"That's exactly what I don't like about him," Julia murmured, glancing out the window toward the barn.

India stared solemnly at her daughter, then at the papers in her hand. "It's your decision, of course, but I hope you'll reconsider and let Marsh look at these."

"I don't think that's the right thing for me and Pete." She massaged her pounding temples. "Please say you understand."

"You must handle it as you see fit."

At her mother's disappointed look, Julia's heart sank even though she was grateful she wouldn't be badgered further. "Thank you."

India hugged her daughter fiercely. "I love you."

"I know." Julia gave a shaky smile.

Her mother rose and briskly folded the bloodstained trousers, placing them in the crate. She and Julia finished in silence, then India walked out to start supper.

Julia picked up the crate, staring down at the papers her mother had left on the bed. There should have been no visible reminders of John or his death or his job.

If you had to write something down, John, why did it have to be this? How could she ignore that these papers might be important?

How could she bear for her son's life to be threatened again? To risk every foundation she'd struggled to rebuild this last year?

Pete's awkward footsteps sounded across the porch, and she reflexively stuffed the papers into the crate. Hefting it up, she marched out to the barn and climbed the ladder into the loft, storing the box in the far corner under a tuft of hay.

Then she made her way down the ladder and walked out of
the barn.

She wouldn't be drawn into the web of the past, seduced
by the hope of justice or the promise in Marsh Tipton's silver eyes. The significance of those papers, if ever there was
any, had diminished.

She wanted to believe that. She did believe that. So why
couldn't she dismiss the cold knot of dread in her stomach?

CHAPTER FIVE

Marsh couldn't stop thinking about the scene in the barn with Julia Touchstone. For the first time since Beth, he'd felt the need to protect someone, and Julia had made it clear she didn't want his "protection."

Whereas India was direct with an easy manner, there was nothing easy about her daughter. Yet a compelling part of her reached deep inside him and tied him in knots.

Was it the sadness in her green eyes? He understood that sadness, had lived with his own for three years. But there was also a tug of desire, totally physical and potent.

Despite her loudly voiced objections, excitement had stirred low in his belly at the emerald fire flashing in her eyes. Fire that licked at him even now.

He shoved away the feelings, disgusted because he knew the pull was more than physical. He could get physical release anywhere. He felt an emotional connection to Julia, probably forged by their common association with Pinkerton, but there all the same. Marsh didn't like it.

Do your job and stay away from her and the kid. He had no problem doing that. All day Sunday he cut down trees on the twenty-acre plot of land that India Blackwell wanted cleared. Just before sunset he and Gyp made their way to the creek he'd spotted behind the house.

Even taking time for the bath, he'd be able to reach town

before dark and have a look around the area where Gordon's
body had been found.

Stripping out of his sweat-dampened shirt and grimy
Levis, he waded in and washed. Gyp jumped in and paddled
to the opposite bank, then back. After guzzling a noisy
drink, he clambered out, shaking himself dry before flop-
ping down on the warm grass.

In the creek Marsh lazed on his back and smoked a cigarette. Red and gold washed the sky. The sun burned orange
as it dipped lower, and crystal water glittered fiery gold in
the glare of the fading afternoon sun.

The gentle lap of the water formed a rhythm in Marsh's
mind, and he gave himself over to the gentle peace of the
place. The creek twisted between a wooded area and an
eight-foot wall of rock that jutted out the side of a hill, its
bluff face stripped of thick grass and dark Missouri dirt by
the elements. Though a clearing stretched beyond the
bank, Marsh was obscured by a thick stand of trees and
bushes.

Bluejays bickered overhead. He could hear the occasional
plop of a surfacing fish and the throaty croaking of a bull-
frog. Smoke from his cigarette curled upward, and Marsh
watched the vibrant sunset through slitted eyes.

With its smooth mud floor, the creek was perfect for
swimming or bathing. Rocks and pebbles dotted the bank
and tiny green shoots scattered in unformed patterns. At its
deepest spot, the water hit Marsh at the middle of his
chest.

Cool water lapped at his body, sliding over him like liquid silk, soothing muscles that ached from overuse. Though
he definitely preferred being outdoors, he hadn't done hard
physical labor in a long time.

He relaxed in the buoyant cradle of water, noticing that
the green of a new plant exactly matched Julia Touchstone's
eyes.

Hell, why did he care about the color of her eyes? Or anything about her, for that matter? He shoved himself out of

the water and walked over to a flat rock, jerking up the towel he'd brought.

He was drawn to her despite her resentment, despite his reason for being there. Because, as much as he disliked it, he understood her anger toward the job.

He'd felt that same blind, desperate rage after Beth had died. Conflicting feelings of damnation and grace. Because of his job, Beth had turned to another man, so determined to leave Marsh that she had taken a careless risk and died. He lived with that guilt every day.

But the job had also saved his life. After Beth, he'd had only the job, and if his life was more one of survival and quiet desperation, he never questioned it. He was able to do some good in the world, and when he no longer was, it would be time to go.

Julia Touchstone had a deceptive strength which enabled her to go forward with almost blind optimism. Until she'd been faced with him.

She had a legitimate right to her anger, and he wanted that anger to be the only connection they had, wanted that to work to his advantage as well as erect a natural distance between them, for everyone's safety. He'd have only minimal interaction with them, less than even a hired hand was expected to have. Which should be easy enough.

He pulled on his Levis, leaving them unfastened as he shrugged into his shirt.

Gyp emitted a low growl and rose slowly, facing the trees. Marsh heard a noise at the same time. Someone strode through the brittle grass, hesitantly but loudly. The hair on the dog's neck rose.

"Hi!" The boy, Pete, emerged from a thicket and lifted a hand in greeting. "My gran says you're gonna work at the farm for a while."

"Yep." Marsh kept his voice cool and uninviting. He looked over the kid's head for signs of his mother. Julia Touchstone would have a fit if she found the boy with him.

Pete limped closer, his progress stilting and slow. Today

he didn't favor his right leg overmuch. He stopped in front of Marsh and extended his hand. "I'm Pete."

He switched his smoke to his left hand and shook. "Marsh Tipton."

"Nice to meet you." Pete smiled and stuck his thumbs in his waistband. "It's nice to have another man here. It can get a little overwhelming with two women."

"I guess so." Bemused, Marsh's lips twitched.

If he packed up his duds, the kid would probably get the hint. Now that his idyll had been interrupted, he was eager to get to Spinner.

Gyp trotted through the tall grass, coming over to sniff the bottom of Pete's trousers.

"Hey, is this your dog?" The boy's eyes widened with pleasure, and he reached out a hand, allowing Gyp to get his scent. "He's huge. What's his name?"

"Gyp." Marsh bent and ground his cigarette into the wet mud of the bank. He gazed out over the wooded meadow, wondering how long it would be before Julia came looking for her son. "Where's your ma?"

"In the house with Gran." Pete sat down on the ground and tugged off his shoes and stockings. "They're arguing about you."

"Is that right?" Surprised, he turned to the kid. Julia Touchstone had obviously been frightened last night. Was she frightened of *him?*

"I wouldn't fret." Pete stood up and unfastened his pants, then pushed them down. "They argue about me all the time. My gran says Ma doesn't let me do enough." The shirt came off, muffling his voice. "You know, because of my leg."

"Yeah. Mind if I ask why you're takin' off your clothes?"

"I'm gonna swim." The boy smiled blindingly. "Like you."

"I took a bath," Marsh offered absently, scanning the clearing and the trees beyond.

Pete cocked his head. "Are you from around here? You talk real slow and thicklike."

He grinned. "I was raised in Tennessee. I moved to Missouri only a few years ago."

"Is that where your ma is? Tennessee?" Clad only in knee-length drawers, Pete scratched behind Gyp's ears.

"Not anymore. Now she and my father live in St. Louis. They moved there after the war."

Pete waded into the creek. "Do you have creeks like this in Tennessee?"

"Some, but close to my house there's a big lake called Reelfoot."

"Reelfoot? What's that mean?"

"Legend has it that the lake was named for a Chickasaw Indian chief who was born with a club foot. Does your ma know you're down here?"

"She doesn't like me to come down here alone. But you're here, so I'm not alone."

"I don't think she would like that any better," Marsh muttered, wondering if he should coax or order the kid out of the water.

Pete glanced over his shoulder. "She's been kinda skittish since last year, when my pa died."

"I can understand that. She might not want you swimming right now, hmmm? Especially with—"

"My pa was a Pinkerton detective. Do you know what that is?"

"Yeah, sure." Tension stretched across his shoulders. He thought about rolling another cigarette but suddenly felt uncomfortable about smoking in front of the boy.

"He was the best detective ever. Mr. Pinkerton said so at his funeral last year." Pete waded in until the water reached his slender waist. "Anyway, that's when my leg was hurt. And Ma was hurt too."

"What happened to her?" Marsh stepped closer to the bank. He hadn't heard that Julia had been injured.

The boy frowned. The sun shimmered on the water, ringing him in liquid gold. "She wasn't hurt like me. She was hurt on the inside. Know what I mean?"

"Yeah, I think so." He rubbed his chin, wondering what to do. He couldn't leave, especially now that he knew Pete wasn't allowed to be there alone.

"My gran says sometimes invisible scars are the hardest to heal. I don't see how you can have scars if they're invisible, but Gran says I'll understand someday."

A sweet ache squeezed Marsh's heart.

"Watch this!"

Before he could respond, Pete dove beneath the surface. Marsh's breath lodged in his chest and he lunged toward the water. How well could the boy swim?

A splash sounded a few yards in front of him and Pete broke the surface. Waving, he swam toward Marsh with strong, even strokes.

"I'll be," he muttered. "Are you hidin' a pair of gills?"

Pete grinned. "I can dive too. See that rock over there?" He pointed to a flat-topped boulder that jutted out from the face of the hill. Graceful willow branches dipped into the water. "I can jump off and pick up marbles from the bottom."

"Pretty good trick." Marsh could just imagine Julia Touchstone's reaction to that. "Your ma must be proud."

A shadow passed over Pete's face, and Marsh guessed that Julia had no idea of her son's activities at the creek. "I practice a lot."

"A lot that she doesn't know about?"

Pete bobbed up and down in the water, watching Marsh with apprehension. He knew he should make the kid get out and get dressed, but Pete was in no danger, and now he couldn't bring himself to cut short the boy's fun. Another few minutes wouldn't hurt, and Julia would never know.

"Watch how fast I am!" Pete shot through the water to a point several feet away, executed a swift turn, and arrowed back, all with barely a splash.

"Is that good for your leg?" Marsh didn't want to be responsible for the boy harming himself.

Treading water, Pete scraped his wet hair out of his eyes. "It doesn't hurt when I swim."

It made sense, Marsh realized, since there was no weight on his leg during swimming. Perhaps it might even help to regain some strength.

The boy stood and walked toward the bank. "Does your dog do tricks? My gran's horse does."

"He can shake hands."

"Really?" Pete's eyes lit up. He slogged through the water and onto the bank, dropping to his knees in front of Gyp, who wagged his tail exuberantly.

"Shake, boy," Marsh commanded.

Gyp immediately sat and lifted one large paw.

"Wow!" Pete breathed, taking the dog's foot.

"Good boy," Marsh said.

Pete grabbed Gyp in a hug and the dog rested his head on the boy's shoulder, his tail thumping in joy.

"I've always wanted a dog. Ma said we could probably get one after we start our herd. What kind is Gyp?"

"German shepherd."

"He looks like a wolf."

"I guess so." Marsh raised his eyebrows, stifling a smile.

Gyp nudged Pete on the shoulder, then swiped at him with his tongue. Pete pushed playfully at the dog, who barked, then tore wildly back and forth across the bank, spattering them all with mud and water.

Gyp darted past the boy, then spun and lunged. Pete laughed, a full, uninhibited sound that made Marsh smile, and moved out of the water, chasing Gyp into the tall grass of the clearing. The dog flattened himself to the ground, hiding his brindle-colored body. He wagged his tail as Pete advanced on him, emitting a playful growl.

He rolled over on his back and pawed the air, then jumped up and barked again in his excitement. Pete clapped, urging the dog higher. Marsh braced one bare foot against the rough bark of the tree behind him and settled back. Watching the two of them, he pulled out his cigarette paper to roll a smoke.

Barely limping, Pete hurried back over to throw on his clothes. Gyp waited patiently until he was finished, then nudged a stick at him. Pete grinned and threw the stick into the meadow. Barking, the dog tore through the grass, a blur of black, brown, and gray.

When Gyp returned with the stick in his mouth, Pete reached for it. The dog growled playfully and clamped his jaws together. Pete tugged, laughing. Gyp planted his rear on the ground and resisted with all his weight, a playful growl coming from his throat as he battled for control of the stick.

Pete reached up with the one hand, tickling the dog behind the ear. "Give me that stick," he growled at Gyp. "Give me—aaaahhhh."

Eager to play, Gyp released the stick. It shot out of his mouth, then flipped through the air. Losing his balance, Pete tumbled backward into the creek, his scream of surprise changing to a gurgle as he disappeared under the surface.

Marsh's heart thudded painfully. In a flash of panic, he dropped his cigarette makings and lunged, reaching the water in two steps and plowing in heedless of his dry clothes.

A sharp scream split the air and Julia's heartbeat stuttered. *Pete!*

She grabbed up her skirts and bolted out of the woods, her gaze darting over sun-drenched hills and the gold, red, and blue of wildflowers to the clear water beyond. She faltered at a hole, but steadied herself and ran on.

For thirty minutes she had been looking for her son. Expecting him to be in the barn with Marsh Tipton—exactly where she had told him not to go—she had looked there first.

She neared the creek, and in a blur took in the scene. Pete stood at the water's edge. A streak of gray and brown fur—

a wild animal—launched itself straight for him, knocking him into the creek. Marsh Tipton hit the water at a run, and before Pete's head disappeared beneath the surface had snagged his arm and hauled him up.

Cold sweat slicked her nape. She flew over the uneven ground, her heart pumping through her chest. The animal—was it a wolf?—yelped, then stood transfixed as she raced toward him.

Please, Lord. Please, Lord. Her heartbeat drummed the rhythm of the words as she ran. *Please let him be safe.*

With Marsh's help, Pete regained his footing. He sputtered and coughed, water streaming down his face as he watched Julia's approach with dread. Not panic or fear, she realized vaguely. He wasn't drowning, thank goodness.

She planted herself between Pete and the animal, clawing a cabbage-sized rock out of the muddy bank.

The animal's eyes grew wide and it scrambled behind a tree. She could see now that it was a wild dog, not a wolf. She brought back her arm to throw the rock and found her elbow seized in a bruising grip.

"Don't throw that rock."

"Let me go." She pulled against Marsh's unyielding hold. "That beast attacked my son!"

"That *beast* is my dog." He tightened his grip, drawing her closer. Rage shimmered in his eyes, lethal and savage.

"He's a wild animal!" Her gaze shifted to the woods, but there was no sign of the animal. "He can't stay."

"He stays." His words were flat, offering no reassurances, no pretense at even asking permission.

She considered whacking Marsh with the rock, and her muscles tensed again.

"Don't do it, lady," the detective said in a dangerously low tone. "You won't run me behind a tree."

"He almost killed Pete!"

"It's okay, Ma. Honest." Pete shook his head, flinging droplets of water all over her and Marsh as he moved out of the creek. "We were just wrestling."

Her chest hurt. She swallowed, trying to ease the bone-chilling fear she'd felt when she'd seen the dog go for Pete.

"It's the truth," Marsh said quietly, his gaze holding hers. The ferocity in his silver eyes dimmed, but she knew it would return if she threatened the dog. She looked at Pete, who stood on the bank, glancing uncertainly from her to Marsh. "Are you all right?"

He nodded, though he eyed her uneasily. A quick glance confirmed that there was no blood, no cuts, no mark from the animal. He didn't look frightened, merely apprehensive.

Marsh Tipton's bruising hold slackened, and she pulled away, holding out her arms to her son. "Pete."

He came to her, mud sucking noisily at his bare feet. Her breath shuddered out in relief, and Julia hugged him, heedless that his wet clothes soaked her bodice and his fair hair dripped water down her back. Her hands molded his slender shoulders as she breathed in his clean scent.

Marsh stood on the bank beside her, hands braced on his hips. Wet Levi's were plastered to his thick calves. Otter-dark hair, still damp from his bath, gleamed black in the sun, and silver glinted at his temples. Strong hair-dusted toes curled into the mud.

The sight of his bare feet elicited a flutter of sensation in her belly. "Are you all right?" she asked her son.

He nodded.

She set him away from her, looking him over with a critical eye. He was barefooted as well, so his shoes had been saved. "What are you doing down here, young man?"

"That's my fault," Marsh said.

Julia's gaze shot to him. How dare he! She had made her feelings on their association perfectly clear. "You invited Pete down here?"

"No, Ma," her son put in quickly. "He didn't even know I was coming. I followed him from the barn." Pete cast a nervous glance at Marsh. "I waited until he got done with his bath, then I came out. You always said don't come to the

creek alone, and since he was here, I figured it was okay."
He smiled hopefully. "It was, wasn't it?"

She leveled a steady gaze on him. From the corner of her
eye she saw Marsh's dog peeking out from behind a tree.
She could barely reconcile this timid-looking animal with
the beast she'd seen flying through the air moments before.
"Pete, Mr. Tipton has probably been working all day. He
would like to relax."

"He wasn't botherin' me." Marsh flashed a quick smile at
Pete.

Annoyed, Julia continued. "Besides that, you aren't familiar with Mr. Tipton's dog and he could've hurt you."

"We were just playin'," Pete insisted.

"Just playing!" she cried. "You could've drowned."

"No, he's a good swim—" Marsh began to say.

"I'm okay," Pete interrupted with a pleading glance at
Marsh. "It was an accident. Look, the water isn't even deep.
You can see the bottom." He gestured to the creek behind
him. "Besides, Marsh was here. He would've saved me."

Marsh! Marsh didn't seem to mind that Pete called him
by his first name even though tension coiled through his
body. He snapped his fingers and motioned to the dog.
"Come on, Gyp. It's okay, boy."

The dog crept out from behind the tree and made a wide
circle around Julia to Marsh, keeping a wary eye on her. He
eased down on his haunches gingerly, poised to make another quick escape.

"He's a good dog." Marsh's measured tones told Julia
how much she had angered him. "He's a hell of a lot more
trustworthy than most men I've known."

"If you associated with the kind of men my husband did,
I'm not reassured."

Feeling the dog's watchful gaze, she looked down. Dark
eyes stared unblinkingly at her and she frowned, feeling outmaneuvered by all three males. "What does he want?"

"He's trying to figure out if you're safe."

"If *I'm* safe!"

"He's good with people, especially kids." His words were taut but not sharp. "He would never do anything unless I told him to. He would certainly never hurt Pete."

"He'd best not," Julia said firmly.

The dog tipped his well-shaped head, and she could swear a pleading look passed through his eyes.

Staring up at her with that innocent puppy face, he did look almost harmless, but she couldn't forget the sight of him leaping through the air. "He looked pretty dangerous when I came out of those trees."

Marsh glanced toward the woods, as though trying to see what she had seen. "Maybe, but they *were* just playin' around."

"I'm okay, Ma. Really." Pete put an arm around her waist and hugged her tight.

Not ready to forgive him for scaring the life out of her, she said dryly, "Yes, I see that."

Gyp shifted restlessly and gave a high-pitched whine, as though he were asking a question. He lifted a paw and stared expectantly at her.

She frowned.

"He wants to shake your hand." Pete knelt between the adults and took the dog's paw. "See, Ma? Like this."

Still uncertain about the animal's trustworthiness, she hesitated.

Pete scratched Gyp's ears, looking up at her. "He's real smart. He can tell if you don't like him."

She glanced at Marsh, who watched the whole thing with a stoic face. Then she bent and tentatively gave the dog's rough, furry paw a quick shake.

"Hello, Gyp." She felt silly talking to a dog, though she'd done so plenty of times with the horses. She ran a damp palm down her skirt. "There."

Excitement quivered through his body, and his eyes lit. A smile tugged at her lips.

"He likes you!" Pete cried, beaming. "Doesn't he, Marsh?"

"Looks that way." The detective's lips were flat and grim; his silver gaze burned into her, hinting at more than anger.

Julia shifted, unable to look away from his carved features. His gaze drifted down her body, then snapped back to her face, which caused her to realize where he was trying *not* to look.

The water from Pete's wet clothes had easily soaked the light cotton of her bodice and chemise. She glanced down and saw that her nipples had puckered and now strained against the damp material.

Had Marsh seen that? The thought caused a fine burn to inch beneath her skin, and her hand spread protectively across her chest.

His gaze dragged over her like a slow hand, resting on her lips. Desire and denial mingled in his eyes. Julia's lips parted on a ragged breath and a warmth eddied between her legs.

Fierce longing tightened his angular features for a brief instant before they became unreadable. A muscle flexed in his jaw, and he looked away, staring over her shoulder.

Her cheeks burned. Eager to be away from Marsh's disturbing presence, she wagged a finger at her son. "You know you shouldn't have bothered Mr. Tipton."

She preferred that Pete wasn't *anywhere* with Marsh Tipton, and by the sardonic lift of his eyebrows, the detective knew she felt that way.

"He said I wasn't botherin' him, Ma," Pete wheedled. "Remember, I told you?"

"We'll talk about that later." She tugged at his ear. "It's time to get washed up for supper. Go get your shoes."

"Marsh, you can eat with us!" Pete's features lit with excitement. "You haven't eaten yet, have you? Can't he eat with us, Ma?"

She hesitated, not wanting to seem ungracious, but neither did she want the man's unsettling presence at her dinner table.

"Thanks, Pete, but maybe another time." Marsh's gaze shifted to Julia, and she could tell by the unflinching stare that he knew she didn't want him in her house.

While Pete fetched his shoes and stockings, she said through gritted teeth, "You're here only a day and already my son is doing things he's not supposed to."

Marsh's brows snapped together. "I can't stop the kid from going where he wants." Pete rejoined them, and Marsh said roughly, "I'll be heading into town, Miz Touchstone."

She hated the way he said her name, so formally polite yet mocking. "That doesn't concern me."

"I do work for you, ma'am." A slow grin split his features and white teeth flashed in his sun-weathered face. "Thought you'd want to know."

"Of course." She flushed, annoyed that she had forgotten the role he was playing.

"Besides, I didn't want to alarm you when I returned."

No doubt he was going into Spinner to snoop around, just as John used to do when he would disappear at all hours.

Her disdain must have shown on her face, because his grin grew wider as though he knew it vexed her. "How's the food at the restaurant?"

"Very good," she said stiffly, irked that Marsh Tipton had read her so easily. "Especially the pot roast."

"Sounds good. I'm pretty hungry," he murmured, his silver gaze locking on her mouth.

Julia drew in her breath at his audacity. Awareness clicked along her nerve endings and she became uneasily aware of the secluded spot, the faint whispers of the breeze against her heated skin.

It didn't help that the man stood there with his legs splayed as though claiming territory. His stance was undeniably that of a conqueror, and sensation tiptoed up Julia's spine like a secret caress.

His open blue shirt, thin and faded from use, bracketed a broad, sculpted chest. Dark hair dusted the hard muscles of his chest, then disappeared on his ridged abdomen. Worn Levis hung low on his lean hips.

Naked hips, she realized with a start. The man had on no underclothes! A slow heat unfurled in her belly, and her breasts grew heavy, acutely sensitive. The damp bodice chafed her turgid nipples. Alarmed, Julia reached for Pete's hand. "Let's go, honey."

"Good night, Pete," Marsh called in that sinfully dark Tennessee drawl. "Good night, Miz Touchstone. Enjoy your dinner."

A faint hint of mockery colored his tone, and she flushed, ashamed that she had been so inhospitable. He had, after all, gone straight into the water to save her son.

She turned and said stiffly, "Thank you for helping Pete."

Surprise flashed in his silver eyes. "You're welcome."

She thought she detected a softening in his voice and stared at him for another second before turning away to walk through the clearing and toward the house.

Pete twisted around. "Have fun in town, Marsh. See ya tomorrow."

"You betcha."

Julia tightened her hand on Pete's and walked faster. She wanted that man to stay away from her son. His very presence put Pete at risk. Guilt twinged at that judgment, but she pushed it away.

She wanted to forget about Marsh Tipton. She wanted Pete to forget about him. She wanted the man gone.

CHAPTER SIX

Determined to forget the frankly sensual look Marsh Tipton had given her, Julia seethed all the way back to the house. In spite of herself, she couldn't dismiss the tingle in her nipples or the awareness that still stroked up her spine.

He had completely unnerved her; she'd forgotten about his sham as a hired hand and very nearly blurted out the truth in front of Pete.

Wanting to put as much distance as possible between them, she stepped up her pace.

"Ma?" Pete tugged on her hand, breathing hard. "Wait. I can't—"

"Oh, honey, I'm sorry." She slowed immediately, ashamed to have let Marsh Tipton affect her so much that she had forgotten her son.

Pete caught up to her, his limp more pronounced than usual for this time of day. That was her fault for walking too quickly and tiring him. She hugged him, then took his hand, walking slowly though a restless energy crowded through her.

"Are you gonna spank me?" he asked eagerly.

She drew back in alarm. "No, of course not."

"Oh."

She frowned. Why would he be disappointed not to get a spanking?

"He's nice, isn't he?"

"Am I walking too fast for you?" She didn't want to talk about Marsh. Or think about him.

"He didn't act like he wanted to get rid of me or anything," Pete said happily.

"Hmmm." Julia considered the best way to handle this. She didn't want Pete around Marsh Tipton, and most likely the detective didn't want her son around.

"Gyp is a swell dog. Marsh taught him all those tricks. When we get a dog, I'm gonna teach him some tricks. I bet Marsh would help me."

"Honey, he might not be here then." Disappointment tugged at the realization, but Julia decided it was because Pete would be sad to see the man go, not because she would.

"Oh, yeah. Well, if he is, he can help me, right?"

She glanced at her son, noting his heightened color and the excitement in his bright eyes. Already he was too fond of Marsh Tipton. "Pete, you need to be careful about bothering Marsh."

"Bothering him how?" He stared up at her, his eyes wide with confusion.

She hesitated, torn between how to caution him without telling him all the reasons she didn't want him to associate with Marsh. She wouldn't forbid Pete to spend time with the man. It wasn't fair, plus he would want to know why. Resentment rose at Marsh Tipton for putting her in this position.

"He's here to work, you know," she said gently. "It's all right for you to see him sometimes, but you shouldn't make a nuisance of yourself."

Her son digested that quietly. "Do you think he thought I was a nuisance, Ma?"

"Oh, no, sweetheart. That wasn't what I meant." Julia's heart squeezed at the hurt he was trying to hide. "What I meant was that sometimes after people work a long day, they like to spend some time by themselves. We should respect that."

"But he was takin' a bath."

She bit back a smile. "All right, Pete. Just remember what I said, hmmm?"

"Okay, Ma."

She opened the gate, grimacing when it squealed. The hinge needed to be oiled and the gate, fence, and house needed a new coat of whitewash. With her recent bonus from Tully, she might be able to spare enough for repairs.

Pete walked slowly up the stairs, favoring his leg more than he had in a long time, and a fresh pang of guilt tripped through her.

She picked up a linen sheet her mother had left to dry on the porch rail and folded it, following her son into the house. The smell of toasty bread and savory meat floated through the air.

"Time for dinner," India called from the kitchen.

Julia placed the folded sheet on one of the rockers in the front room and walked into the kitchen. Pete was already in his chair at the table that comfortably seated four people. Her mother pulled a pan of biscuits from the stove and placed them in the center of the table as she took her seat next to Pete.

"What did Gyp do then?" India poured Pete a glass of milk.

"He jumped up in the air and barked, like he was telling me to give him the stick." Pete's eyes sparkled. "I understood exactly what he wanted, like he was really talking to me, Gran."

"He probably was." India smiled at Julia. "I didn't know Marsh had a dog."

"Neither did I," she said dryly.

Her mother grinned.

They bowed their heads and Julia offered grace, adding a silent request for forgiveness of her earlier inattention to Pete's handicap.

She filled her plate with green beans, chicken, and biscuits, forcing all her attention to her meal.

Pete slathered butter on his biscuit and popped it in his mouth. "I bet Marsh would really like these. Can I take him some, Gran?"

"Certainly." She glanced at Julia, who kept her face carefully blank and continued eating. "Why don't you fix three or four of them?"

"Okay." Pete gulped down a drink of milk. "He likes to go barefoot, just like me."

"A man after my own heart." India reached for more green beans.

Julia wished they would stop talking about Marsh Tipton, but she was determined to remain silent on the subject. She didn't want to give Pete the impression that the detective was forbidden. That would make the man too alluring to her son.

"Gyp looks like a wolf, but he's a German shepherd."

"I bet he's beautiful," India said. "I can't wait to see him."

"What's a *German* shepherd?"

"It's a type of breed that originated in Germany."

Pete paused, his fork poised halfway between his mouth and the plate. "Germany. I've heard of that. Where is it, Gran?"

She explained that it was across the ocean and on another continent.

"Is it in Europe?" he asked excitedly. "We studied that in school. I saw Europe on the globe."

Tension pounded behind Julia's eyes.

"Gosh," he breathed. "I wonder if Marsh went to Germany to get Gyp. I bet he's been everywhere."

Julia wished the detective was anywhere other than here. She couldn't escape that heated moment at the creek when his silver gaze had stroked over her with blatant lust. At the memory, her breasts grew heavy.

His look of leashed desire aroused and frightened her, but mostly it annoyed her. Almost as much as hearing his name incessantly throughout her meal. She wanted to scream at her son and mother for being so taken with the man.

"You should've invited him to dinner," her mother said. "Perhaps you can take him a plate."

"No," Julia said emphatically, then shifted restlessly when Pete and India frowned at her. "Er, he's going into town and said he would eat at the restaurant."

"Oh, yeah, Ma told him to get the pot roast."

"I see." India's voice tightened in disapproval. "When he returns, you can take him a piece of pie, Pete."

Julia sighed. Was everyone going to be mad at her today because of Marsh Tipton? "He said he probably wouldn't be back until late."

Her mother nodded, curiosity replacing the irritation on her face.

Through the remainder of their meal, Pete and India discussed every tedious facet of Marsh Tipton, from his dog to his cigarettes. The pounding in Julia's head steadily increased.

She rose to clear the table. "Pete, you have an hour before bed."

"Can I swing on the porch?"

"For a while." She kissed the top of his head and watched as he limped out the door.

She turned to find India watching her, lips flattened in disapproval. Julia picked up her plate and carried it to the drysink.

"What's the matter? Are you still angry that I let Marsh stay?"

"I don't like it, Mother, but no, that's not the problem." She hesitated, unwilling to relive the total fear that had gripped her when she'd seen that dog leaping for Pete. "That dog pushed him into the water."

"On purpose?"

"No, not to hear Pete and Marsh tell it. But I thought Pete was going to drown." Her hands shook as she explained about mistaking Gyp for a wild dog. "I don't want Pete around that man. I mean, he's put us all in danger by coming here and that dog—"

"Julia," India interrupted. "I think *you're* more afraid of that dog than Pete is."

"Well, he doesn't have the sense to be frightened."

"Daughter, the boy has a way with animals. Besides, Marsh was there the entire time. You don't really think he would let anything happen to Pete?"

"Pete isn't his son." She clenched her fists, disturbed at the image of Marsh protecting her son, or any of them, for that matter. "Marsh isn't going to watch out for him as though he were."

"The man is good, Julia. He's honorable and single-minded and smart."

"How do you know all that? He's been here only a day."

"I just know," India said with certainty. "You know too. He's not going to let anything happen to Pete."

"I suppose, but I still don't like the idea of Pete spending time with him."

"It was one time, Julia. Half an hour, at most."

She felt silly, but couldn't ignore the protectiveness toward her son that had grown even greater with the detective's arrival.

"Pete's curiosity has been satisfied. As Marsh becomes more familiar, the novelty will wear off." India carried a stack of dishes to the sink. "Things will settle down. But you can't expect Pete not to associate with him. They live within yards of each other and they are both male."

Julia's mother, in her less-than-subtle way, was pointing out that Pete needed a masculine influence in his life. Julia agreed, but didn't want Marsh Tipton to be that influence. The sooner the detective finished his business, the better. Before her son was in danger of losing more than his heart.

"Do you think you can finish up here?" India untied her apron and draped it across a straight-backed chair.

Julia glanced up from pumping water into the sink. "Of course."

"I need to go into town."

"This late? Why don't you wait until tomorrow?"

"I have plenty of time before dark. I'm determined to finish more quilt squares this week than Dorothy Webster."

"All right. Be careful."

"I will." India turned at the door. "Everything will be fine, honey. I promise. One day you'll be glad Marsh Tipton showed up in our barn."

"I don't know about that." At her mother's mildly disapproving look, she smiled sheepishly. "Sorry about before. You know how I get tied up in knots sometimes."

She said the words to reassure her mother, but she herself wasn't reassured. It was Julia, not India, whose mind kept replaying images of Marsh Tipton half-naked at the creek. It was Julia who kept reliving the feel of his sharp silver gaze on her bodice, burning her skin into awareness. Who kept smelling the heady odor of clean male heat and musky skin.

India couldn't reassure Julia about any of that. Assaulted by such tantalizing images of the man, it was nigh on impossible for Julia to be reassured. Or to forget.

Savage want razored through him. All the way into town, Marsh kept flashing back to the image of her wet bodice, those taut nipples straining against thin material. His arousal throbbed and he shifted in the saddle.

He'd tried not to look, but damn, he couldn't help it. He'd wanted to haul her up to him until the soft points of her nipples drilled into his chest. He wanted to weigh her breasts in his palms, delve into the softness between her legs with his hardness. Ravage her mouth until she surrendered to him.

Stupid, stupid, stupid! The woman couldn't stand the sight of him, and her opinion certainly hadn't changed when she had found Pete with him at the creek. Hell, what was wrong with him? Why would he want a woman who blamed him for the past?

Best for him to uncover a link to the Thompson gang, and fast, before he found any distance from Julia hard to maintain. Determined to investigate the place where Gordon's body had been found, he had a quick dinner at Lil's House of Boarding and Fine Dining.

India, bless her, had taken it upon herself to tell everyone about her new hired hand, and several people, including Lil, had greeted him upon his arrival.

As he finished his meal, Sheriff Kisling walked over. Marsh pulled a couple of bills from his pants pocket and laid them on the table. "Good evening, Sheriff."

"Mr. Tipton." The lawman's hazel eyes glittered like broken glass and he lowered his voice. "Did some checking on you for Julia."

"Is that right?" Well, well. The widow appeared less in need of protection every day. He said lightly, "Have you come to arrest me?"

"The bank in Crowley confirmed that you worked there, but they said for only three weeks."

"Is there a law against short-term employment?"

"Nope." Kisling weighed Marsh for a moment. "You know, I was the one who found Gordon's body."

"Who?" He kept his tone casual, but tension lashed his nerves. He had the uneasy feeling that Robin Kisling knew *exactly* what Marsh was doing in Spinner.

Kisling's gaze probed. "The telegraph operator who was killed."

"Oh, yes." Marsh returned the lawman's stare, revealing nothing. "I heard something about that."

"I don't know for sure why you're here, but I got a theory." Comprehension darkened the man's eyes and he extended his hand. "If you need anything, I'm glad to help."

"Thanks." Marsh shook hands with the sheriff, battling the frustration that ripped through him. Hell, he might as well have taken out an advertisement in the Kansas City paper for all the anonymity he had on this case.

The sheriff clapped him on the back. "Don't worry. I know how to keep my mouth shut."

How trustworthy was Kisling? Marsh gave a vague smile,

as if humoring the man, and walked out the door. What else could possibly happen to jeopardize this case?

Less than fifteen minutes later he slipped along the inside edge of the woods to the south of Spinner. He'd returned to town unnoticed and concealed Sarge in a stand of stunted oak and hickory trees on the back side of the forest.

As he walked, Marsh scanned the dry, rutted road. Though late in the day, heat still shimmered from the ground. The air hung heavy, perfumed with the scent of yellow honeysuckle and bruised grass.

There was a calm in the woods, a stillness that beckoned to his mind and replayed taunting images of Julia as he'd seen her at the creek. Despite the presence of her son, he'd wanted to rip that modest cotton daydress from her and bare her body to his eyes, his hands, his mouth.

Want flicked against his nerves like a whip, and his erection surged against his britches. Damn, he wanted her.

For just an instant, while he was alone and shrouded by darkness, he let himself imagine running the rough pads of his fingers over her smooth porcelain skin, turning her green eyes smoky with desire. His muscles twitched as he envisioned her small hands moving over his chest, his flanks, cupping his arousal. Her skin would be magnolia-white against the copper of his, and she would taste like sugar and cream.

Marsh halted. The hair on the back of his neck prickled in warning, and he turned, gazing intently into the woods behind him. Pearly gold light wove through the thick tree branches and cast dancing shadows on the ground.

He saw no one and exhaled in relief. Hell, he'd been so wrapped up in thoughts of Julia that an army could have approached him unaware.

Moving cautiously, he set off again. He slipped from oak to hickory to scrub elm, his boots making near-silent whispers on the dirt floor. He shoved away thoughts of Julia and concentrated on the things around him.

The scent of loamy earth and rich grass floated to him. Late-day heat clung to him like damp wool, and he rolled up the sleeves of his blue linsey shirt. The sound of approaching hoofbeats caused him to halt, and he watched from the trees as a man and woman drove south in a wagon laden with supplies.

Again he sensed another presence. The squeak of the wagon wheels faded and he waited, listening.

The crackle of a twig echoed in the closed space and his head swerved toward the noise, his nostrils flaring. His gaze probed the hazy shadows, but he saw nothing. Who was there? Had someone followed him into the trees?

He palmed off his hat and slipped behind a slender elm. The fecund odors of grass and trees and clean air floated to him, but he could smell nothing that hinted at a human. Overhead, a squirrel pitter-pattered across a branch. A twig plopped to the ground. Marsh's low, controlled breaths came at steady intervals.

His gaze swept the area behind him. The low branches of a hawthorn shrub jiggled with the movement of an unseen lizard or rodent. Marsh eased out from behind the tree and slipped on his hat.

He walked slightly faster but kept his body loose, as though unaware of being followed. He knew someone was behind him, and finally the noise came, an airy *thud,* a swift intake of breath.

On guard now, he eased behind an oak and placed his hat on a branch above him. Without taking his gaze from the woods, he slipped the slender five-inch blade from his boot.

He heard a tentative footstep, then another. The air grew weighted with the feel of an unidentified person and he smelled sweat underlined by the scent of lilac toilet water. Toilet water?

Sunlight fingered through the trees, hazy light mixing with the shadows, and he saw a single shadow separate itself, move closer. Marsh tightened his grip on the knife, his muscles clenching. He didn't move even an eyelash, his breath so shallow in his chest that he could barely hear it himself.

Footsteps scuffed softly on the soft dirt. He heard a barely audible swishing, the slide of fabric on fabric, and frowned. Whoever tracked him must be brushing against every bush and tree in sight.

The person neared and Marsh drew back slightly. A shoulder appeared, and he hooked the guy with one arm around the neck, pinning the knife against his side.

His captive squealed and Marsh dropped his arm, spinning the person around. "India!"

"You scared the daylights out of me!" Julia's mother pressed a hand to her heart. "Must you jump out at me like that?"

"What in hell are you doing?" He lowered his voice with an effort, sliding the knife back into his boot.

She took a deep breath, calming herself. "I'm here to help."

It was then he noticed her dark dress and the loosely woven black shawl draped over her hair. He rubbed his forehead, fighting down his irritation. "Help how?"

She glanced behind her and lowered her voice to a husky whisper. "Aren't you looking for clues?"

"Maybe," he answered tightly, not liking the sudden suspicion in his mind.

"I've come to help you find some," she announced as casually as if she were assisting him with directions.

"You?" He snorted. "Mrs. Blackwell—"

"India."

"This is not a game."

"It certainly isn't."

"What I mean is, I'm here. It's my job. There's nothing you can do, so you needn't concern yourself."

"John was my son-in-law!" Protest flared in her green eyes. "I would say his murder is something I should be concerned about."

It was easy to see where Julia got her stubbornness. After

that earlier scene with Pete at the creek, he could just imagine her reaction if she discovered he'd allowed her mother to help him. "Why don't you go on home? It's not likely I'll find anything out here, but I'll let you know."

"No."

"India, I don't need your help."

"I would say it's rather that you don't want it, but you've got it anyway. Two heads are better than one."

"Maybe in some cases. Not this one. I don't need to worry about keeping an eye out for you, when I should be doing my job."

She was quiet for a moment. He had hoped using guilt would send her along, but he suspected by the set of her jaw that she wasn't considering going home, rather, telling him something.

"I want to help you, Marsh. Please try to understand. Like Julia, I believed that Allan wasn't going to continue looking for the Thompsons, but now that he is, I *need* to help. I tried to be like Julia, put it behind me and move on, but I can't. I need to do something."

"I understand what you're saying. I do, but this could be dangerous. Besides, involving more people only increases the chance of disturbing any possible clues." Not that he expected to find any there—it had been too long since Gordon had been found and the area was too well used.

"I'll be extremely careful." She raised her right hand as though swearing in court. "I won't touch anything or walk anywhere unless you tell me to."

"Walk home."

"Except there." She pursed her lips. "You might as well let me stay, because I'll just come back after you leave."

Marsh's initial surprise was matched by irritation. Since she was now there, any possible evidence, and herself, would be better protected if they were together. "All right, but you have to do everything I say."

"Yes, yes."

"Come on, then." He turned on his heel and scanned the

empty road. He heard no approaching horses or wagons. Keeping to the trees, he moved closer to the road, heading south and carefully searching the dark earth, grass, rocks, flowers, for any signs of disturbance. He looked for blood, clothing, jewelry, animal droppings—anything that drew his attention.

"This is where they found Hamp Gordon," India informed him absently. She followed slightly behind and to his left, stepping gingerly to peer at the ground. "Did you know that—oh, my goodness!" She grabbed Marsh's arm, turning him toward her. "Was he a detective?"

"India," he growled. "Keep your voice down."

"Sorry." She glanced nervously up and down the road. "I'm right, aren't I?"

He refused to endanger either her or his case by confirming her suspicions. "Just concentrate on finding something."

"He was, wasn't he?" she whispered.

Marsh exhaled and continued alongside the road. The sun had long since dipped behind a hill, and lingering rays of red light spread over the trees. The sky turned dove blue. He halted at the fork in the road. India stopped beside him, rubbing her hands up and down her arms.

He looked carefully over the road, seeing no indication that anything had ever been there, much less a body.

"Maybe there's something in the grass?" She pointed to the center, where the fork veed.

He knelt, hoping the better angle would reveal partial hoofprints, broken twigs, anything out of place, but there was nothing. Circling the outside of the fork, he knelt again and painstakingly ran his fingers through the grass that grew next to the road.

Though daylight dimmed to dusk, he made out a broken twig at the base of a bush. Judging from the distance and angle of where he guessed Gordon's body had been found, the twig could easily have been broken by passing wagons or people or animals.

Marsh stood and repeated the same tedious search on the

opposite side of the road. Allan had said that Gordon had been interrupted while sending the wire.

Who had known of Gordon's wire? Who had known he was at the telegraph office in the wee hours of the morning when Allan had received the partial message? Who had access to the wire office at that late hour?

The obvious answer was Bundy, Spinner's long-time wire operator, but John Touchstone and Hamp Gordon had watched the man closely. Both had dismissed him as a suspect. Besides, anyone could break into the telegraph office if they wanted to badly enough.

Besides the link to Pinkerton, what else was common to the murders?

It couldn't be the wire itself. Touchstone and Gordon were the only two who'd sent wires; the other three had been found out in some other way.

Marsh had learned nothing here. He and India walked across the road and into the woods. Marsh knew that he needed to get word to Allan that he had gotten on at the Touchstone place and he didn't particularly want to send a wire.

"Did you find anything?" India followed close behind him.

"Not really." He glanced thoughtfully at her. Perhaps India *could* help.

"What's next?"

"Are you sure you really want to do this?"

"Yes." She hurried to catch up. "Are you going to actually let me do something?"

"I want you to send a wire to your old friend, Mita Harland."

"I don't know any Mita Harland."

He grinned, pushing aside a low-hanging branch so she could pass in front of him. "You do now."

"Who is she?"

"A woman."

She huffed in disgust and he bit back a smile.

India's voice rose in excitement. "Is she a detective?"

Only one of Pinkerton's best. She would be able to get a message to Allan and a reply to Marsh. "You're not supposed to ask the questions. I am."

"Oh, pooh. She is, isn't she?"

When he didn't answer, she gave him a satisfied smile. "Hah! And you didn't want me to help you."

"*She's* trained, India." He grinned at her obvious pleasure. "You tell her you've been thinking about visiting her on the twenty-eighth of September."

"Where will I be going?"

"Nowhere."

"It's a code," she breathed. "What does it mean?"

"India," he warned. "Don't get carried away."

"All right, you don't have to tell me, but don't try to get rid of me either."

"It's a deal." Marsh hoped that the tedious part of his job— examining evidence that often turned up nothing, tracking down every lead no matter how ridiculous, asking questions that had to appear aimless—would discourage India.

They emerged from the woods, and Marsh saw that her roan mare was staked next to Sarge.

"So, does Mita travel around like you do? What about her family? Does she have one?"

"It's best if you don't know."

She made a face at him but asked no more questions.

Marsh couldn't tell her about Allan's secret headquarters in Kansas City, where Mita Harland posed as a war widow though she had never been married. No one in Kansas City suspected that the genteel woman was in reality a Pinkerton agent.

When he and India reached the outskirts of Spinner, she halted. "Marsh, do we need to tell Julia about this?"

He reined up and glanced over his shoulder. "You mean that you followed me?"

"Well, that, and the fact that I'm going to help you." For

the first time since he'd met her, she appeared ill at ease about her daughter's disapproval.

Amused, he rested one wrist atop the saddle horn and stated for effect, "She wouldn't like it."

"No. Most definitely not."

"Okay, I won't tell her."

India sighed in relief.

"As long as you do what I say. Don't go sneaking off on your own or pulling any stunts."

"Why, that's blackmail!"

"Yep." He kneed Sarge into motion.

"Hmmph," she groused, but he heard a hint of grudging relief underneath. "Should I ride in alone?"

"No. If somebody asks, you can say you asked me to ride into town with you."

"All right." She saluted smartly.

In town, she spoke to the few people they encountered before they dismounted at the telegraph office.

At the door, Marsh reached for the knob and tucked a piece of paper into her hand. "Here's Mita's address. And we'll wait for a reply."

"All right."

They walked inside, and Bundy, a thin man who stooped like a wind-bent stripling, rose from his chair. "Good evenin', India. Need to send a wire?"

"Yes, please. To a friend of mine in Kansas City."

"Okeydokey." The older man removed a stubby pencil from behind his ear and licked the tip, poised to write.

After she gave him the message, he rolled his chair over to the metal equipment and tapped it out. While India chatted amicably with him, Marsh waited by the door. If he'd been afforded the opportunity in the army to learn Morse code, he could translate Allan's message as it came back over the transit.

"This is my new hand, Marsh Tipton." India gestured to him with a smile. "He's helping us clear another twenty acres for alfalfa. Marsh, this is Hal Bundy."

"Hello there," Bundy said gruffly, peering around India.

Marsh doffed his hat and stepped up to shake the man's hand. "Hello."

"You from around here?"

"Crowley." At least if people in town started talking about him, they would all compare the same information.

In less than an hour the machine began to click and Bundy sat down in his chair to scribble the message.

"Sorry, India. Your friend is planning to be gone. I guess you won't be able to go for that visit after all."

Don't risk contact again. Marsh got that part clearly.

"Oh, bother." India slid a sideways glance at Marsh, seeking direction.

He nodded slightly in encouragement.

She reached across and took the message from Bundy. "Oh, she's going on a trip herself, the last part of September."

Allan would send someone to him. Perhaps by the time his contact showed up, Marsh would have learned something.

"And I won't be able to visit again until next year." India looked truly disappointed and Marsh silently applauded her. "Thank you, Bundy."

"Any time."

Marsh opened the door and India preceded him outside.

She unlooped the reins from the hitching post, whispering, "Now what?"

"You did just fine, India. Really fine, in fact."

"I suppose you were able to make something of that nonsensical reply."

"Yep."

"I don't suppose you're going to tell me what."

He simply smiled and swung into the saddle.

"I didn't think so," she grumbled. "Oh, wait!"

She still stood in front of the telegraph office and he motioned at her. "India, come on."

"I need some embroidery thread."

"Huh?"

"I need it for my cover." At his blank stare, she sighed impatiently as though he should already know what she meant. "I told Julia I was going into town for thread."

"Oh." He took her reins. "All right."

"Thanks, boss." She grinned and hurried across to Henner's store.

Despite India's lightness regarding the situation, Marsh had no intention of really involving her. By letting her believe she was helping, he could keep an eye on her.

He snorted in disgust. So much for his plans to keep to himself and away from Julia's family. First her boy, now her mother. Too bad Julia wasn't so enamored of him.

CHAPTER SEVEN

A week later Julia still couldn't erase the image of Marsh Tipton rushing in to save Pete. He had not hesitated, had not paused to remove his clothing. He had simply reacted.

She stood beneath a mammoth oak in the north pasture, savoring the coolness of the shade. Late-afternoon sunlight splayed across the field and heat clogged the air, crowding her lungs as surely as the fear. Alfalfa, grass, and hay grew in mixed clumps. Black oak saplings and mature stumps scattered through the pasture, their bases clustered with climbing milkweed and Virginia creeper.

As the trees were cut, the trunks were split into firewood or rolled close to a gulley that served as a natural fenceline. That wood would be sold or given away later.

Her hands tightened on the papers she had retrieved from the crate in the barn. Though she resisted believing that they were significant, she was reluctant to release this last piece of John to a stranger, a man whose very presence could jeopardize her and her son.

Because of the recurring memory of Marsh diving in to save Pete, she couldn't keep these things to herself. Her conscience wouldn't allow it. Even so, she couldn't help hoping that Marsh would find nothing of benefit and he would leave.

Her reasons for wanting him to leave had nothing to do

with the ridiculous reaction she had experienced at the creek, looking at his half-naked body. Nothing.

Rather, he needed to leave because of Pete. The detective had promised to protect her and her son, but he couldn't protect Pete from a broken heart. And she very much feared that was what Pete would suffer.

The uncommonly quick bond they'd established seemed to strengthen every day. This week Pete had spoken only of Marsh, despite the birth of new kittens and his growing fondness for the now infamous Gyp. Julia couldn't allow him to become any more attached to the detective.

Pete, Marsh, and India thought Julia was unaware that the boy and the man spent quite a lot of time together. She wasn't, and it alarmed her.

So now she stood watching that man from the cover of the trees, determined to show him John's papers and prove that there was no significance to them.

She hesitated, partly to gather her courage and partly because she couldn't tear her gaze from him. He worked industriously. Whatever else she said about Marsh Tipton, laziness was not among his failings.

He wore his hat but no shirt, and even from her distance of several yards Julia could see the sheen of sweat between his shoulder blades, the sleekness of his bronze skin. He was bulk and muscle and iron-hewn sinew.

She felt awakened and frightened and physically stirred. Hidden as she was in the trees, it didn't seem wrong to admit that she'd been thinking about him all week. About the startling silver of his eyes, the unhesitating way he had gone after Pete when her son had fallen into the water.

Marsh hacked at a stubborn root. Muscles flexed in his back and arms and the tendons in his neck corded with strain. The sweat-soaked waistband of his Levis was dark against his tanned skin.

His torso was broad and his waist lean, but he wasn't narrow in the hips or legs. He was big and unbreachable. Muscles in his buttocks and thighs flexed with his steady movements.

The powerful rhythm of his body mesmerized her, and she watched the slow-timed glide of arm to muscle to sinew, each part operating in the fluid motion of a silent melody.

Heat fluttered in her belly—the same heat that had taken her by surprise at the creek last week—and she pressed a calming hand to her stomach. He dropped the hand ax, reaching for a bandanna to wipe his brow.

He saw her and straightened slowly, his gaze locking with hers. For a moment she saw alarm there, then nothing as his gaze traveled carefully over her features.

She moved out of the trees, determined not to acknowledge that she had been standing there longer than for the moment he had spotted her. "Hello."

"Everything all right?" He slipped on his shirt, quickly fastening the middle buttons so that only a wide wedge of chest hair and tanned skin showed. His gaze skipped over her and awareness nudged, but Julia squashed it.

She glanced at the papers in her hand and forced herself to keep walking. She skirted an uneven furrow in the ground; sharp rocks jabbed but didn't penetrate the sturdy shoes. "I have something for you."

He met her gaze expectantly. She halted a few feet from him, reluctantly close to his tantalizing masculine scent. Why had she ever brought these papers? Ever allowed herself to think about them again? *Ninny,* she admonished herself. *Just give the papers to him.*

He thumbed back his hat, his gaze shifting to her hand.

"I thought you might want to look at these." She offered the papers to him, not realizing until he tried to take them how tightly she gripped.

"Miz Touchstone, you sure you're okay?"

Take these and leave, she wanted to blurt out. The scent of clean sweat drifted to her, underlined by a hint of cigarette smoke and dirt. She released the papers reluctantly, only then realizing that they had kept her tied to John.

Marsh wiped an arm across his perspiring forehead, then looked at the things she had given him. Sweat trickled down his right temple and traced the strong column of his neck. Julia swallowed, looking away.

He shifted the map to study the partial telegram and the newspaper notice, then glanced up. "You were all-fired set against helping me last week."

She didn't answer, just watched him, trying to read his reaction. Or lack thereof.

His chiseled features tightened, pulling at the healing scrape on his cheekbone. "If you'd given these things to Allan last year after John died, we might already have caught these bastards."

"I didn't find them until the day after you arrived," she defended herself.

A muscle flexed in his jaw. "And you held on to them for a week?"

"I told you from the first that I didn't want to be involved in this."

"Or with me?" His gaze pinned her.

She refused to squirm beneath his razor-sharp regard. "I've made no secret of that."

"I'm not the enemy here, Julia."

"Anyone or anything that threatens my son is an enemy, *Mr. Tipton*. Or whoever you are."

"You can call me Marsh and I promise to answer," he taunted in a wicked rumble that sent a shiver through her.

She braced herself against the flutter of awareness. "It won't be necessary to use your given name. I doubt you'll be here that long."

"So, you brought me these to hurry me along?"

Irritation flared. "Are you saying they won't help you?"

"Hell, you sidestep more than a mare in a breeding chute. Are you helping so I'll leave?"

She glared, nonplussed by the warmth that unraveled inside her. "Pete is already getting attached to you."

"At least you didn't say it was because you'd decided I might be able to help you." He rubbed his chin, his beard stubble now grown into a short beard and mustache. "I never would've believed that."

"You can believe whatever you like," she said stiffly.

"Don't go all prickly on me," he said in a lazy drawl, his gaze skating over her with unnerving thoroughness. His features sharpened again, and she sensed his sudden withdrawal as he stroked the bloodstained paper he held. "I think your husband left a clue in here, and if we're lucky, we can still use it."

"But, but—" He was supposed to return the papers in disgust, admit that perhaps he should move on. "There's nothing there. That notice about the bank robbery—that happened three weeks after John died!"

"That's true." Marsh carefully folded the papers and slid them into the back pocket of his Levis. "Once I'm able to get a better look at these things, I'll let you know what I find."

She curled her hands into fists. "Didn't I just tell you that I don't want to be involved in this?"

"The choice was taken away from you last year. When John was killed and Pete—"

"That choice was taken from me when John decided to work for your . . . your blasted agency." Anger sharpened her voice, and she turned away, fighting quick tears.

Green and brown-edged leaves fluttered in the gentle breeze. She stared at the woods, tired of the fear and the anger but not knowing how to escape either. "Do you think you can keep us out of the investigation? Or at least apart from it?"

He moved up behind her. His heat caressed her back and his breath skimmed her nape, eliciting a flood of warmth. "Julia, I know you don't trust me, but I swear on my life that you'll be protected."

"I didn't ask for your stupid protection." She wrapped her arms around her waist. Fear snaked through her, bringing echoes of the past. "I've been taking care of myself and my son for a long time. Better, I might add, than John did when he was around."

"You don't have to do it alone anymore."

"Don't you understand?" Clenching her fists, she whirled, and her skirts swirled against his legs. "You can't promise what you can't control!"

"I've controlled this so far." His gaze held hers fiercely. "I *will* continue."

"John thought he could too." A dull ache throbbed in her chest. "He was taken completely by surprise. That can happen to anyone, even you."

"If it does, it will happen to *me*. Not to you or Pete or India."

"I think you believe that." She pushed away a stray tendril of hair and stared up at him, trying to fathom why anyone would willingly put themselves in jeopardy. "Why do you do this? Who are you really?"

"You know I can't—"

"I don't mean your real name," she said impatiently. "I mean *you,* the man underneath."

Pain and regret flitted through his eyes. "Just a man doing his job."

"No." She studied him, wishing she could peel away the layers of flesh and muscle and secrecy to see his heart, his soul. She very much wanted to see inside that secret place. "It's more. The job is what makes you *who* you are, *what* you are. You *live* it. My husband was the same way."

"And you hated that," he said in clipped tones, showing more emotion than she knew he wanted.

She eased closer, less than an arm's length away, and stared into his shrewd silver eyes. "No, I didn't. At least, not the passion or the integrity. But sometimes I hated the dedication, the utter selflessness he possessed." Her gaze traveled over Marsh's wind-burned features and she whispered, "I never understood that."

He stilled, as if he could hear the frustration and the grief that she hadn't shared. When his gaze moved slowly to her, there was no mockery in his eyes, only sincerity and frank interest.

At his avid regard, a traitorous heat fluttered low in her belly. She recognized the renegade part of him that was so like John, the disregard for danger, the craving for excitement. Did every agent possess those traits? Were these the qualities that made them bigger than life, bigger than the people who loved them, the people they saved?

"Ask me," he rasped, the dark tone of his voice slipping over her. "Ask me what you would never ask John. What you always wanted to understand."

He looked as surprised as she at the demand. Though she might try to deny it, she felt connected to him in some elemental way. Was it only that he shared traits with John? Or was it something more?

She wanted to refuse, but his urging tempted her. Would he let her see what made a man like him? What drove him? "How can you go from place to place, knowing that you'll never belong anywhere?"

He paused, as though he'd never thought about it. "It's a price that comes with the job, but I believe in what I do, that it's ultimately for the better good of people."

"The better good! And what about your family?" she asked bitterly. "Your wife? Or have you ever been in one place long enough to have one?"

He stiffened, his eyes tormented.

Did he have a wife? She'd never considered the possibility until then. From his silence she knew she'd hurt him. "I'm sorry. I shouldn't have—"

"My wife is dead."

Julia winced. "I'm sorry."

In a quiet voice he said, "Explain what you meant about the job hurting the family."

"Well," she began, unwilling to hurt him again. "I just meant that it uses you up so that when you finally have the opportunity to give something to your family, you have nothing left to give."

"Is that what happened with John?"

She blinked. "We're not talking about John."

"Aren't we?"

"No." She turned away, realizing that she had indeed been talking about her dead husband. "Maybe."

The sun loitered on the horizon, a ball of red-gold fire, and Julia realized that a lot of her anger was directed at John for leaving, not at Marsh for coming.

He shifted behind her, one hand settling on her shoulder. "Julia, don't you believe in sacrifice for the cause of higher good?"

"I used to." She stood frozen, affected in spite of herself by his gesture of comfort. His heat lapped at her, coaxing her to trust him. "Maybe I still do, but it seems that the price is too high."

"In what way?"

"What you take from those who love you." She faced him, noting the tight lines of strain around his mouth and the fatigue in his silver eyes. "What you never share or experience. A baby's first steps or first words. Being a part of something or someone outside of yourself, watching growth and change and endurance and knowing you made it that way. Being part of the cycle. Haven't you ever wanted that? Don't you ever miss it?"

"I've never thought about it," he said hoarsely.

There was genuine bafflement in his eyes, and sadness shifted through her. Julia shook herself, astonished at her passionate reaction. "Yes, well, neither did John and I imagine Allan Pinkerton ever has either."

"No. He hasn't."

The quiet certainty in his voice caused her to stare up at him. "You sound as if you know from experience."

A fleeting emotion crossed his face—a hint of remorse, of understanding? An ache lodged in her chest, a certainty that he, too, had once questioned the merits of the agency. Had he done so because of his wife? If so, why was he still working for them?

Julia stepped closer, seized with the urge to offer comfort. "I'm sorry about shooting at you."

"Are you?" Marsh's gaze moved slowly over her features and lingered on her lips.

Julia's insides melted. She considered putting more distance between them, but she couldn't move. Her skin felt lit from within; her nerves tingled with excitement and anticipation. She wanted to feel his lips on hers and was shocked at herself.

He wanted it too. She could tell by the way his clear silver eyes changed to smoldering steel. He moved slightly. Or did she? Her heartbeat kicked up and a tingle skimmed her body. Her gaze locked on his lips, and he closed his eyes, shutting her out.

When he opened his eyes, his face was carefully blank. Disappointment stabbed and she fought against it. He was right to pull away. She should have done the same.

He stared over her head into the fading sunset, a mixture of rage and hopelessness settling over his features.

She knew that look. She'd suffered it during the endless nights when John was away from home, through the infinite days of his absences, the horrible fleeting moment before his death. Marsh wasn't supposed to understand how she felt, and she wanted to touch him, to take his hand in comfort, but she laced her fingers together.

His gaze shifted from the landscape to her. Tapping at the papers in his pocket, he said coolly, "Thank you for these."

Whatever emotional connection Julia had thought she felt was gone now. She wished that she had never brought him the papers. She wished she could talk to someone about this, but she already knew she couldn't talk to her mother. And she didn't dare risk involving Riley.

"I think I'm finished here for the day." Marsh reached for the hand ax and slid it into his back pocket. "May I walk back with you?"

"Of course." Her gaze moved to his shirt pocket, where

the papers were hidden. If he discovered something, the possibility of danger was almost certain. Her chest ached.

"I'm starvin'," he said as they started toward the house. He removed a match from his shirt pocket and stuck it between his teeth. "Wonder what Lil's having for supper tonight."

"I'm not sure—oh, no!" Julia groaned and grabbed up her skirts, walking briskly over the uneven terrain. He quickly caught up to her. "What's wrong?"

"I forgot about Riley."

"Riley? The preacher?"

"He's supposed to come for me at six o'clock." She fumbled for the watch pinned inside her apron pocket. "Oh! Thirty minutes ago!" Ashamed that Marsh had made her forget the preacher, she stepped up her speed.

"I take it he's not married?"

"Of course he's not married!"

His lips twisted in a reluctant grin. "Is he courtin' you?"

"That is none of your business!"

"Hmm, guess he's not. Seems like if he was, you wouldn't mind if people knew it."

She frowned at him and walked faster.

"If you forgot he was comin'," Marsh said softly, his breath tickling her ear, "maybe he's not the man for you."

Unnerved by the caressing heat of his breath against her skin, she snapped, "Don't make me regret missing that shot in the barn."

He threw back his head and laughed, a rich, full sound that summoned an involuntary smile from Julia.

She wished she could ignore this man who made her feel giddy and uncomfortably aware of him all at the same time.

CHAPTER EIGHT

He'd almost kissed her, still wanted to. Judging from the plea in her eyes and the slight parting of her lips, Julia had wanted him to. But he'd turned away.

Hell, had it been so long, he'd forgotten what to do with a woman? He smiled mirthlessly. No, he'd backed off because he knew he shouldn't get further involved with her or her family.

Restlessness shifted through him. For the first time in his life, *the case* wasn't uppermost in his mind. Marsh stood in the barn doorway, watching Julia drive away with the preacher. Her soft laughter faded as the buggy disappeared into the night.

With a ferocity that startled him, Marsh swore. He wanted to be the one sitting beside her, the one who made her laugh. He wanted to tell her his real name. He wanted . . . her.

There, he'd admitted it, for all the good it would do either of them. It would be better to feel the way she did.

She wanted him to leave, and the day would come when he would. If he remembered nothing else, he should remember those two things, but the faint scent of wildflowers that clung to her like a fine mist still teased him. He could still see the sadness in her green eyes, feel her anger and regret.

With a curse he strode out of the barn and around the corral, intent on a bath at the creek. He hadn't lied to Julia out in the pasture. Always he'd been a man just doing his job.

And, as she'd pointed out, *living* his job. It had driven Beth into the arms of another man, and finally to her death.

Oh, yes, he understood Julia's anger, but working for the agency was the only thing that made him feel alive. He had never wanted any other kind of life, and since Beth's death he had never cared if the job caused his death as well.

Until that afternoon, when he'd looked into Julia Touchstone's eyes and recognized a common pain.

She made him think of things he never had before; even so, he had no business wanting her. He was part of something she hated. His very presence here invited danger.

He took a leisurely bath, refusing to allow a single thought of her. Nearly an hour later he put on clean clothes and returned to the barn, his thoughts focused on the papers Julia had given him in the pasture.

Sitting at the small wash table next to his bed, he pulled a flat piece of paper from his pocket. After creasing it with two fingers, he sprinkled aged Virginia tobacco into the fold. His beard itched and he reached up to scratch his chin.

Suddenly he wanted to be rid of it, wanted to look and feel like his old self. He dug out his shaving mug and razor and a small square of mirrored glass his mother had given him long ago. He retrieved some water from the pump outside the corral and lathered up.

With quick smooth strokes he scraped away the beard stubble, leaving his face clean and naked and cool. He lit his cigarette and again picked up the papers.

He toed off his boots, stuffed his stockings inside, and set them in the corner. Wriggling his toes, he took a last drag from his cigarette, then ground it out against the barn wall.

He lit a fat candle on the edge of the wash table. The pale yellow flame fluttered, then grew stronger, spreading light over the table and cot. Marsh eased down onto the floor, his muscles stiff and strained from a day of chopping wood and hacking vines. Rolling his shoulders to release the tension, he unfolded the papers.

The map could depict any of a hundred caves in the re-

gion. There were no notes of nearby towns or landscape
marks to guide a man. The only distinguishing characteris-
tic was a rendering of what looked like a cluster of boulders.

He put the map aside and studied the message. *Thompson
contact suspected in Spinner. Not yet sure who.* The day
after sending it, John and Pete had been ambushed.

Marsh stared at the handwriting for another moment, then
read the newspaper release regarding the bank robbery that
had occurred in Spinner three weeks after John Touchstone's
death.

From talking to Allan, Marsh knew that no one in Scotty
Thompson's gang could read or write until John had joined.
Once Thompson found that John could do both, the outlaw
had ordered his newest member to prepare newspaper notices for the towns they robbed.

There had been three robberies, three public notices just
prior to the Spinner robbery. Obviously that robbery had
been planned well in advance, enabling John to write the notice far ahead of time. Had he done so per Thompson's in-
struction? Or had he known they suspected him of being a
detective and tried to leave a clue?

Gyp scrambled up from the floor, his tail wagging vehemently. Marsh looked up as Pete's voice echoed in the barn.

"Marsh, you in here?"

"Back here." He folded the papers and his gaze froze on
the back of the newspaper release. The pencil marks weren't
a continuation of the notice, but . . . hell, it looked like . . . it
was. Morse code. Identifying dots and dashes covered the
page.

"Whatcha doin' back here?" Pete appeared at the foot of
Marsh's cot, holding a bundled-up towel with both hands.
"Hey, you shaved!"

"Yep. Those whiskers were starting to itch." He stuffed
the papers in his shirt pocket.

"I brought you and Gyp some of Gran's peach pie." The
scent of warm, sugary fruit and pastry crust wafted to

Marsh. Pete glanced over his shoulder, and Marsh suspected he was making sure India hadn't followed him from the house. "It's not my bedtime yet, and I thought y'all might be hungry."

"Smells mighty good. Think it's okay for you to be out here?"

"Sure. Gran don't—*doesn't* care." Pete smiled, and Marsh smiled back.

The boy sat on the edge of the cot and Gyp crowded at his knee, sniffing the pie hidden in the towel and licking Pete's hand in greeting. After scratching the dog behind the ears, the boy lifted the cloth. He plucked up a piece of pie, offering it to Gyp before turning to Marsh. "Want some?"

"Couldn't risk getting a plate or forks, huh?" He chuckled, reaching for a bite.

Pete popped a piece in his mouth and grinned. "Gran and me already washed the supper dishes. I didn't want to do them again."

Marsh nodded, savoring the sweet yet tart taste of the fruit and the thick, syrupy filling. The flaky crust melted on his tongue, and he wished for a good cup of coffee to go with the snack.

The boy licked his fingers and looked over at Marsh. "I'm not being a nuisance, am I?"

"Nope." He grinned.

"So it's okay if I stay and talk to you for a while?"

"Sure, I'm not doing anything special." He reached for another piece, and the two of them ate in silence for a few moments. "You're not going to get into trouble by being out here, are you?"

"Nah. Ma's gone. Besides, I never get in trouble, at least not real trouble. She didn't yell or nothin' about finding me at the creek." He peeked at Marsh from beneath lowered lashes. "Did she yell at you?"

Marsh shook his head, licking the last of the sticky dessert from his fingers. "I don't think she was mad, Pete. Just worried because she couldn't find you."

"Oh, she was mad all right. At you." He balled up the towel and wiped his mouth. "She practically ran all the way back to the house. I could hardly keep up." He added matter-of-factly, "She walks real fast like that only when she's mad, and she said she wasn't mad at me."

"Yep, sounds like she was mad."

Pete placed the towel on the ground beside Gyp, and the dog sniffed at it eagerly before shaking it open with his teeth. "I asked her if she was going to spank me since I disobeyed. I bet anybody else would've got spanked."

Marsh laughed. "You asked for a whippin'?"

The boy nodded, his expression sheepish and wistful at the same time. "I've had 'em before when I did something wrong."

"Why would you—"

"If my leg wasn't like this, she would've tanned my hide for disobeying." Pete shifted on the bed so that he faced Marsh and crossed his legs Indian-style, not appearing in the least uncomfortable.

At the anguish on Pete's face, Marsh's heart tugged. "She hasn't spanked you since your leg was messed up?"

The boy ducked his head and plucked at the linen on Marsh's cot. "I guess I should be glad that I don't get licks like other kids, but I'm not. I mean, I don't really want a lickin', but, but . . . I don't know."

"You wish she wouldn't treat you any different from how she did before you were shot?"

"Yeah." He leaned forward, his voice fervent. "She acts like I'm gonna break or something. I'm tough. Even the doctor said so. I've been shot and I'm still here!" His voice rose in frustration. "She won't even let me go swimmin'. I'm a good swimmer. You've seen me."

"You are one good swimmer," Marsh agreed, suddenly ambushed by a bleak realization. There was more to life than courting death every day, than living in the dark recesses of wrong, than inviting hell to take him. There were joys and trials and love and . . . forever.

In the three years since Beth's death, he had committed totally to his job, a commitment he hadn't made in his marriage. He had never wavered from his job, never questioned it, never considered that there might be another way, a better way. Until now.

Pete flopped down on his belly and cupped his chin in his hands. "I bet your ma gave you whippings all the time."

"I certainly got my fair share."

"Was she always following you around, telling you not to do stuff?"

"Just the regular things, like don't get dirty and don't run in the house." His own mother had encouraged him to try everything in life, but he hadn't been crippled either. "You know why your ma is that way, Pete. She's just trying to be careful of you."

"It's because of my dumb ol' leg. I hate it!" He smacked the offending limb. "She acts like it got shot off. I still have it even if it doesn't work as good as it used to."

"Seeing you hurt had to be hard on her."

"I guess." He sobered. "She's had this scared look in her eyes ever since. That's why I don't want to worry her. I have to take care of her. We take care of each other, but sometimes—" His voice broke and he brushed at his cheek. Gyp edged up to the bed and rested his head close to Pete's hand, as if offering comfort.

"Sometimes, I just want—" He swiped angrily at the tears trickling down his cheeks and lifted sad green eyes to Marsh. "I just want to do things like other kids."

Marsh's throat burned.

The boy threw himself off the cot and into Marsh's lap. Gyp whined and padded over to stretch out beside him, resting his head on Pete's leg and gazing up at the boy.

Marsh's arms tightened around the child and his heart ached as he let the boy cry. Shortly, Pete's sobs eased and he relaxed against Marsh's chest.

Beneath his broad hands, the boy's shoulders felt as thin

as twigs and he smelled of peach pie and the clean sweat of a child.

Pete stroked the dog's nose and mumbled into Marsh's chest, "I'm not always such a big baby."

"Hey, I don't think that. There are some things botherin' you and you don't understand why."

"Do you always understand when things bother you?" He lifted innocent eyes to Marsh.

"No, sir." Marsh hugged the boy to him. "And sometimes I feel like doing exactly what you did."

Pete was quiet for a moment. "Have you ever cried?"

"Sure." Agony rolled inside him as he remembered the pain and devastation he'd suffered after finding Beth and realizing that she had risked death in order to escape her life with him. "Sure."

The boy exhaled shakily and burrowed his head under Marsh's chin, keeping one hand on Gyp's head. Marsh's chest tightened. He had grown too close to the boy, but how could he resist Pete's game spirit and refusal to be a victim despite the circumstances that had made him one?

He'd become too involved with this entire family. How had it happened so quickly?

Pete's breathing deepened and Marsh realized he was asleep. He touched the boy's silky blond hair and wondered what it would be like to have a child, to have this child. A challenge surely, probably more so because of his handicap. What did Marsh have to offer a child like that? Hell, any child.

For the first time, he wondered what kind of legacy he would leave behind. He had affected no one but his parents and perhaps Allan. Yes, he'd saved lives, thwarted crimes, but other than that, what had he contributed to society? What did he have to offer anyone?

"I thought I heard you two in here."

Julia's voice startled him. He hadn't heard the buggy or even her approach into the barn. He glanced at Gyp, who appeared not to have heard her either since he was still sprawled lazily on the floor, thumping his tail in greeting. Some watchdog.

Julia stood at the open end of Marsh's makeshift room, her hand resting on the top post of the last stall. She looked fresh and sweet in a green-and-white-striped shirtwaist. "Pete?"

"Shhh." He shifted so that he could rise without disturbing the boy. "He's asleep."

Her eyes softened, and he felt a knot of heat unravel in his belly. What would it take to make her look at him like that? A hell of a lot more than that earlier promise of a kiss.

"I'll take him." She held out her arms and her full skirts brushed Marsh's leg. As she stepped closer, a faint spicy scent floated around her.

Hell, she smelled like Riley. Whatever her relationship with the preacher, they had obviously gotten close enough tonight for the man to stake his claim on her. Marsh held Pete tighter.

The boy stirred and opened one eye. "Hi, Ma. I was talkin' to Marsh."

"I see that," she said softly, keeping her eyes averted from Marsh.

He couldn't tell if she was annoyed about Pete being there with him, but he definitely read a new wariness in her eyes. He sensed that was about him and that near-kiss rather than the threat of danger he represented. Since the incident at the creek, she had stayed quietly out of his way, and it bothered the hell out of him.

Pete snuggled against his chest. "Can Marsh carry me to bed?"

Alarm chased through Julia's eyes, and she opened her mouth. To protest, Marsh knew. He didn't want to hear it, so he stepped around her and started out of the barn. Pete was already asleep again.

She hurried to catch up. At least out there he couldn't smell Riley's scent as strongly. The rational part of Marsh's brain said it was a good thing he hadn't kissed her, but right now he wanted to ignore common sense and do it anyway.

She pushed open the gate and he walked through.

"The gate didn't squeak," she exclaimed.

At the bottom of the porch steps he glanced back. She stood at the fence, looking over the gate. "I worked in some axle grease."

She walked toward him, her eyes flashing. "I didn't ask you to do that."

"No." He frowned at her obvious displeasure. "You didn't."

She took a deep breath, her lips clamped tightly together.

He shifted Pete in his arms and said in a low voice, "Sorry if it bothers you, but I can't very well undo it, now, can I?"

Irritation flashed across her features, and she picked up her skirts, sidestepping him.

"Julia?" He stepped in front of her, angling his body so Pete wouldn't bump into her. "What's the problem?"

"I'm not the one who pretended to hire you!" she whispered roughly. "I know why you're really here, so you don't have to . . . to fix things just to keep up appearances."

Would he ever understand women? Why had greasing the damn gate gotten her so riled? "It needed to be done, so I did it."

"Well, don't." She marched up the steps. "I'm perfectly capable of doing such things around here, and I don't need you to do them for me."

"All right." At a complete loss, he shook his head. How had the conversation gone from fixing a gate to questioning her independence? "Why don't you just consider it repayment for giving me John's papers?"

"Hmmmph." She opened the door and motioned him inside.

Marsh clenched his teeth, battling the urge to set Pete down and find out exactly what had Julia wound up so tight. As he passed in front of her, he caught another whiff of Riley's shaving lotion, and his irritation flared higher.

What exactly had Julia and the preacher done? How far

progressed *was* their relationship? Marsh told himself he shouldn't care, but too damn bad. He did. "You weren't out very late," he growled, hating the envy that gnawed at him. "Did you have time for dinner?"

"Yes."

"Is that all?"

She opened the door, giving him a flat stare as he walked past her into the house.

Except for a light burning in the parlor and a thin reed of light from the open bedroom, the house was dark. He padded on bare feet down the hall, past a closed door and a partially opened one to Pete's room.

He hated imagining what she and Riley might have done, but the man's spicy scent lingered in his nostrils. How intimately had they touched if *she* was wearing his damn shaving lotion?

Julia turned back the sheet and thin blanket on Pete's bed, then drew aside the curtain so that Marsh could see. Moonlight filtered into the room, washing the bedlinens and headboard in soft silver. He laid Pete gently on the bed and waited while Julia quickly removed his shoes and socks.

Pearly light gilded her delicate features, and his throat went dry. He wanted to press his lips to her neck, run his tongue over the velvet of her skin and his hands over her breasts—

He started, realizing she was waiting for him at the door. He mentally shook himself and walked out, following her to the front of the house.

Her back was drill-sergeant stiff and her steps jerky as she glanced back. "I hope Pete wasn't bothering you."

Her new wariness, the jealousy he'd felt about Riley, the damn arousal he was getting just by looking at her slender curves, all combined to snap Marsh's control.

In front of the open bedroom he snagged her elbow and spun her to face him. "Pete *never* bothers me, and I'm startin' to resent you saying that."

Surprise widened her eyes, and she stiffened. Her gaze

dropped to his lips, then bounced away, causing fire to knot in his belly. She tugged on her arm. "You know how I feel about him spending time with you."

"Oh, yes, I know, Julia," he hissed. Tightening his grip, he drew her closer until he could feel her breath against his lips. Blood surged in his veins and his heartbeat kicked into a wild rhythm. "If Pete did bother me, it sure as hell wouldn't be as much as you do."

She jerked away from him and marched to the door, yanking it open. "Since you find me so offensive, why don't you leave?"

"I don't mean that kind of bother, and you know it." He halted on the threshold, facing her.

"How can I bother you?" Her gaze slid away. "I hardly see you."

"Oh, sugar," he groaned. "You're woman enough to know the answer to that one."

Her gaze flew to his face, and she must have read his savage desire, because she wrapped her arms around her waist as though afraid he would ravish her.

And he wanted to. Violent need for her slammed into him, and a slow burn inched under his skin.

Marsh knew he should walk away while he still could, but he had to know if she tasted as sweet as he imagined, if he could again spark the want in her eyes that he'd glimpsed at the creek. *He wanted to know if he bothered her as much as she bothered him.*

Even in the pale light he saw color burn her cheeks. Her chest rose and fell rapidly, and he was reminded of her wet bodice at the creek, the tight bud of her nipples.

She tightened her arms and lifted her chin. "Have you found anything of help in those papers I gave you?"

He studied her, intent on the pulse that fluttered in the hollow of her throat, the way she worried her bottom lip. She was nervous, not afraid.

Excitement pulled taut in his belly even as he told himself

to say good night. "I thought you didn't want to know what I found out."

"I don't really care one way or the other." Her gaze challenged him, but he could feel the uncertainty vibrate from her.

She wanted him too. Tension cracked between them, ensnaring him in a velvet net of heightened sensation. Instead of stepping onto the porch, he nudged open the door until it bumped the wall behind her.

She jumped like a trapped doe. "What are you doing?"

"If you really want to know what I've found, Julia," he said caressingly as he eased closer to her, "ask me nice."

"If you want to tell me, that's fine," she said haughtily, then ruined the effect by biting her lip.

He clenched his fists, fighting the tease of desire. His gaze locked on hers, finding uncertainty and curiosity and the beginning embers of the same desire he felt.

He hooked one arm around her waist and slowly pulled her into him, giving her the chance to refuse, to break away. To slap his arrogant face. He couldn't help himself. He was driven by the burning need to rid her of another man's scent.

Alarm widened her eyes and she stood motionless, staring warily into his eyes as if trying to determine his next move.

Her skirts flattened against his thighs. He could feel the outline of her legs beneath her skirt and petticoat and his nostrils flared.

"What are you doing?"

"Isn't it obvious?" He lowered his arm from her waist but pressed close, savoring the sweet torture of her breasts against his chest, the throb of his arousal straining toward her heat.

"You . . . You . . ." She angled her chin at him, and he could see her tremble. "You can just let go of me right now."

"Sugar, I'm not holdin' you."

Her gaze flew to his hands at his sides, then her eyes widened.

Before she could speak or he could reject the notion, he cupped her jaw and covered her lips with his.

Sweet, aching relief. Wicked, ripping frustration. She stiffened against him in surprise, and he knew an instant of regret. Then her lips parted under his.

His hands bracketed her hips, pulling her into him and against his throbbing arousal. He was courting trouble, the very same as if he touched a torch to gunpowder.

If she had resisted or cried out or remained passive, he would have pulled away, but she surrendered. With a growing hunger her mouth opened for him, and she touched the tip of her tongue to his.

That single action destroyed every rational thought in his head, every ounce of honor. Even knowing full well that they would both regret it, he couldn't stop.

She was like dark honey, and he wanted to lap her up. Fire nicked at him, but he was able to gentle the kiss. His tongue dipped inside her mouth, stroking the sleek velvet heat; she moaned and gripped the front of his shirt.

Savage need hooked into him. He wanted to lift her skirts and part her thighs. Tongue her nipple to turgid attention in the same way her restless movements were stroking his erection.

Wanting to touch her everywhere, he lifted her from the floor and brought her flush against him, fitting the hot V of her thighs to his throbbing arousal.

He wanted to lick and nip at every inch of her body, knowing she would taste like sweet cream. "Oh, sugar," he groaned, changing the angle of his kiss. "I could just eat you up."

She whimpered low in her throat, her hands sliding into his hair to pull him closer. She met his thrusting tongue with her own, and sleek heat ricocheted through his body.

Suddenly he was assaulted by a strange sense of déjà vu. As though they'd done this before, he knew that her skin would feel like liquid velvet, that she would taste like musky sugar, smell of warm wildflowers in her secret place. He knew to drag kisses down her jaw and neck, tongue the spot behind her ear that made her buck in his hands.

Her dress was high-necked, but beneath the silk gauze ruching of her bodice he could see the shadow between her breasts, feel the frantic pulse of her heart against his chin.

Want curled in sharp points through his body. He burned to feel her naked breasts against his bare chest. He knew what she wanted, and shifted her so that his teeth could skim the swell of her breast.

His lips moved toward the fullness he ached to taste. She gasped his name and arched her back, nudging the peak to his mouth.

His mouth closed over her and he began to shake.

"Marsh," she moaned in a shaky whisper, tossing her head back and forth. "Oh, my goodness."

The wet heat of his mouth dampened her bodice and the chemise beneath. The rasp of the cloth on his tongue made him frantic. He suckled her until he could feel her nipple pearl.

She moved against him and her knee brushed his arousal, caressing it to an even fuller throb. "Marsh—please. Marsh—Marsh."

Her panted words finally penetrated the roaring in his head. Heat thundered through his veins with the force of a locomotive. Dazed and breathing hard, he looked at her.

Her lips were swollen from his kisses. Desire turned her eyes a smoky green, but there was also fear and a sadness that immediately sliced through the haze of lust. What in the hell had he done?

He lowered her, wincing as she slid down his sensitized body. She locked her arms around his neck as though afraid she would fall. His arms trembled and he felt the same trembling echo in her body.

Her breath shuddered out, and she pressed her fingers to her lips, passion clouding her eyes. "What was that?"

"I believe that was a kiss." His attempt at levity came out hoarse and rusty. He struggled to corral his rampaging lust, but it was difficult since her quivering body was still pressed to his.

She looked alarmed, disoriented.

"Julia?" He wanted her to dismiss it or laugh it off or move back into his arms for more, but she stood unmoving, as though carved from wood.

Her face looked as pale as ice in the moonlight, and fear darkened her eyes. Was she afraid of *him*? An alien fear fluttered in his chest. "Julia, did I hurt you?"

Her fingers traced shakily over her mouth.

"Julia? Tell me."

"No, you didn't—" She drew in a deep breath and her eyes filled with sudden tears. "Didn't hurt me."

His heart lurched. *Damn!*

She glanced away, shame and shock and disbelief crumpling her delicate features, but she didn't pull away. Searching for control and trying to calm them both, he stroked her back. Her arms tightened abruptly around his neck, and the slight movement pressed her breasts even more firmly against him.

"Sugar, if you want me to stop, that's not the way to go about it."

Tension lashed her body as tight as a drawn bowstring, and she whispered shakily, "Marsh?"

"Hmmm?" His voice was husky with restraint.

Her nails dug into his neck. "There's someone out there."

After a second, her words sank in. Wary now, he turned his head and scanned the yard, the fence, the corral. "Where?"

"It's a man." Her voice, still a whisper, rose in panic. "I can't tell . . . Oh, no! He went into the barn."

Marsh focused on the weak light that flowed out the barn door, but he saw no sign of an intruder. "Where's your rifle?"

"Here." She unwrapped her arms from around his neck and reached behind the door.

Ignoring the sudden ache he felt at her absence, he took the gun and shifted it to check the chamber.

"It's loaded."

"Stay here." He paused, listening for a sudden noise or a warning from Gyp, but there was nothing. Dread knotted his gut.

"Oh, no. Gyp!" Julia moved toward the door.

He grabbed her wrist. "He'll be fine. Don't move. Don't make a sound. I don't want them to know I'm comin'."

She nodded, worry sharpening the features that moments before had been soft with desire.

Marsh stepped onto the porch, glad he was barefoot. Fighting every ounce of protectiveness that welled up in him, he glanced back at Julia.

"Be careful," she whispered.

He nodded, then crept off the porch, the chill of reality spreading through him. It could be his fault the intruder was here.

CHAPTER NINE

Apprehension mingled with desire, causing a flutter in her belly. Even as alarm pounded through her, Julia attempted to tamp down her body's reactions to Marsh. She had soaked up his touch like brittle ground in need of rain, and sensation poured over her.

Her body quivered as if his mouth still tugged on her nipple, as if his rough velvet tongue caressed hers. Struggling to shake off the drugging effects of his kiss, she took a deep breath.

The scents of soap and water and faint cigarette smoke clung to her, and her muscles pulled tight in reaction. She watched as Marsh blended into the darkness. After a few seconds she made out his shadowy form as he slipped silently along the barn wall toward the door.

Reason slowly returned though her skin still tingled where his broad, gentle fingers had touched her jaw, her hips, her waist. She wanted to explore him with tongue and hands the way he'd done her.

She should have pulled away, but she hadn't considered it once his lips had touched hers. And when he had taken her breast in his mouth, she had given herself up to the glorious fire raining through her. The memory caused a tug of sensation low in her belly, and moist heat gathered between her legs. She had never felt such abandon, such reckless freedom.

As she watched, Marsh eased up to the door of the barn, silhouetted in a weak streamer of candlelight. Tension knotted her shoulders. Who was in the barn? What was Marsh walking into?

If he thought she was going to stay there while he was ambushed or worse, he was wrong. Hurrying over to the fireplace, she took India's Sharpe rifle from above the mantel. The weapon was longer than her gun and heavier, but she balanced it under her arm and headed out to the barn.

Keeping to the shadows, she eased silently through the gate that Marsh had left ajar moments earlier. No noise came from the barn, and she hoped that was a good sign.

Each step was traced with memories of Marsh and his mouth. Flashes of hot lips on her skin, suckling at her breast. Coaxing her will right out of her.

With quick careful steps she crossed to the corral and slipped between the fence posts. Noonan looked up, then poked her head between the fence posts and resumed chomping grass. But Ginger, her mother's roan, neighed softly and walked over.

Julia stroked the mare's muzzle and strained to hear inside the barn. The low pitch of voices rumbled out, and she inched up to the side door that hung partially open.

Where was Marsh? And Gyp? The dog had been silent for too long, and dread coiled through her.

A blast of hot, sour breath hit her neck, and Julia jumped away from the wall in time to prevent smacking it with the rifle. She turned around and glared at Ginger. "Go away."

The mare nudged Julia's arm with her nose, then nibbled at Julia's skirt.

She placed a firm hand on the horse's jaw and turned her head away. "I don't have an apple. Go on."

The mare stood stubbornly, and Julia shoved against her side, urging her toward the other horse. Ginger swung her head around and eyed Julia balefully, then lumbered over beside Noonan.

Julia stepped back up to the door and peered inside. A

candle squatted on the small table, its light flickering over Marsh's cot. There was no sign of him or Gyp.

Her heart rushed in her ears. The only other sounds were the croak of crickets and the monotonous *chump chump* of the horses eating grass. Alarm skittered up her spine and she eased through the open door.

Something brushed her leg and she stifled a gasp, looking down. Gyp stood in front of her, tail wagging joyfully, his eyes bright. She frowned. Surely the dog would sense if there was anything amiss, but where was Marsh?

A low chuckle rumbled through the barn, and she tensed, moving toward the sound. Through the posts of the stall she could distinguish two masculine shapes and hear the resonant mumble of voices.

She rounded the end of the stall and leveled the rifle at the man with his back to her. He was taller than Marsh by at least three inches, and wiry. His britches bagged as though weighted in the seat.

She glimpsed a shoulder and the side of Marsh's face. He laughed warm and low, then shook the other man's hand. What exactly was going on?

Gyp darted past, running a figure eight between the men. ". . . looked like you were getting cozy with the lady," the stranger said.

Marsh shifted, his face half hidden in the shadows. "That better go no farther than this barn, Brill."

They were discussing her! Heat flushed her body as she recalled the way she had yielded to Marsh.

Realization slammed into her. This man was Marsh's friend. Was he also a detective? With stunning force Julia was reminded of exactly what Marsh was and why he was there. Rage and humiliation exploded inside her.

She cocked the gun. At the sharp sound, both men whirled to face her, their faces lax with shock and surprise as they fumbled in unison for their guns. Perverse pleasure shot through her.

"Julia." Marsh lowered his borrowed rifle. "I thought you were back in the house."

"Obviously," she said coldly.

The other man grinned and holstered his revolver, flashing a dimple. "Hell, lady, you scared ten years off my life."

Anger started a slow build inside her. This new man *was* another detective. Why else would Marsh be so cozy with him? And they were discussing her as if she were a prize in a card game.

She was a fool. She had been a fool to kiss Marsh and a fool to come to the barn. Obviously there was no threat to him here.

He stepped around the taller man and walked to her. "Julia, everything's okay. I just need to talk to Mr.—"

"You're having some kind of detective . . . meeting out here, aren't you?" She didn't want him to be this close to her, even though moments ago she had thought he couldn't get close enough.

He frowned. "Detective meet—"

The other man's lips twitched and he looked away.

"Don't ever do this on my property again." She pushed past him, enraged and sick and feeling like a naive schoolgirl.

Strong fingers closed on her upper arm. "Wait."

Gyp growled. Thinking the dog meant to threaten Julia, Marsh snapped, "No, Gyp!"

But a glance down showed that the dog was plastered to Julia's side and baring his teeth at *Marsh*! He blinked. What the hell!

Julia pulled away and leveled a hard green gaze on him, all trace of softness and desire gone. She cradled India's rifle in the crook of her arm and plucked her own out of Marsh's grasp. Her back ramrod stiff, she marched out the barn door.

Marsh automatically started after her and found his path blocked by Gyp. The shepherd braced himself as though for attack, and a ruff of fur bristled down the middle of his back in warning. He growled, then wheeled, padding out behind Julia.

Marsh stared after them dumbly.

"Isn't that *your* dog?" Brill walked up beside him.

Annoyed, he huffed out a breath. "I thought so."

Julia had obviously been concerned that he had met with trouble and had come out to help. Regret pinched that she had found him with Brill, but he didn't go after her.

"I didn't mean to scare her. Please apologize for me."

"It's not you, it's the whole thing," he said darkly. "She resents the hell out of me and the agency."

"After that bungled attempt to capture the James brothers last spring, that seems to be the mood of half the country these days."

"Yeah." But he didn't care about half the country, only one hot-blooded widow who'd just turned him inside out.

"If she dislikes the agency so much, how'd you get on here?"

He explained about India's willingness to help as well as Julia's wariness of the agency.

Brill let out a weary sigh. "I saw the two of you, uh, on the porch when I walked up. I had no idea she would come out here. Do you think she heard what I said?"

"Probably."

"Hell." The other man slapped his hat back on his head and shifted restlessly.

Marsh glanced at his friend. "How'd you know where to find me, anyway?"

"Allan told me."

"I didn't know who he'd send. Or when." He wished that Julia had never learned of his meeting with Brill. Guilt twinged at the look of angry disappointment he'd seen in her eyes. What did he have to feel guilty about? He was just doing his damn job!

Brill thumbed his hat back farther on his head and folded his arms. "Scotty Thompson and his boys robbed the train between Poplar Bluff and Sikeston."

"That's pretty far east for them."

"Nowhere's too far for them," Brill said dryly. "Have you had any luck finding anything?"

"Only these." Marsh pulled the papers from his shirt pocket, explaining how he'd come to have them. He showed Brill the dots and dashes he'd found on the back of the newspaper release. "I haven't had a chance to look at them very closely."

His body still stung from the feel of Julia's sweet heat, the anticipation of her mounting him and taking him inside, erasing all the loneliness and guilt he'd felt since Beth's death.

What was wrong with him? He was there to catch the Thompson gang and that was all.

"It looks like Morse, all right." Brill paused for a moment. "I'll copy it down and take it to Kansas City, see what Allan comes up with."

"Good."

Marsh read the release aloud and Brill wrote. Then while Brill copied the Morse symbols, Marsh paced.

Even though he answered Brill's questions, Marsh's mind centered on Julia. Touching her had only intensified his craving for her. Had it affected her the same way?

She might have yielded to his kiss, but that didn't mean she wanted more, the way he did. He wanted to merge his body with hers and tap deep into her soul. Wanted her eyes to soften for him. Wanted to hear her call out for him. Damn foolish notions every one.

Brill returned the paper to Marsh. "I hope my coming here doesn't cause problems with the case."

"No." He knew it would and wondered what kind.

The other agent eyed Marsh speculatively, then walked out the door. "Allan will send someone down every week, probably me."

"Good."

Brill glanced toward the house. "Think it would be a good idea to meet somewhere else?"

"Yeah."

"I'll be in touch." The other man touched his hat and disappeared into the shadows.

Marsh paused in the doorway of the barn, studying the house. It stood like a solitary sentinel, silent, with no hint of light or warmth. Julia was in there, most likely cursing him. He wanted to apologize to her. For Brill. For the kiss. Hell, even for coming here.

He walked back inside and sat on the edge of his cot. Loneliness and regret surged through him.

Gyp trotted in, edging along the far wall of stalls. Directly across from Marsh, he eased down on his haunches and stared unblinkingly.

Marsh frowned at him. *Traitor.*

He never should have kissed her. He'd known that even as he was coaxing her surrender, trying to get closer to her soft heat. Julia Touchstone could easily break his heart, he realized soberly.

Feeling the dog's intense stare, Marsh glanced up. Frustrated because he wanted Julia and couldn't have her, he growled, "What are *you* looking at?"

Gyp snorted as though disgusted and flopped down in front of the empty stall.

"You sleepin' over there?"

In answer, the shepherd looked away and rested his head between his paws.

"Ungrateful whelp," he muttered, lying back on the cot. Even the damn dog was angry at him.

Sugar, I could just eat you up. A shiver stroked over her and evoked a tingling warmth between her legs. Julia closed her eyes, savoring a desire that she hadn't felt in too many months to count. Why had she kissed him like that? Why had she kissed him at all?

She flopped onto her stomach and buried her face in the pillow. Inside her room, the air was stifling and clammy, but she wouldn't open the window. That would make Marsh somehow closer, and he had already gotten too close for her peace of mind.

Restless and aching with need, she tried to forget about him. But if she closed her eyes, she felt his mouth on her breasts. If she opened her eyes, she saw his features drawn sharp with desire.

Never had she been so swept away by a man, so out of control. So absolutely frightened of her feelings while wanting to experience more.

She punched the pillow. Why couldn't she feel this way about Riley? Though the preacher had never done more than kiss her hand, she instinctively knew he wouldn't spark this treacherous coil of fire through her belly. Nor would she have to wrestle with this damnable choice between what she wanted and what she should do.

Why did she have to feel this unbridled aching need for Marsh Tipton? Or whoever he was.

She didn't even know his real name! Choking off a groan of frustration, she flopped over onto her back. What a fool she was. Like John, Marsh was a man whose job and duty came first. Invariably his job put him and those closest to him in danger, but he would never give it up.

He had come here to get the Thompsons, and she had no business wanting him.

Wanting him?

She sat straight up in bed, her long-cloth nightdress tangling around her thighs. It was true, she realized. That kiss had unleashed a surge of power, a lust she had never experienced with John or anyone.

Marsh's kiss had burned away all thought to the degree that she hadn't known her own name, and the realization brought a flush to her cheeks.

Before his death, John had been absent over a year with only two short visits in between. At the time he was killed, they hadn't been intimate in almost nine months.

All that time she had slept alone, unstirred, unchallenged, uninterested. *That* was why she had responded so uninhibitedly to Marsh, not because he held any sway over her. Women had needs too, and she was simply starved for the physical act of lovemaking.

But her reasoning rang of denial. It didn't matter what name she put to the scorching need that budded to life inside her, she had behaved like a wanton the first time another man had touched her. Not just any man, but a man who represented everything in her past she had tried to escape.

Moaning in frustration, she fell back upon the mattress and stared up at the ceiling.

Stay away from him, Julia. Stay away from him.

Just stay away from her, Granger. Through the night, Marsh chastised himself with a little help from Gyp. Damn dog.

The next morning he cleared out of the barn at first light, planning to avoid Julia as long as possible. *He never should have kissed her.*

By midday Gyp finally forgave him and showed up in the pasture where he cleared trees. Despite the steady pace Marsh set and the burn of his muscles, thoughts of Julia invaded his mind.

Had she lain awake all night tortured by images of him as he had of her? Each time the ax cleaved wood, he imagined his body stroking between her thighs with the same steady purpose. Penetrating her soul and heart the way she had penetrated his.

A sharp pain twinged in his hand and he glanced down. A blister had burst in his palm and blood mingled with sweat to trickle down his wrist. Marsh buried the ax in a tree stump and dragged an arm across his sweat-slicked forehead.

Physical labor couldn't distract his thoughts from Julia, but perhaps mental labor could. As he rode back to the house, he catalogued every scrap of information he had on the Thompsons.

At the barn he dismounted, stifling a groan. If possible, he ached more than yesterday. Hell, even his bones felt bruised. After a quick wash, he would go into Spinner for a turn of daytime surveillance, perhaps pay a visit to Tully. The man seemed to know something about everyone.

Every day last week, Marsh had put in a full day's work on the farm, then ridden into town. After supper, he visited with various townspeople either at the saloon or Henner's General Store, and once he had spoken briefly with the sheriff. Most often he simply hid in the shadows and observed. So far, he'd seen nothing suspicious.

India had followed him a couple of times, but only to sit quietly with him in the shadows. Since there was no danger, he didn't protest, but he preferred that she stay clear of his investigation. Though he enjoyed her company, it made him edgy and nervous and mindful of responsibilities he didn't want.

A clean pair of Levis lay on his cot, and he silently thanked India, who had taken to washing his clothes. Placed on top of the denims was a tissue-wrapped package three inches square.

He picked it up and ripped off a corner of the tissue to discover a fancy soap that smelled dark and woodsy. Stuffing the soap in his pocket, he grabbed up his clean clothes and a towel.

Half an hour later, he returned from the creek feeling refreshed and better able to control his wayward thoughts of Julia. After towel-drying his still-damp hair, he slid on fresh stockings, then his boots, and began buttoning his shirt.

"Marsh?"

He turned at the sound of India's voice. "Back here."

He stuffed his shirt into his Levis and fastened them, rolling back the cuffs of his shirt as Julia's mother walked up.

She halted at the corner of his makeshift room and Gyp padded over to her. "Going somewhere?"

"Into Spinner. Need anything?"

"No." She scratched the dog behind the ears. "Did you and Julia have a fight?"

"A fight?"

"She told me you had a visitor last night, and when I asked who she nearly bit my head off."

"I'm not surprised." What else about last night had Julia told her mother? He picked up his hat and settled it on his head. "He was another detective."

"Have you learned something about the case?" She stepped closer, eyes eager.

"Not specifically." Was she aware of the kiss between him and her daughter?

"What about those papers from John? Julia told me—" India broke off, a quizzical look coming over her face. She wrinkled her nose. "What's that smell?"

"It's not me," he said indignantly. "I just had a bath."

She laughed. "It smells good. Oh, you borrowed Pete's new soap."

"Pete's soap? I found it on my bed and thought—you didn't give it to me?"

"No. It smells very nice though."

"Yeah." What was going on?

"My grandson must really like you." She smiled, her eyes softening. "He begged for that soap the entire time we were at Henner's yesterday."

"Why would he give it to me?"

"Maybe he thought you needed it."

He pinned her with a flat stare.

She grinned. "He's a very generous child. Now, what about the papers Julia gave you? Will they help?"

"It's a little early to tell."

"Did you recognize anything on that map?"

"No, did you?"

"Not right off." She tapped her chin with her finger. "But there's something familiar about that cave. I bet I could find it."

"India, I don't want you going off by yourself. Scotty Thompson is a walkin' talkin' version of hell you don't want to meet. Exactly what have you been up to since we sent that telegram?"

"Nothing." Her gaze slid away.

"Tell the truth." Unease slithered up his spine. He didn't

want to find out that she had indeed been running around on her own, trying to dig up information on the Thompsons. "What have you been doing?"

"Nothing, I swear." She planted her hands on her hips. "Are you planning to look for that cave?"

"Maybe." He ran a hand over his denims as though dusting them off, making certain that the derringer was strapped in place on his calf and within easy reach. "You promised not to do anything without me. Remember?"

"Yes."

"Yes, you promised?" Marsh leveled a stern gaze on her. "Or yes, you remember?"

She rolled her eyes. "I don't even have the map. How could I find the cave without it?"

He studied her for a moment, then stepped around her, pulling the reins over Sarge's head.

"You never answered my question."

"Stay, Gyp." Marsh swung into the saddle. "What *was* your question?"

"Did you and Julia have a fight?"

At the reminder of the kiss, he bit back a groan. "Not exactly."

"Then what *exactly* did happen last night?"

He searched the green eyes so like Julia's. India seemed to be sincere in her question, but he had the uncomfortable feeling that she had guessed about the kiss. "Let's just say we came to an understanding."

"Meaning?"

"You're something else, India." His lips twisted in a wry smile. "Just like a bloodhound."

"Meaning you're not going to tell me." She crossed her arms and eyed him balefully.

He tipped his hat and wheeled Sarge toward the barn door. "Yep."

CHAPTER TEN

On the way to town, Marsh wondered if Julia had for-
given him yet. For the kiss and for Brill showing up. Even
though Brill had asked him to apologize for frightening
Julia, Marsh had no intention of doing so. The detective had
done no harm, and Marsh was tired of feeling as if he had to
apologize for everything, even breathing the same air.

Just forget about her.

Glancing over his shoulder to make sure India hadn't followed him, he considered what he'd observed about the res-
idents of Spinner. Every night Tully worked the bar. Henner
unfailingly swept his porch with the same north-to-south
motion before locking up. Bundy stayed in the telegraph office until eight, and Sheriff Kisling checked the bank every
hour on the hour, then returned to the saloon for a drink or a
hand of cards.

No one left town and no one unfamiliar arrived. Marsh
hoped to see a variation of that behavior during the day.

Once in town, he reined up in front of Henner's General
Store and picked out a new pair of work gloves. From what
Marsh had observed, Bob Henner and his wife, Jeanette,
worked the store and lived upstairs with their three chil-
dren.

After finishing at the store, Marsh walked over to the
saloon. A steady stream of customers moved in and out
of the bank. The telegraph machine clicked like a busy

woodpecker, growing louder as he neared. He called a hello through the open door and Bundy's voice echoed in return.

He wanted a beer, but would forego it if Julia were still working inside. Peering over the swinging double doors, he saw only Tully, who sat at a table in the middle of the room, puffing on a cigar and dealing cards so quickly, his movements blurred.

Marsh had never seen such speed, even from a riverboat dealer he'd met in the war. He pushed through the doors. "You open?"

The barkeep plucked the cigar out of his mouth and waved Marsh inside. "What can I do for you?"

"I wanted a beer."

"Sure. Help yourself. Use the big mugs under the counter."

"Thanks." He walked behind the bar and located the glasses, filling one from a keg. Dark gold liquid foamed to the top, and he took a long swallow, sighing in pleasure.

The saloon owner looked up, deftly cutting the deck with one hand. "How do you like Spinner?"

"Pretty well." Marsh took another swallow of beer and moved around the bar.

Tully kicked a chair away from the table in invitation for Marsh to sit. "I guess it's due to India that you got the job at Julia's place?"

"Yeah." Why had Tully assumed India was responsible? Marsh warily eyed the saloon owner.

"Julia doesn't usually change her mind about things," the man said by way of explanation. "Is she treating you okay?"

"Well enough." The awareness he'd tried to dodge all morning sent a quiver of tension through him. "I like the kid."

"Pete's one tough little son of a gun."

"Yeah. Did you know him before the accident?"

"Yeah, since I moved here about five years ago."

"You native to these parts?"

Tully flicked a glance at Marsh. "No."

"Me neither." He took another swallow of beer. "I came west after the war."

"Yeah, me too." With a flick of his wrist, Tully fanned the deck in a perfect circle, then snapped the cards back into place.

Thinking of Tennessee, Marsh fondly recalled the fog that hovered over Reelfoot at daybreak. Dense forests of cypress, oak, and cottonwood surrounded the lake that had been formed by the earthquakes of 1811 and 1812. "These hills remind me a little of home. It's peaceful here."

"Yeah," Tully agreed, flashing a smile. "No factory noise, no soot. I never knew the sky was so blue."

"You worked in a factory?"

The saloon owner removed the cigar and exhaled. Smoke clouded the air between them, then floated away in thin wisps. "An ironworks."

"Did you work cannon during the war?" Marsh kept his tone casual.

Tully pursed his lips, eyeing the cigar. "No."

"See much action?" He finished his beer and set the glass on the table, wondering at the hard look that passed through the man's eyes.

Tully fanned his cards again, his eyes carefully blank. "Enough."

"Know what you mean." Marsh had begun the war working undercover for Pinkerton but had transferred by the end of the second year to the Army of Tennessee, feeling that he could help more in the cavalry.

Light footsteps sounded on the stairs behind Tully and Marsh glanced up. Hell! What was Julia doing here? He'd thought she had finished with her work, or he never would have come in.

She hadn't noticed him yet and glided down the stairs with easy grace, carrying a balled-up rag in one hand and pushing wayward curls from her forehead with the other.

As though they'd touched only seconds ago, his skin tingled. Heat traveled through him with the fierce power of an August storm, shattering his defenses. Memories erupted of her tongue stroking his desperately, their bodies fitted together as though they'd been molded from the same clay.

"Tully, could I get some rags and maybe a tin of soda crackers for Hazel?"

"I think I've got some left." He rose and strode behind the bar, removing a key from his shirt pocket. "How's she doing?"

Julia stopped at the bottom of the stairs and glanced over. When she saw Marsh, horror widened her eyes and she quickly looked away. "A little better, but weak."

He rose, his gaze moving helplessly over her. Despite both dreading and aching to see her in the last twelve hours, pleasure shifted through him.

He glanced over to Tully just as the saloon owner disappeared through a recessed door that Marsh hadn't noticed before. Annoyed at seeing Julia, he scowled.

"I had to ask him to get those things for me," she said defensively, her back rigid. "He doesn't like anyone to go in there. What are you doing here?"

"Hello, Miss Julia." He edged around the table for a better look at the door, warning her with his eyes to be cautious. Why would Tully invite Marsh, a near-stranger, to serve himself at the bar but fetch something as innocuous as soda crackers from his office for Julia, who cleaned the place every day?

From the next room came the sounds of Tully shifting furniture, opening a drawer. Marsh contemplated the open door of the office while speaking to Julia. "How are you today?"

Her gaze shot to the door where Tully had disappeared, and she said coolly, "I'm fine. And yourself?"

"Fine, thank you." His gaze stroked over her and he hungrily committed to memory every detail.

Her moderately low-cut daydress was saved from being improper by a stiff edge of ruffling. The pale butter color turned her hair the color of sun-whipped honey and deepened the green of her eyes. Her lush breasts swelled slightly over the V-shaped décolletage, and his hands itched to follow the path of his eyes. Want pulled taut in his belly.

"Here you go." Tully closed and locked the office door, then walked toward them, giving Julia the requested items.

"Thank you." She placed a hand on his arm. "Could we put Hazel in the front room?"

"You know the blue room's for special customers."

"If she's contagious, the other girls might catch it."

"That girl has been sick this year more than anyone I know," the saloon owner grumbled. "And now you want me to put her in the blue room. She costs more money than she makes."

"Tully!" A hint of rose stained Julia's cheeks. She stood stiffly at the bottom of the stairs, keeping her gaze averted from Marsh.

"All right, all right." Tully strode back to his office, opened the door, and reached inside. "Does she need help getting there?"

"Yes, she's pretty weak."

He slammed the door and headed up the stairs.

"Thank you."

Julia turned to follow, but Marsh snagged her wrist. She jerked at his touch, her gaze flying to his.

The memory of the kiss surfaced and started a heavy throb in his veins. Once Tully was out of earshot, Marsh released her, but moved so close that her breath brushed his cheek. "What did you mean, he doesn't like anyone in his office?"

She shifted as though ill at ease, eyeing him warily. "Nobody goes in there. He likes things a certain way."

"Don't you clean the place every day?"

"No. *Nobody* goes in."

Marsh slitted a narrow look toward the office.

She made a sound of exasperation. "Are you suspicious of everyone? Tully has his own way of doing things and he doesn't want it messed up. That's all."

"Then why did it take him so long to find a key?"

"I didn't say he was tidy, just that he has a system." She glanced away, looking trapped.

Uncertainty tugged at Marsh. Instead of easing, her nervousness seemed more pronounced. The fresh spring scent of her webbed around him, strumming his nerves. "Brill wanted me to convey his apologies for slipping up on us last night. He didn't mean to alarm you."

Her gaze touched his lips, then bounced away. She stepped back and crossed her arms below her breasts. Was she afraid of him? Or was it what he'd done last night?

Hell, *he* was afraid of how shaken he'd been after that kiss. Regret and self-loathing crawled through him. He wanted her trust, not her fear, and cleared his throat, hoping to reassure her. "Julia, I know you don't like me—"

"That's not true!" Denial flared in her eyes.

"Maybe that's too strong," he conceded, eager to have his say before Tully returned. "But I know you don't feel comfortable around me, and I want to apologize."

Her gaze moved over his features, and a tiny frown creased her brow.

"I'm sorry for, uh—" He clenched his fists and fought the urge to duck his head. He'd never apologized to a woman for wanting her. "Last night. I was out of line when I kissed you, and I'm sorry."

Astonishment spread through her eyes, followed by a flicker of pain. "No need to apologize," she said coolly. "Nothing happened."

Nothing? She called that foray into ecstasy *nothing*? Marsh strangled the urge to kiss her again and force her to admit she'd felt the want as strongly as he had. But doing that, while pleasurable, would only make her harder to forget. "Well, *nothing* won't happen again."

"She's settled, Julia." Tully started down the stairs, stuffing the key into his pants pocket.

Julia spun and rushed up the stairs as if escaping a noxious odor.

Tully pressed against the railing, giving her room, then turned to Marsh with raised eyebrows. "What'd you do?"

"Nothing." He shrugged and picked up his glass.

The saloon owner rested his elbows on the railing and leaned over, eyeing Marsh curiously. "Trouble already?"

"Let's just say Miss India is the only reason I have a job."

"You know, Julia's pretty tough to a degree." Tully's gaze rested on Marsh, hard and measuring. "But she could easily be hurt, and I'd hate to see that happen."

The saloon owner was warning Marsh off Julia? He would have expected that behavior from the preacher or the sheriff. Marsh met Tully's gaze. "Yep, that'd be a shame."

After another moment Tully relaxed and shot a rueful glance up the stairs, giving a bark of laughter. "Man, I sure wouldn't want to be caught between two women in the same house. Not unless it was under the most arousing of circumstances."

Marsh nodded in wry agreement and pushed his way through the doors. "Thanks for the beer."

"Any time."

He wasn't sure if he'd gotten any useful information from Tully, but if Julia hadn't come downstairs, he might have missed seeing that door.

He walked around to the back side of the saloon, curious to see if he could discern Tully's office from the outside. Surprisingly, there was another door on the back wall, located right about where Tully's little room met the telegraph office.

Saloon chairs bumped against the wall, punctuating the steady click of the telegraph machine and the barely audible hum of voices. A crow squawked, wheeling close to the roof of the building.

What was in Tully's office that he didn't want disturbed? Was he hiding something? Or was he simply particular about his things, as Julia had said?

Marsh wanted inside that office. But how would he know when Tully was gone unless he stayed in town night and day?

He couldn't ask Julia for help. It might jeopardize her job, and he wasn't entirely certain she would help him. He smiled as a thought occurred. He could ask India.

Though piqued at his apology, a traitorous warmth fingered through Julia as she stepped inside the blue room. She closed the door, leaning against it as if he might follow her inside. Her heart thundered in her chest and an alien anticipation stroked at her belly.

She wanted him. And despite her limited experience with men, she knew he wanted her. Just now, at the bottom of the stairs, she had wanted to feel his hands, his hot, tempting mouth, lose herself in the dark, smoky scent of him.

He had apologized, then made it worse by swearing that he would never touch her again.

"Miss Julia?" Hazel croaked from the expansive four-poster across the room.

Julia pushed away from the door, hurrying over to the girl. She took a clean shift from the foot of the bed.

Purple shadows rimmed the girl's brown eyes. Her face was chalk-white, drawing attention to her few faint freckles. Thin pale skin stretched over her protruding collarbones. Julia eased an arm behind the girl's slight shoulders and helped her into a sitting position.

"Did you tell Tully?" Hazel's eyes widened in apprehension.

"No." Julia opened the tin of soda crackers and forced one into the girl's hand. "Eat this. It won't be long before he'll guess."

"I know." Hazel nibbled on the cracker, worry sharpening her angular features. "I'm afraid of what he'll do."

"He wouldn't hurt you?" Julia dipped a clean rag into the water basin that sat on the bedside table, then wrung it out before lifting Hazel's limp, dark hair and placing the cool cloth on her neck.

The girl looked down at her still-flat abdomen and placed a protective hand there. "He won't hurt me, but he won't let me keep the baby neither."

"Surely he wouldn't make you give it up!"

"What's he gonna do with a baby, Miss Julia? Even if Tully was willin', which he won't be, this ain't no place to raise a baby."

"I suppose you're right about that." She glanced around the spacious room with its sky-blue counterpane and flocked blue and white wallpaper.

The mahogany bedside table was draped with a blue floral-and-ribboned fabric. A dainty gaslight lamp with a frosted white globe rested in the middle of the table.

This room was nice and clean, hardly outfitted with the gaudy decor one would expect of a brothel. But even if Hazel were allowed to move in here with her child, there was no denying the purpose of the place.

The other rooms contained a bed, a lamp, and a table with a chamber set of basin, pitcher, cup, and pot, rudimentary items placed there only for the most basic purpose.

Hazel sniffed. "I don't want to get rid of it."

"Of course not!" Julia gasped. "Surely Tully wouldn't make you?"

"I don't mean to offend you, Miss Julia, but it's been done before. Not to me, but one of the other girls."

Julia covered the girl's clammy hand with her own. She remembered the wonder, the awe, and the excitement of carrying Pete, and wished for Hazel all those same feelings. "Hazel, you're not going to get rid of your baby, are you?"

"No, I'm not." She firmed her lips and squeezed Julia's hand in return. "I won't."

"I'll help you any way I can."

"Oh, Miss Julia, you done too much already."

"I've done nothing except bring you crackers and wipe your face," she said with a smile. "I want you to let me know if you need anything."

"Thank you, ma'am. Thank you." The girl's grip tightened and her eyes filled with tears.

"Would you like to change your shift now?"

The girl nodded and set the tin of crackers on the bedside table. She pulled the old shift over her head and traded Julia for the fresh one.

"That Mr. Tipton sweet on you?" Hazel's voice was muffled beneath the garment.

Julia gave a nervous laugh. "Don't be silly."

"I seen the way he looked at you the other night when you was playin' the piano. I know what that look means." Experience beyond her eighteen years colored her voice.

A blush heated Julia from her neck to her toes, her skin prickling as though Marsh were in the room with her. How could she feel it simply by hearing his name? "He works on the farm, for my mother actually. I hardly ever see him."

"I don't get to see my Bill much, but I think about him all the time."

"Bill?" She asked the question in order to shift attention from herself, but she also wondered if Bill was the father of Hazel's child. Of course, in Hazel's line of work, how would she know for sure? "Bill Young?"

The girl chewed her bottom lip before nodding reluctantly. "You cain't tell Tully, Miss Julia. He'd shoot Bill for sure."

"I won't. It's your place to tell Tully, and you must do what you think best."

Hazel nodded. "Don't worry. I won't tell nobody about Mr. Tipton."

"There's nothing to tell," Julia said airily, but her chest tightened.

"You looked—I don't know, scared or somethin' just then. Are you scared of him?"

"No, of course not." It wasn't Marsh she feared, but her own reactions to him. "Why would I be? I told you, he's our farmhand, nothing more."

He was so much more, and Julia suddenly wanted to know everything about him. What made him smile, what regrets he carried, if he had dreams beyond capturing the next outlaw.

The man went out of his way to reassure her, to make sure that she wasn't involved in his nefarious activities. She had known he wanted to go inside Tully's office, but he had asked her nothing except why Tully insisted on fetching things himself.

". . . just lie here for a while. I'm not feelin' so queasy now, but I don't think I can face Tully yet."

"Rest for a while. He knows you're ill." Julia gathered up the used rags and the shift. "You'll let me know if you need anything else?"

"Yes, ma'am." Hazel snuggled under the sheet and smiled, her eyes as round as nickels in her pale face. "Thank you."

Julia let herself out and quietly walked down the stairs. Hazel's words echoed in her mind. Could other people tell Julia was so affected by Marsh? After her response to his kiss, Marsh certainly could.

How could she not be affected by a man who treated her son with genuine affection and kissed her as though she were the only woman on earth who could ease his hunger?

Whatever defenses she'd possessed had been shattered by his kiss. How could she resurrect a wall against a man who was so obviously concerned for her? In spite of herself, she was charmed, and Julia feared it was becoming obvious to him.

She didn't want to be involved with him, and yet she was piqued that he had apologized. That kiss had renewed an awareness of herself and of men that she hadn't felt in years. It had turned her bones to water, and she gladly would have allowed more. Not an admission she was proud of, but true all the same.

She had wondered if he had been struck with the same reckless abandon she had, the same willingness to be seduced. Instead, he had apologized and sworn never to kiss her again.

He was right to draw the line at intimacy of any kind. Even so, Julia ached at the loss.

John's job had forced choices she never would have made. Forced her, however unwittingly, into the line of danger. It had crippled her son, deprived him of a father and her of a husband.

Marsh Tipton offered nothing different from what John had, certainly not security or stability or peace. Things that Julia had sworn she would give Pete and herself.

Yes, Marsh was right to retreat behind an invisible line that never should have been crossed. No matter how much she wished things to be different between them, she knew they couldn't be.

"We're having fried chicken." Pete sat on the cot and watched Marsh scrub a towel over his damp hair. "That's Ma's specialty. And biscuits. You *know* how good Gran's biscuits are."

Marsh grinned, poking playfully at the boy's ribs. "You must be pretty desperate for company to be bribing me with your gran's biscuits."

"You gotta come. This'll be the first time you've had supper with us."

He was tempted. There was little he could do tonight on the case. From India he had learned that Tully would be at the saloon all evening for his biweekly poker game, so there would be no chance to snoop around the barkeep's office.

There had been no word yet from Brill concerning the in-

formation Marsh had given him. And the idea of a home-
cooked meal tugged at him something fierce.

"*Everybody* wants you to. Please."

He doubted that "everybody" included Julia. Not after the
way she had bolted from him at the saloon. He didn't know
if she'd been angry or embarrassed, but instead of reassuring her, he'd sent her running.

"You wouldn't be foolin' with me, Pete? Just so I'll eat
your share of greens?"

"No sir." The boy shook his head vehemently. "I like
greens. We only wanted you to come to supper."

"Well," Marsh drawled, watching hope light Pete's young
eyes. "All right."

"Yippee!" The boy pushed off the cot and started toward
the door at a fast hobble.

"Hey, thanks for the soap!"

"You're welcome!" the boy yelled. "Hey, Marsh, don't
smoke in the house, okay? Ma doesn't like it."

He smiled as Pete limped quickly outside. Gyp trotted
next to the boy, his tongue lolling out in happy abandon.
Marsh tugged on his boots, then followed, anticipating the
meal and the sight of Julia with a growing excitement.

Gyp was waiting when Marsh reached the porch. He
knocked on the door. "Sorry, boy, you'll have to stay out
here tonight."

The dog grunted in protest, but flopped down obediently
onto the porch.

India opened the door and pleasure warmed her eyes.
"Hello, Marsh."

"Hello." He removed his hat and handed it to her.

She placed it on a small table in front of the window,
where a jar of blue, yellow, and orange wildflowers splashed
color against the snowy white of the window curtain. "Pete
tells me you accepted his invitation. Hope you like
chicken."

"Yes, ma'am. And your biscuits too."

She smiled, wiping her hands on her blue-and-white

checked apron dusted with flour. "Come on in. We're almost ready. Julia's just washing up."

How would Julia receive him since their discussion at the saloon? He walked through the cozy parlor, noticing things he hadn't before. Of course, at the time he'd been focused solely on Julia, the scent of her, the feel of her.

A Sharpe rifle hung over the mantel of the stone fireplace. In front of the hearth were twin rocking chairs, one draped with a lacy white shawl. A glass-front cabinet full of tiny figurines and pewter frames stood in the corner behind him.

A trestle table covered with a daintily crocheted white cloth stretched in front of the window, its chairs pushed underneath for easy access. An unlit kerosene lamp sat on one end of the table, and a small student lamp burned softly in the middle.

The room was cozy but not suffocating. Julia's flowery scent lingered in the room, a hint of sweetness under the smell of aged firewood. Marsh moved into the kitchen.

The rich odor of savory spiced meat and vegetables permeated the air, and his mouth watered. "Smells good."

Pete smiled at him, painstakingly placing forks and knives at each place. At the stove, India forked chicken onto a platter, then covered it with a towel. She placed the meat on the table and urged Marsh to have a seat.

Four chairs circled the oblong table. The pecan wood was carefully tended though well used. Peg lamps burned in candle sockets behind him, and a window behind the stove stood open to relieve the heat.

Pete poured milk from a pewter pitcher, his arm wobbling slightly, and Marsh reached out a steadying hand.

"I made coffee." India wrapped the bottom of her apron around the handle and moved to the table, filling cups. She returned the pot to the stove. "We're ready as soon as Julia gets here."

"Here I am." She walked into the kitchen from the hallway, buttoning up her bodice.

Marsh could see only a smooth expanse of skin below her collarbone and the edge of her chemise, but desire lanced his gut.

She looked up and froze, her hands poised on the second button. Surprise and pleasure flitted through her eyes, then they shuttered against him. "Marsh."

Even though he had tried earlier to reassure her about his intentions, his gaze snagged where her hands rested on the swells of her breasts. Her sweet scent twined around him and his nerves tingled as he rose. "Hello, Julia."

Her gaze shifted to her mother, and he read bewilderment, then a stark flash of panic. *She hadn't known he was coming, and didn't want him here.*

Loneliness stabbed through him. Had the dinner invitation been strictly Pete's idea? Julia stood rooted to the floor as if she would bolt.

Pete broke the stiff silence. "Ma, Marsh is comin' to supper with us. I told him about your fried chicken."

"Good." Her forced smile strengthened Marsh's feeling that he wasn't wanted.

Before, he had felt welcome, even comfortable in the house; now the ceiling seemed to press in on him and the air grew sparse.

"You know, I just remembered something I should do before Henner closes the store." He rose and squeezed Pete's shoulder, his voice husky. "I appreciate the invitation. Maybe another time, okay?"

He didn't wait for an answer but moved slowly toward the hall, giving Julia time to step out of his way.

"No, Marsh, please stay." Pete scooted out of his chair and limped around the table.

India chimed in. "Everything's ready and you'll need to eat sometime tonight."

Julia said nothing. Whether because she wanted him to go or was still stunned at seeing him, Marsh didn't know.

Feeling caged, he strode toward the door. "I'll get something in town. Lil's serving pot roast tonight, I believe."

"You've eaten in town every night since you arrived." India followed him out of the kitchen. "It'll be all over town that I can't even set a table for my farmhands."

He smiled as he knew she expected, but inside, his chest squeezed tighter. He didn't want to cause Julia any pain, and he obviously had, simply by showing up.

He reached the front door and opened it. Light footsteps rushed behind him, and Julia said breathlessly, "Please, Marsh. Don't go."

"You're just being polite." His voice was low, for her ears only, as he stepped onto the porch. "It's all right, Julia. I shouldn't have come in the first place."

"Nonsense!" She followed him out, pulling the door shut.

Her scent tormented him with images best ignored, and he eased back a couple of steps, trying to put some distance between them.

She gave him a tremulous smile. "Please stay. You surprised me, that's all. I . . . I didn't know you were coming and I wasn't . . . as you could see—" Her hand went to the throat of her bodice and her skin flushed pink in the late daylight. "I was just embarrassed."

"You're being kind," he said flatly, rubbing his chin.

"I want you to stay." Her gaze locked with his. "Really."

"Yeah," he said dryly. "I thought you would swoon with joy when you saw me."

"Stop it." Her blush deepened. "I was surprised, not irritated. It's true I didn't know you were invited, but stay. Please. I'd like it."

What harm could come of it? He and Julia would be chaperoned by her mother *and* her son. "I don't want to disappoint the kid."

Julia smiled, and his insides warmed. "Good. And from now on you'll take all your meals with us."

"No, I can't do that." He couldn't curb the surprise in his voice.

Julia stared at him in bewilderment and placed her hand on his arm. "You signed on to work for room and board and I'm afraid we've, *I've,* provided very little of the latter."

"It's not necessary." Her touch sent a fine shiver under his skin.

She withdrew her hand, looking vexed.

"I do appreciate the gesture."

"But?"

He swallowed and rubbed his chin. "I don't think it's a good idea to get too involved."

"You mean . . . with Pete?"

Hell, no, I don't mean with Pete. "Yes."

"I see." Her eyes searched his, the green depths layered with yearning and confusion and curiosity.

He felt the same dangerous things, but he couldn't make himself turn away from her tonight. Just once he wanted to feel the warmth that had been freely offered to him.

"You will stay?"

He nodded. "I'd like to."

"Good." Relief and genuine pleasure warmed her eyes. She opened the door, glancing back over her shoulder. "Coming?"

"Yep." He smiled, and when she smiled back, he clenched his fists to keep from reaching for her.

Except for one incident, dinner was relaxing. Julia was full of laughter and impish exchanges with India. And Marsh was fascinated.

Her eyes glowed like heated emeralds, and for the first time, she seemed completely relaxed around him. Well, not completely.

She'd caught him staring raptly and blushed, squirming in her chair as though he'd tickled her. A delicate pink had stroked up her neck and he imagined that she blushed that delightful shade all over. His blood heated and he hadn't been able to look away.

Prudently, he took his leave soon after supper.

"You don't have to go yet!" India exclaimed.

Julia echoed her mother. "Can't you stay for a while longer?"

"Please, Marsh," Pete chorused the loudest.

Though it was difficult to walk away, Marsh couldn't foster a relationship that he knew he'd have to forget. He smiled and walked to the front room. "Thanks for the meal. I enjoyed it."

"I meant it when I extended the invitation for every night," Julia said.

He shook his head, his gaze holding hers. She knew why he couldn't accept.

India glanced from Marsh to Julia, then took Pete by the hand. "Help me with the dishes, Pete."

"But, Gran—"

"Good night, Marsh," India called, pulling Pete along.

"Good night. Thanks again."

"Bye, Marsh!"

"Bye, Pete."

He smiled, his gaze shifting to Julia.

"I'm glad you stayed," she said quietly.

Uncertainty thrummed up his spine. "Me too."

He stood only inches from her. Her gaze skittered away and color stained her cheeks. Walking past him toward the window, she lightly fingered the flowers on the table.

"They're lovely."

"Yes, they are." He gazed hungrily at her, remembering the open smile she'd given him moments before.

She cast a glance over her shoulder, then looked quickly away, almost shyly. "You certainly didn't have to go to all that trouble. Pete said you picked them before dinner."

Marsh pulled his attention from the flare of her hips. She thought he'd given her the flowers? "Uh, Julia?"

"Yes?" She turned, her eyes lighting eagerly.

He inwardly cringed, reluctant to tell her he'd never seen the flowers until he'd arrived for supper.

Realization unfolded. Pete had given Marsh the soap in an effort to gain Julia's attention. Had he given Julia the flowers in an effort to make her believe that Marsh was interested in her? Yes, the less-than-subtle efforts *were* Pete's.

"I think you've been set up. Both of us actually."

"What do you mean?"

"I didn't give you the flowers."

Despite his gentle tone, she colored in embarrassment. "You didn't?"

He shook his head.

"Then who—Mother?"

"Pete."

She glanced down at the blooms. "Why would he say they were from you?"

"He gave me soap."

"Soap?"

Marsh explained about finding it on his cot. "I think that was supposed to help me get *your* attention."

"Oh, yes, I noticed today at the—" Her gaze skittered away, and she added with quiet dignity, "You smell very nice."

At the compliment, pleasure warmed him, but he ignored it. He knew he should leave, but was reluctant to do so.

She glanced at him. "So this dinner was Pete's idea?"

"I think so."

"I'll talk to him."

"Aw, come on. He didn't do any harm."

"You're defending him?" She gave a small laugh. "I'm surprised."

"If you bring it up, he might be embarrassed. As long as *we* know where we stand, it's okay, isn't it?"

She studied him, her eyes full of questions. "I suppose you're right."

"Good." He grinned. "Don't worry. I know the soap doesn't mean you have designs on me."

She smiled, but it lacked her usual warmth.

He sobered. "If Pete asks me to supper again, I'll say no."

"I don't want that." Her gaze, rife with uncertainty, searched his.

"It would probably be wisest," he said with a firmness of purpose he didn't feel.

Disappointment chased across her delicate features, and she glanced away. "Of course. Whatever you think best."

He didn't know what was *best*. He did know that he'd have to be extremely careful about spending time with Julia.

CHAPTER ELEVEN

Julia. Excitement fringed with a sense of the forbidden rippled through him. Since last week, thoughts of her had lurked on the edge of his mind like a secret addiction.

Hell, he was already half in love with her—her strength, her beauty, her unflagging devotion to Pete, but he wouldn't pursue her. Through Julia, Marsh had finally understood the desperation that drove Beth to leave him.

The day Julia had given him John's papers, he had glimpsed the pain, the rejection she'd suffered because of John's job. With bitter regret Marsh realized he'd resigned Beth to those same things.

And Marsh knew a relationship between him and Julia would yield the same heartbreak. His job as a detective was his life, and she had made it plain that she wanted no part of that life.

He couldn't act on his feelings and was seized with a fierce sudden urge to solve this case and move on.

Half an hour later, he stood in the woods just south of town. Late-afternoon sun glared through the trees. Even in the shade, heat shimmered, and sweat trickled down his spine. The scents of bruised grass and flowers mixed with manure and horseflesh and the slight odor of a rotting carcass. Overhead, a hawk cried harshly and a group of sparrows chirped frantically.

Marsh wore his oft-used disguise of a shapeless charcoal hat and sack coat, a well-mended pair of gray trousers and a specially made pair of soft-soled boots.

A mixture of ashes and powder turned his hair and eyebrows to steel gray. He wore the hat low on his forehead. The overly large coat hung loosely from his broad shoulders, making him appear frail. Special pads sewn into the lining gave a roundness to his back that depicted an elderly man.

A pair of black woolen gloves, minus several fingers, concealed the calluses on his hands and helped camouflage his strength.

An old belt hitched up the sagging trousers, creating the illusion of a slender frame and brittle bones. Marsh knew that he now appeared thirty years older and forty pounds lighter.

He tugged off his boot and dropped a pebble inside, then pulled the boot back on. Taking a deep breath, he closed his eyes and pictured in his mind the image he wanted people to see. Anyone he met today would not see Marsh Tipton, hired hand, but a stooped, gray-haired man with a pronounced limp.

Thanks to India, he knew he had at least thirty minutes before Tully returned. She had ridden back from Spinner with the news that the saloon owner had gone to the neighboring town of Osceola for a liquor purchase.

He put a leather pouch around his neck and over one shoulder, adjusting it beneath the coat so that it rested at his right hip. He crossed the rutted dirt road, edged up to the livery and around the back of the saloon.

From the street he heard the clippety-clop of horses and the clatter of wagon wheels. Wind whistled through the alley between the livery and the saloon, dimming the sound of footsteps and voices.

A padlock secured the back door of the saloon. Removing a wire-thin tool from the pouch, Marsh set to work. In seconds the lock snapped open, and he slipped it into his pocket.

He took a tin of lard and smeared it on the door's double hinges, easing the door open soundlessly. Daylight slanted over his shoulder into the windowless room.

Stepping inside, he closed the door and removed a candle stub from his pouch. Stale cigar smoke and the tang of liquor hung in the air. He lit the candle, and a ring of gold light rippled through the room.

His first impression was that he had found only trash. Paper fluttered from the wall, was strewn across a curve-legged table at the south side of the office and stacked atop a shoulder-high cabinet, spilled from a desk against the north wall.

The cluttered room measured about ten by twelve and was surprisingly clean of dust. A broom leaned in the corner next to the cabinet. On the jamb of the door that opened into the saloon hung a trio of keys. Marsh moved silently to that door and pressed his ear against it. He could hear nothing.

Footsteps vibrated on the second floor and he glanced up, assuming they belonged to Tully's girls. Urgency wound through him, and he walked over to the table at the south wall, his soft soles rubbing faintly against the wooden floor.

Thumbing through a stack of papers, he made out scribbled notes for liquor, an order for mugs, a bill of sale for the chandelier. He moved to the desk on the other side, which shared a wall with the telegraph office.

A round stool shoved under the desk was the only thing in the room free of paper. On top of the desk were receipts and ledger books. He pushed aside a box of Virginia cigars, exposing worn green felt glued on top of the desk.

The corner of an envelope protruded from beneath the felt covering, and Marsh pulled it out. It was addressed to *Jms.*

M. Tully, but Marsh's attention riveted on the return address. *Tully Ironworks, Pittsburgh, Penna.*

Hell. Did *Tully Ironworks* belong to Tully, the saloon owner? Marsh ran his fingers inside the envelope but found no letter.

Cautiously, he moved the candle lower and flipped through another stack of papers, finding an order for the saloon's piano and the saloon's bill of sale dated 1871. Five years ago, just as Tully had said.

From next door, the telegraph machine clicked an annoying rhythm. Marsh tried to focus on the room. He wasn't sure what he was looking for, but something that explained why Tully was so protective of this cluttered office.

The candlelight shifted, slanting Marsh's shadow across the wall to reveal deep scratches in the wood. Pausing, his gaze inched over the portion of the wall just above the desk. Frowning, he moved the candle closer. Something bothered him about those scars in the wood.

They weren't scars at all, but words and numbers written in pencil. Wax rolled down the side of the candle and stung his hand, but he was barely aware. Anticipation flicked at him, and he pulled out a stubby pencil and a piece of cigarette paper to make notes.

5:00. 623. May. 1:00. 12160. Nov. Noon. 9700.

Months he could recognize—May, November. Some were obviously times, but for what?

Frustration burned through him. Were these scribbles significant to his case? Tully might or might not have made these notations. Why would he write on the wall, when he had all this paper within easy reach?

The resuming click of the telegraph machine prompted Marsh to return to the worktable for another look. Footsteps clattered up the saloon stairs, and he tried to determine if the person headed up or down.

Behind him, the telegraph machine clicked in rapid succession, then paused. Footsteps vibrated on the floor above.

These were heavier, different from those he'd heard before. Did they belong to Tully?

Wary now, Marsh's muscles clenched. A *thud* sounded on the saloon wall and adrenaline shot through him. Voices filtered through from the telegraph office, then were drowned out when the machine resumed its bothersome clicking.

Damn that infernal telegraph! He strained to hear over the rapid-fire rapping, but could hear only an irritating *tap tap tap*. After a few seconds he was able to distinguish some of the signals. *Short long. Long long short. Short.*

Too bad he didn't know Morse, he thought dryly. He'd be privy to someone's message. Marsh took one last look around and moved toward the door, the annoying click of the telegraph swelling in his head.

Suddenly he pivoted, his gaze boring into the wall that was littered with undefined messages. The wall shared by Tully and Bundy.

If Marsh could clearly make out the length of Bundy's signals, so could someone else. By knowing Morse code, outgoing and incoming messages could be translated from right here in Tully's office.

Anticipation shot through him. Did Tully know Morse? Marsh again studied the scribbles on the wall. Why were there so many numbers? Could some possibly be dates? Amounts of money? Would any of them correspond with information from past robberies?

The faint scratchings could have been there since before Tully owned the place, but the pull in Marsh's gut told him they hadn't.

Tully had served in the war. Exactly what duties had he performed? Another agent would be here within the next two days and Marsh would have Tully's background investigated. Tully Ironworks was the perfect place to start.

A voice, definitely masculine, drifted through the wall, and Marsh straightened. Boots thundered across the floor, then quieted. Bottles and glasses clinked against each other. The stairs creaked again and Marsh opened the door that led outside. A glance around assured him he was still alone. He slipped out, carefully pulled the door shut, and replaced the padlock.

He crept north, behind the buildings, then padded along the wall of Carl Monday's barbershop until he emerged at the corner. Just as he moved into the street, a man stepped down from the barber's porch.

"Whoa!" Riley Carmichael recoiled to avoid a full collision.

Before he could check his movement, Marsh rammed into the preacher. He ducked his head as he grabbed the corner of the building. Hell!

Riley's hands closed on the shoulders of Marsh's ill-fitting coat to steady him. "Are you all right?"

"Fine, fine," Marsh mumbled, making his voice frail. "Just a little startled."

"I apologize." Riley released him and stepped back. "I'm afraid my mind was elsewhere."

On Julia no doubt, Marsh thought darkly. He patted clumsily at the reverend's shoulder. "No harm done."

"Good."

The preacher peered at Marsh, but before he could say anything further, Marsh gave a close-mouthed smile and hobbled off. "Good day to you, then."

"Yes, good day." Curiosity colored Riley's words.

Aided by the pebble in his shoe, Marsh hobbled across the road. Even though he could feel the preacher's gaze bore into his back, Marsh forced himself to keep a slow, steady pace as he passed Henner's store and the row of houses behind.

Damn! Carmichael hadn't recognized Marsh, but the accidental meeting had unleashed the memory of Julia's open-mouthed surrender to his kiss.

Did she respond the same way to Carmichael? Marsh instinctively knew she didn't, but what did it matter? The preacher offered stability, security. Marsh offered risk, uncertainty, and unreliability.

Frustration sliced through him. *Keep your mind on the case and get the hell out of Spinner.*

As long as we know where we stand with each other, it's okay, isn't it?

Perhaps Marsh knew where they stood. Julia didn't. Confusion and arousal and an unfamiliar restlessness churned inside her. She dipped her paintbrush into the bucket of whitewash and slapped it against the fence, her strokes impatient and short.

Whitewash flew through the air, speckled her wrist and hand. She cared less and less about Marsh being a detective. In his arms she forgot entirely his real reason for being at their farm. She was starting to fall in love with him and felt helpless to stop it.

She knew what life with him would be—always alone, always uncertain of his whereabouts or his safety, always second to his job. She couldn't endure another life like that. She *wouldn't.*

Yet despite that determination, her feelings toward him had changed. His defense of Pete's matchmaking had touched her. Even though her son had been disappointed at Marsh's recent distance, Julia understood that the detective was trying desperately to protect Pete from being hurt in the end.

She knew Marsh would leave, knew that was best, but she wanted him to stay, wanted to explore the feelings he'd evoked with his kiss.

Uttering a low sound of frustration, she wiped her perspiring brow. Perhaps he knew where they stood, but Julia had no idea. She was confused and surprised at herself because of it.

She knew nothing about the detective, not even his real name. But the man? He was stubborn and protective and would deny himself to the point of pain before breaking a promise.

Which explained why she was drawn to him, but not

why only a glance from his silver eyes could infuse her with feather strokes of heat and cause her breasts to grow heavy.

None of those traits justified this newly discovered emptiness in her soul and the realization that she didn't want to go through life alone anymore.

She felt suddenly overwhelmed. Hadn't she vowed to herself and to Pete that she would never become involved with someone like John? That she would never willingly participate in the unpredictable?

Marsh had destroyed her willpower as easily as rain eroded loose soil. Vexed, Julia tugged the bucket along the fence line and slopped whitewash on another picket.

"Need some help?"

Marsh's smoky midnight voice caressed her, and sensation skimmed along her nerves. She swallowed against a knot of desire and turned with a smile. "Hello."

"Hello."

His lips curved, but her attention was captured by his silver eyes, edged with the same desire she felt. Peripherally she was aware that his hair was damp and the V of his buff-colored work shirt was wet at the throat.

Despite wanting such attention from him only moments before, the frank sexual interest in his eyes intimidated her. She glanced down, dunking her brush in the chalky liquid again.

"Got another brush?"

Her gaze swiveled to him. "Haven't you already put in a full day?"

"Hey, I'm the hired hand. It's my job." He stepped closer, his warmth reaching out to her. "Why don't you go in?"

She should have felt crowded or threatened at his nearness, but instead she felt sheltered and somehow liberated. She inhaled the tantalizing scents of sun-warmed male skin and woodsy spice. The soap Pete had given him?

That renegade giddiness tickled her stomach again, and she ached to know if her response was caused by him or simply the hunger of her body for a man.

"Go ahead and take a break. I'll finish it, Julia."

Could she cause the same restless longing in him? "Did Pete put you up to this?"

"Nope." He grinned. "It's all my idea."

She smiled. "It will be faster if we both work. There's another brush in the barn."

He returned shortly, taking a position on her right about a foot away. A comfortable silence descended, broken only by the rasp of paintbrushes on old wood, the occasional *splat* of whitewash in a jostled bucket, and the lazy drone of insects.

Julia's gaze strayed to his broad hands and strong, corded forearms. They were smooth of hair and the color of wet birch, like his chest. She recalled that his upper chest was lightly dusted with hair, and a heavier line arrowed from his navel to disappear beneath his britches.

Want prickled her skin and her breathing became shallow. From the corner of her eye she could see him working diligently. He focused on the fence post in front of him, but she sensed that he was as aware of her as she was of him.

She gave a final stroke to the post in front of her and lowered her arm, bumping elbows with Marsh.

"Sorry." They spoke in unison.

He smiled, his silver eyes tempting her with heat and light and sultry promise. Tension rippled through her, and she turned back to the fence.

Marsh whistled tunelessly and Julia concentrated on the motion of her stroking hands, hoping to take her mind from the temptation that nudged.

They worked quietly for several minutes. She dipped her brush into the bucket and straightened just as Marsh turned. His arm brushed full across her breast. Her nipple puckered and her breath caught in her chest.

Before she thought, her gaze lifted to his. A muscle flexed

in his jaw and he jerked his gaze away. His grip tightened on the paintbrush until his knuckles blanched white. Leaning down, he thrust his brush into the whitewash and moved several feet away.

She told herself to ignore him, but finally Julia gave up and her gaze locked on Marsh. She painted the same fence picket at least four times. Without his beard, she could see the clean, sharp angles of his cheekbones, the sculpted jaw and chin. His features weren't exactly handsome, but they were compellingly, blatantly male.

Entranced by the subtle rhythm of his movements, she watched him paint. He balanced the brush loosely between two fingers. Long, smooth strokes down the fence post, slower, fluid ones back up.

She imagined those hands stroking her body with the same thorough care, and her throat ached. She wanted to be the focus of his intense silver gaze, wanted to explore the heat flaring to life inside her. Her tongue slid out to moisten her lips, and sensation fluttered between her legs.

Julia, stop. A flush crawled up her neck. Mentally shaking herself, she dipped her brush into the bucket that sat close to his feet.

He reached into the pail at the same time and their knuckles bumped. Her gaze riveted on their hands, his broad and dark against the pale rose and white of her skin.

Marsh didn't move. Hunger ravaged his features, carved the angles of his face into sharp relief. His gaze tracked over her as though memorizing every detail.

Her chest tightened and she could scarcely breathe. She wanted to feel the rough velvet of his hands glide over her skin. She wanted him to kiss her and brand her with his scent.

Longing darkened his eyes to gunmetal gray, and she could tell he struggled against wanting the same thing. For an instant she feared he would step away. Then, his movement seeming involuntary, he reached out with one finger.

As lightly as the kiss of the wind, he stroked her cheek. His finger was coarse but gentle, and her skin felt like a lush rose petal against it. She locked her gaze on his, letting him see how badly she wanted him to kiss her. Did he feel the same urgent need to merge their bodies, their scents, their hearts?

His hand poised at her cheek. Uncertainty clouded his eyes and his muscles locked, as rigid as granite. He wanted to walk away. At the realization, Julia's throat tightened. His pulse tapped frantically in the hollow of his neck, and she knew he was as affected as she.

She told herself to pull away, but her hand pressed against his in eager petition, knuckle to knuckle, pale skin to bronze, dainty to sturdy.

He dropped his brush and she heard a liquid *splat* as though from a distance. With a shaking hand he cupped her cheek and his gaze burned over her features. "Your skin is so soft."

She closed her eyes and dropped her own brush, savoring the feel of his hand on her. He took his hand away and she opened her eyes, wanting to ask him to stay for a few seconds more.

His gaze, hungry and devouring, captured hers. His fingers slid into her hair, loosened her chignon. Butterfly touches and the wicked scent of aroused male tested an invisible wire that ran between her legs to her breasts.

Kiss me, Marsh. She wanted it so desperately, her throat ached. *Kiss me.*

Desire flared in his eyes, and he leaned toward her. Eager to meet him, she lifted her chin, but he hesitated.

Impatient desire erupted inside her, and she cried out, "I want you to kiss me, Marsh Tipton."

"The name's Granger," he growled just before his lips covered hers.

Triumph swept through her, then melted away under the onslaught of relief and desperation. She rolled up on tiptoe and met his ravaging mouth with her own. Tongues caressed, slipped sleekly against each other in a desperate attempt to satisfy the desire coiling through their bodies.

He pulled away, slanting his head to the left now, and caught her moan with his mouth. He tasted of mint and coffee and a dark sweetness reminiscent of herself. One strong arm hooked her around the waist, drawing her nearer, until her breasts nudged his chest. Sensation streamed to her toes.

Julia trembled as though buffeted by a storm, and she held on to him, cradling his palm against her face and gripping his forearm with her other hand. His heart thundered against her breasts and his arousal swelled against her belly.

She couldn't breathe, couldn't reason and didn't care. Marsh was kissing her, filling her with light and promise.

Abruptly he pulled away and choked out, "No. Julia, no."

"Marsh?" She wobbled at the sudden loss and blinked against the burn of frustrated tears. "Marsh?"

"We can't do this, Julia."

"But—"

"Sugar, please." Agony lashed his features and he bowed his head.

"It's not wrong." She meant the words to be defiant, but they were quiet and broken. "It's not."

His gaze shifted to hers. Desire flushed his features and his eyes glowed like tempered steel. "I wish we'd met under different circumstances," he said hoarsely, then gave a wry laugh. "What am I saying? All I ever do is work. If it weren't for this case, we never would've met."

"Marsh." Julia shied away from his deliberate reminder of the case and struggled to control the urge to reach for him.

"You can't ignore it, Julia. The case brought us together and it'll tear us apart."

"Stop. Please." She did reach for him then, and he allowed her to touch his cheek.

He bent his forehead to hers, their breaths mingling. "We, *I,* can't allow this to continue." He stepped back, barely out of arm's reach, but emotionally much farther away.

Fear jabbed at her. "I have the feeling we've wasted a lot of time, that we should—"

"Julia, sugar." He gripped both her hands in his. Pain and yearning burned in his eyes. "Don't forget why I'm here. At best, this case will make you resent me. At the worst—" He broke off, his voice ragged. "At the worst, you could be harmed, and possibly Pete too."

"You would never do anything to harm Pete!"

"Not intentionally, but it could happen. Like it did with John," he ended softly.

Horror widened her eyes. "No."

"You can't ignore what I do, Julia. You can't pretend not to hate it."

It's not you that I hate. The admission burned through her chest.

He lifted her hands and pressed a kiss to her whitewash-spattered knuckles. "I can't be what you want. Or need."

She knew this honesty ripped at his insides as much as it did hers. Tears prickled her throat, and she bit at her lip to keep from crying. "I know you would protect us with your own life."

He closed his eyes, agony creasing his features. "I can't be this close to you, Julia. I won't."

Rejection bit into her, sharp and swift. She nodded and dropped her hands to her sides, struggling to retain a shred of dignity. "You're right, of course."

"I am," he said quietly, and walked away.

She took a step after him, then forced herself to stop. She wanted to curl up in embarrassment for throwing herself at him, for becoming hostage to those treacherous, beguiling sensations. She had completely disregarded his reasons for being there—reasons that could threaten her family.

Though her body clamored for him, Julia forced herself to retrieve her paintbrush. Moving mechanically, she dipped the brush into the whitewash and began to paint the fence. Dip, stroke, stroke. Dip, stroke, stroke.

Remember the Thompsons. Remember the Thompsons.

Julia repeated the words over and over until she lost herself in a blessed net of numbing warmth.

The name's Granger. As Marsh walked away, he bit back a curse. What had he been thinking, to tell her his name?

He could feel her staring after him, and his muscles strained to go to her, but he kept walking. He'd seen her painting the fence and slipped unnoticed into the barn to conceal his disguise. He should have stayed there, but seeing Riley in town had churned up his frustration.

He wanted Julia, wanted to be the one to make her smile, the one in her bed.

He'd been unable to resist the temptation of being close to her, reaching selfishly for what she had unthawed inside him, the exhilaration that confirmed his hunger for another try at life.

He had believed he could simply enjoy her company without giving any of himself. Even hammered by guilt and lashed with desire, he'd been completely aware the entire time that his emotions were involved, and he'd said to hell with it.

He had wanted her to know who he really was, to know the name of the man who wanted her with such gut-burning urgency. To know he was sharing a part of himself that he'd never shared with any woman, even Beth.

An image of Julia flashed through his mind. Her face was flushed with pleasure, her lips moist and swollen from his kisses. Raw energy licked at his skin and his erection throbbed painfully.

His nerves itched for her soft voice; his body burned for her soothing caress. He wanted to make love with her, realizing dazedly that for the first time he'd thought of sex in terms of sharing. Instead of craving a smoke, he craved Julia, but he couldn't have her.

The truth razored through him, leaving a sense of bitter loss. The guilt surged back, as it always did. He couldn't hurt Julia. Nor could he jeopardize Pete the way the boy's father had, however unwittingly.

He would rather live without her than live with the knowledge that he had caused her more of the same pain she had already suffered. For her sake, he kept walking.

CHAPTER TWELVE

He came to her that night.

Naked, he straddled her. He imprisoned her between his powerful thighs and pinned her arms above her head, his long fingers easily circling her wrists.

Warm, callused hands pushed up her nightdress, baring her knees, her thighs, the sandy hair at the apex of her legs. She quivered in anticipation.

Moist lips traced the path of his hands, his hot tongue flicking behind her knees, the cleft where her thigh met her pelvis, dipping into her navel. Restlessness combed through her and she opened her legs wider, impatient to feel his bare skin next to hers.

She wanted to reach for him, but he kept her arms trapped above her head, making her a willing captive of his wicked tongue and mouth and hands.

Warmth bloomed between her legs and she arched on the bed, seeking his heat, his mouth, his hands. Coarse whiskers scraped softly across her belly. He bunched the long-cloth gown higher, skimming it over her breasts. Cool air brushed her skin and his warm, moist breath puckered her nipples.

A constant stream of fire pulsed through her, layering want with need until they became one. She shifted against him, loving the feel of steel-taut sinew against the softness of her breasts. His muscles clenched and power roiled beneath the tenderness.

His tongue ignited wicked sparks of fire on her hip, the underside of her breast, in the hollow of her collarbone. He tugged the gown over her head and his lips closed over one pouting nipple.

She moaned deep in her throat and writhed, desperate to reach for him. The want steepled in her belly, clawing at her until she trembled. *Please, please.*

But her reflexes were stymied due to his fiercely tender onslaught and the words remained locked in her throat. A fine sheen of sweat misted her body. Her heart thundered in her ears, pulsed a sweet torment between her legs. She needed the relief of his body inside her.

His hand dipped between them, and one strong finger slipped inside her, sparking a rain of fire. Desperation clawed through her. She gasped and opened her thighs in full surrender, tilting her pelvis to deepen his thrust. *Yes, yes, yes.*

Tension unraveled, sliding, climbing, charging through her body in a frantic rush until the desire peaked on the edge of pain. Liquid silk spilled from her and sobs tightened her chest. She was slick and hot, aching for his possession. *Now. Take me now.*

She opened her eyes, wanting to see him when he took her. His face was cloaked in shadow and she made a sound of protest. His hands framed her face and he thrust his fingers into her hair, caressing her temples with his thumbs, urging her mouth to his.

His tongue stroked a slow exploration of her mouth until her eyes drifted shut. Ragged breaths tore from her and mingled with his. Her nipples, extremely sensitive, stung.

She wanted his hands everywhere. Fevered heat washed through her over and over, coaxing her passion to a frenzy. He lifted his head, his silver gaze sharp with desire and love.

Marsh. His name ached in her chest. Desperate to touch him as he'd touched her, she struggled against his grip. Abruptly, his hold was broken and she reached for him, but touched only air.

No! No!

Panic woke her, and she sprang upright in bed. The want hammered at her, cutting her breath and clouding her awareness. Dim moonlight crept under the curtain at her window and her gaze frantically searched the room.

Her nightdress lay on the floor; the counterpane and sheets tangled at the foot of the bed. Through the haze of unfulfilled passion, she realized she was alone.

She had been alone the entire time.

The want throbbed to an overwhelming pressure and frustrated tears burned her eyes. Aching to the point of pain, Julia bowed her head.

"Marsh." His name was wrenched from her in a ragged whisper. "Marsh."

Marsh.

He whirled, his heartbeat kicking into a rapid staccato. His hand closed over the butt end of his revolver.

Marsh. The whisper came again, and a shiver slid under his skin. Longing and loss pricked at him.

He expected Brill at any moment, but the broken, pleading voice had belonged to a woman. Julia?

Gyp sat a few feet away, staring at Marsh expectantly, as if he hadn't heard a thing. Odd. Tension stretched across his shoulders and he peered into the darkness, trying to see who called him.

Moonlight splashed over the road, sketching a wild rosebush and a stripling oak, a copse of hickory trees on the other side, but revealed nothing of human form.

Situated in a cluster of oaks, Marsh turned in a slow circle, his head cocked for sounds of Brill's approach. Marsh heard only the steady rhythm of his own breathing, the almost inaudible creak of holster leather as he shifted his gun, and Gyp's shallow panting.

Reassured that he was alone, Marsh relaxed. Who had

called to him? He shook his head, wondering wryly if a continued state of arousal could affect a man's hearing.

Since that kiss with Julia that afternoon, he had been hard-pressed to calm his body or his thoughts of her. No surprise considering what had happened between them, but the imaginary whisper of his name brought thoughts of her flooding back.

Gyp rose and Marsh glanced up just as Brill strolled out of the shadows into a wedge of light between two trees. The two men shook hands and stepped back into the darkness.

Marsh's gaze skated over the dips in the landscape, the lush grass rippling like a midnight-black blanket. "See anybody on your way in?"

"No." Brill plucked off his hat and ran his hand around the inside.

He stared into the trees, defining branches out of shadows, picking out the night eyes of a coon. "Nobody?"

"No." The other man withdrew a piece of folded paper and handed it to Marsh. "Something wrong?"

He gave one last cursory look around. "No."

"Thompson and his boys robbed a train last week, just outside of St. Louis."

Marsh shook his head in disgust. "They sure are gettin' around." He tapped the paper Brill had returned to him. "What did you find out about this?"

"Whoever's feeding information to the Thompson gang can read Morse."

So, he'd been right. "What's it say?"

"At first we thought it was only a translation of the newspaper release, written in Morse to be sent to the paper. But smack in the middle of the article a few words translated 'the source knows Morse.' "

Was Tully the source? Marsh tucked the paper into the bottom of his holster. "That could explain how the Thompsons knew about Touchstone and Gordon."

"If someone had seen the wires they sent, yeah, but how did they know about the others?"

"Maybe one of Thompson's boys followed our men like we've been doing to them." Marsh shrugged, certain that the key lay in whoever could translate the code. "Maybe our men were too obvious, like Lull and Daniels when they closed in on the Youngers outside Monegaw Springs. Got too eager and tipped their hand."

Brill was silent for a moment. "We know it's not Bundy. Who else has access to that telegraph machine? Who can get in or out anytime they want without raising suspicion?"

"Or can hear and decipher the messages that are sent?"

Astonishment spread over the other detective's face. "I'll be damned. Who would ever know that the guy had heard *anything*?"

"That's right."

Brill rested his hands on his hips and spat into the darkness. "Who you got in mind?"

"I want you to check out the saloon owner, Tully."

"That his first or last name?"

"Last. James M. Tully." Marsh recalled the crumpled envelope he'd found on the saloon owner's desk. "Check out Tully Ironworks in Pittsburgh."

"I've heard of it. What kind of connection are you looking for there?"

"I don't know yet." He hoped more that Brill could find a connection between Tully and Morse code, and shared the bit of information he had on the saloon owner, including the year of Tully's arrival in Spinner. "We need something on this case soon."

"Is there trouble? Someone suspicious of you?"

"Not as far as I know."

"More trouble with the woman?"

Marsh had no intention of admitting that he needed to get away from a certain blond widow before he lost control and compromised her. "I'm ready to nail these bastards."

Brill considered him for a moment. "I'll head for the Pinkerton office in Chicago tomorrow. Allan's son, Bill, will probably be able to help. And I'll send word to Allan about our progress."

"Thanks."

"It might take longer than a week."

"If we get something, it'll be worth the wait."

"Okay." Brill walked to the road, checking for passersby. "I'll be in Pennsylvania next week, but someone will meet you here."

"Send Allan."

The man's gaze snapped to Marsh. "All right," he said slowly. "You sure everything's okay?"

"Yeah." He reached into his shirt pocket for his tobacco and cigarette papers. "Just need to fill him in on some things."

After another measured stare, Brill disappeared into the night. Marsh lit his cigarette, snapped his fingers for Gyp to follow, then started down the steep incline that led to Julia's farm.

His need to see Allan was for the sake of precaution. He wanted his boss to understand how crucial it was that Julia, Pete, and India remain safe and uninvolved.

He cursed at the irony of the situation. Because of his growing feelings for Julia, he should leave. Because of his job, he couldn't.

The dream alternately thrilled and appalled her, but she couldn't forget it. Like a secret, she hugged the memory to her just as she hugged the knowledge of Marsh's real name.

It was as though she had a private piece of him that no one else had. Because Marsh Tipton—*Granger*, she corrected herself with a bittersweet smile—certainly had a private piece of her.

Past experience should have kept her thoughts from him. Marsh had forced her to remember why he was there, and just because she no longer believed that he constituted a threat didn't make it so. Because she should, Julia swore to forget about him. Somehow.

That decision had been made several days earlier, and though she had done a lot of thinking about Marsh, she hadn't had the dream again, even though she thought of it just before going to sleep every night.

That morning, after cleaning the saloon, she had accepted an invitation from Riley to attend ladies night on Saturday evening. With a little effort, perhaps she could fall in love with him.

Later that afternoon, Julia stood in the front bedroom, watching Marsh and Pete amble through the pasture and toward the creek. Midday sun spread amber-gold light across the ripening wheat. Her son struggled to match Marsh's long strides, and even from this distance she could tell Marsh tempered his pace so Pete could keep up.

Why didn't he send Pete back to the house? Since their discussion at the fence, Marsh had made himself scarce.

As much as it bewildered Pete, Julia knew it hurt Marsh. He had been alone a great deal in the past few days, as had Julia.

She'd thought a lot about what he'd said about wanting to protect them all. Lately she had realized how much she blamed John for Pete's injury, when John had been more a victim than anyone. Though the realization shamed her, she was relieved that she didn't feel that way anymore.

John's unselfish work had helped many people. He hadn't been able to help their son that awful day last spring, but neither had she, and that hurt.

In spite of knowing that Marsh possessed John's same drive and unselfishness, in spite of the fact that he followed the same path, she still longed to know him. But he worked at staying well away from all of them.

Every time Pete had approached Marsh to spend time with him, he returned quickly to the house. "Marsh was busy," or "Marsh was working and didn't want me to get hurt," or "Marsh was going into town."

Which was why, as she stood looking out the window thirty minutes later, she couldn't understand why Marsh still hadn't sent Pete back to the house.

Irritation wound through her. He had to know that she would worry. In truth, she was vexed more because Marsh was spending time with Pete after he'd said he wouldn't.

"I don't like this." She turned from the window to face her mother, who sat quilting in the far rocking chair.

India bit off a piece of thread. "Julia, Pete couldn't be safer if he were with you or me."

"I know that. It's just that a few days ago—" She clamped her mouth shut, appalled that she had been about to explain her and Marsh's discussion. And the kiss.

India's hand moved deftly over the red-patterned fabric. "A few days ago what?"

"Marsh felt that Pete had, uh, ideas about him staying, and he didn't want to encourage that." She glanced out the window again, seeing no sign of them, and added emphatically, "He won't be staying."

India arched an eyebrow at that.

Her mother always saw more than Julia liked, and she fought the urge to squirm, turning back to the window. "Where *are* they?"

"You sound as if you want Marsh to stay."

"Mother, how can you say that?" She tried to dismiss India's keen observation, but heat crawled up her neck as she recalled being in his arms. "You know how I felt when he arrived."

"Yes, but that was some time ago." India ceased her stitching and watched her as though waiting for an answer.

She couldn't deny wanting Marsh to stay, but neither could she share what had happened between them. The kiss had drawn them together, but learning his real name had brought about a deeper level of trust that had been growing.

"Something's changed, but I suppose you'll tell me when it suits you."

"There's nothing to tell, Mother."

"Whatever you say, honey."

"Oh, Mother, stop." Julia gave a light laugh and opened the front door. "I'm going after Pete. Do you want to come?"

"No, I want to finish this square. Why don't you invite Marsh to supper?"

She almost told her mother about his refusal to share their meals, but India eyed her speculatively, so she shrugged. "All right, but he probably has plans. You know, to spy on someone or sneak around somewhere."

"Oh, Julia, it's not because of the job that you're wary of him."

"What do you mean?" Anxiety fluttered in her chest. Had her mother guessed that she battled feelings for Marsh?

"You'll realize it for yourself, I think. Don't be too hard on him, all right?"

"He was the one who suggested spending less time with Pete. I just intend to remind him."

As she drew closer to the creek, anxiety slowed her steps. She hadn't seen Marsh since the dream. What if he took one look at her and knew every last searing detail? That was silly, of course, but her nerves fluttered anyway.

Her palms were clammy and she fluctuated between irritation at him for spending time with Pete and pleasure that he had established such a rapport with her son.

She pushed through the trees and emerged into the clearing. Pete's laughter sounded on the wind, followed by a splash. She shaded her eyes and scanned the bank, the weeping willow to the right, the flat rocks and the gnarled oak tree that arched over the water.

Marsh and Gyp sat on the rocks, but she couldn't see Pete.

Suddenly he exploded out of the water, surfacing with the energy of a fish fighting a hook. Water sprayed both Gyp and Marsh.

"How long was that?" Pete yelled, breathing hard.

Julia's breath knotted in her chest. She broke into a run, skirting rabbit burrows and ragged seams in the earth. Why had Marsh let Pete in that creek?

Her son flopped backward, water slapping at his back.

"Pete!" Her voice sharpened with panic. "What are you doing?"

Marsh rose, turning. Gyp leapt in the air and barked.

She rushed toward them, barely aware of Marsh's frown as she searched the water for her son. "Help him! He doesn't know how to swim!"

"He doesn't need any help, Julia. He's fine."

She splashed into the water.

"Hey, hold on!" Steely fingers bit into her arm.

She pulled against his hold. "Let me go. He barely knows how to swim."

"Julia—"

"Hey, Ma!" Pete surfaced several yards away and swam easily toward her.

Her body went slack. She blinked and her jaw dropped as he expertly maneuvered the distance between them. "Wh-what are you doing?"

"I'm swimmin'." He flipped over on his back, then dove below the water, resurfacing close to the bank.

"You certainly are," she murmured.

Marsh tugged at her arm. "Julia, you're getting wet."

"He's swimming." Hardly able to comprehend what she saw, she stared at Marsh. She felt torn between ordering Pete out of the water and praising him. "He's marvelous!"

"Julia, your shoes."

She glanced down. Two inches of water covered the tips of her kid boots and lapped at the hem of her skirt. "Oh."

"Here."

She allowed Marsh to pull her onto the bank.

"He's good, huh?" He stared after Pete, pride softening his features, and she was struck by a mixture of fear, panic, and irritation.

Marsh had taught Pete to swim and Pete had kept it from her. With a sharp flick of her wrist, she snapped her wet, clinging skirts away from her ankles. "You shouldn't encourage him to do things like that."

"Why not? He's great at it."

"You might hurt—he might get hurt or something."

"I would never hurt him, Julia." Anger flared in his eyes. "Or let him get hurt."

"What if you weren't here? Or weren't looking? What if—"

Pete traipsed out of the water and hurried past her, his limp barely noticeable. "Watch this, Ma."

"Pete, I don't think you should—where are you going?"

"To the tree." He was already climbing up the trunk of the oak several feet away that arched over the water.

"No." She started toward him and once again found herself halted by Marsh.

"Let him show you, Julia."

"What is he doing?"

"You'll see." He grinned as his gaze followed Pete's progress up the tree.

Nausea churned. That old tree had to be at least fifteen feet tall and eight feet above the water. "Marsh, tell me."

"He's going to swing from the rope."

"Swing?" She craned her neck and found her son moving lithely among the branches. "No, he's not. Pete, you come down right now."

"Julia, let the kid alone."

"He is not your child," she said hotly. "How dare you!"

"You're not helping him by being so overprotective."

"Overprotective? I am not!"

Marsh studied her through narrowed eyes. "What would you call it?"

"I'm, I'm . . . concerned."

"Ready, Ma?" Pete hollered down at her. "Watch!"

Her gaze flew up. He perched on the highest branch of the tree, looking small and helpless.

"He swims better than a fish, Julia."

"That isn't even possible," she hissed, waving Pete down and trying to catch her breath. "He's been here only a hand-ful of times and—"

"The kid can really swim. Hell, the first day I was here, he swam all over the place."

"And you didn't tell me?" Hurt, her gaze shifted to his.

A red flush crept up Marsh's neck and he glanced away. "I promised I wouldn't."

"You're sharing secrets with my son," she said flatly. "You knew I wouldn't like this."

"Hell, you never let the kid do anything. You handicap him more than the damn leg does."

Her eyes burned with quick tears, but she sniffed haughtily. "I didn't know you were so concerned with what he's allowed to do."

"You can't expect him to hang on to your skirts." Marsh kept his gaze pinned on Pete. "It's not fair and it's not right."

She stared at him, speechless at the indignation in his voice. As if her own son needed defending from *her*!

"You can't be with him all the time. You need to let him try things while you're here to guide or console, but don't hold him back." His voice gentled. "If he can't fend for himself, what will he do when you're gone?"

"Well, you won't be there for him, will you?" She turned away.

His hand squeezed her shoulder. "I'm sorry. He's not mine and I shouldn't presume to know anything about kids."

"You know more about mine than I do," she said sadly. Why did she suddenly feel that she wasn't enough for Pete? When had he become so self-sufficient? A sharp pain twinged in her chest and she covertly swiped at a stray tear.

"I shouldn't have said anything," Marsh said quickly. "You've done a fine job with him."

"I can't be both parents to him, can I?" She shifted her gaze to Pete.

"Ma, are you watchin'?"

"Yes, honey." Julia thought she might retch. All she could imagine was Pete falling and breaking his leg or hurting his lame one. The air seemed thin and sparse, and panic stretched across her chest until she could hardly breathe. "Oh, Marsh, make him get down."

"If something happens, I'm right here." Compassion warmed his eyes. "Let him show you."

"I can't watch this."

"Yes, you can. I'm here."

She glanced up as Pete inched farther out on the branch, his features creased in concentration. The end bowed under his weight and his skinny legs dangled above the water, causing her heartbeat to arc painfully. Realizing how much this meant to her son, she kept quiet, but her stomach clenched.

Marsh glanced at her, then looked back at Pete. Frustration raked through her. How easy for Marsh to stand there and calmly watch. He hadn't found Pete broken and bleeding on the ground.

He moved closer to her and she instinctively knew the gesture was meant to reassure her. Apprehension knotted her nerves and dizziness swept over her.

Barely aware of what she did, she reached over and grasped his hand. His muscles tightened in surprise, but he didn't pull away.

Pete latched on to the rope and Marsh squeezed her hand. Her son jumped and swung out over the water, soaring higher and higher into the sun. She edged closer to Marsh, fighting the urge to bury her face in his shoulder. She was plastered to his side so tightly that she could feel the definition of his ribs through his shirt.

He kept her hand tight in his, one iron-thewn arm pressing against her breasts.

Pete let go of the rope and sailed through the air, tucking his body just before hitting the water in a burst of speed.

"Oh, my goodness." Her gaze darted over the water, searching for his blond hair. She clutched at Marsh. "Where is he?"

Pete cleaved the surface in a spray of water and sunshine. "Yahoo!"

He bobbed in the water, almost to the bend past the willow tree. Julia started forward, certain he wouldn't be able to make it to safety.

Marsh held her back. "Wait."

With strong, even strokes, Pete swam toward the shallow water, where Gyp frolicked like a puppy. Her fear eased somewhat, then was joined by a growing pride.

"Look at him." Tears of relief and pride blurred her vision. "Look how strong he is."

"Didn't I tell you?" Marsh smiled at her, and Julia smiled back, wrapped in a net of warmth and belonging. For an instant she imagined that Pete was *their* child, that the incident with the Thompson gang had never happened.

But those thoughts were dangerous, made her yearn for things she shouldn't. It was brought home to her with slicing reality that Marsh would really leave, and the day suddenly seemed bleak. He had changed her life when she had been unaware and forced her to believe in hope again.

Pete climbed out of the water and tossed a stick into the air for Gyp.

Julia turned to Marsh, determined to have her say. "I'm sorry about what I said earlier. I know you would never hurt him or let him do anything to hurt himself. I appreciate what you said." She glanced away. "You know, about being overprotective."

"You knew it, Julia. And you were ready to hear it."

"Maybe, but . . . thank you."

Together they watched Pete and Gyp frolic in the water. His hand was warm and strong in hers. A quiet peace invaded her soul, and she knew it was due to Marsh. "You're good for him."

"He just needs some room." He looked at her, his eyes tender. "You're a wonderful mother."

She met his gaze full on, letting him see the longing in her heart. "He needs a man to look up to."

Naked pain ravaged his eyes, and he looked away, a muscle flexing in his jaw. "You know that can't be me."

Julia realized that she was making it more difficult for him to do his job and leave. Feeling torn, she stared at the ground for a moment, then nodded.

She had meant to upbraid him for encouraging Pete; instead, she had shown Marsh how badly he was wanted. She knew that he cared about them, enough to walk away and insure security for her and her son.

She could help him by separating their lives, the way they had been when he had arrived. Which was what she had already done by accepting Riley's invitation to ladies night on Saturday.

She gently extricated her hand, and Marsh's fingers slid across her palm in a sensual reminder of his hands on her in other places. Their eyes met and heat flooded her body. She walked quietly beside him down to the bank to meet Pete.

Her son's gaze went uncertainly from her to Marsh and apprehension clouded his features. "Ma?"

"I'm so proud of you." Her chest ached as she realized how quickly he was growing up. "Maybe next time you'll let me help you learn something new."

His eyes widened in surprise. "Really?"

"Really."

"Yeah!" He nodded his head vehemently and threw himself into her arms for a tight hug. "Yeah, I will."

Marsh squeezed Pete's shoulder and the boy stared up at him adoringly.

Julia's eyes burned. How could they bear it when he left?

CHAPTER THIRTEEN

Julia lifted the skirts of her Parma moss-colored watered silk and walked carefully out to the barn, searching for her mother. Pete wanted to stay with India rather than go into town with her and Riley.

She walked inside and lowered her skirts. The odors of fallow earth and hay dust and horseflesh tickled her nose. From the back corner, a light glimmered and a long shadow slanted across the back wall. The bitter-root smell of tobacco floated to her, and smoke curled through the air.

"Marsh?"

He rose and peered over the stall. "Evenin', Julia."

"Good evening." Regret twinged that she would be dancing tonight with Riley rather than with Marsh.

Nonsense. This was best for everyone, especially Pete. "I was looking for Mother. She offered to watch Pete tonight."

"Oh. Going somewhere?" he asked in a strained voice, his gaze stroking over her.

Awareness thrummed in her belly and she steeled herself against it, giving a forced smile. "I don't usually wear a dress like this to come to the barn."

"I suppose not." Hunger flared in his eyes and he looked away.

Julia knew he would read the same longing in her eyes if he looked. "Have you seen her?"

"Who? Oh, your mother." His gaze traced from the tips of her green kid slippers to the low, rounded neckline that bared the swell of her breasts and dipped low into the shadow between.

Heat flushed her skin. Though Julia had never thought the neckline immodest before, she suddenly felt she should place her kerchief there.

When finally he looked in her eyes, she was taken aback at the fierce desire she saw. He said hoarsely, "You look beautiful."

"Th-thank you." Awareness tiptoed down her spine and her throat went dry. He might as well have touched her, because her nipples tightened and sensation burned between her legs. She wanted to ask him to kiss her again, feel his callused hand against her breast, but instead she swallowed past a painful lump. "I'm going into town with Riley. For ladies night."

"That right?" His casual tone was lashed by an underlying tension. No emotion flickered in his eyes, but his lips flattened as he turned away and scooped up his hat.

"I believe you were at the last one? When we met for the first time?"

He walked around her and took a harness from the wall.

She smoothed her hair even though it lay perfectly in place. "Everyone's invited."

"You have a good time, then." Marsh tossed the saddle blanket over Sarge's back, then the saddle. "Haven't seen India since before supper."

Julia blinked, then remembered she'd come here looking for her mother. "Oh, well. I suppose Pete can go with us."

"You think that's proper? Takin' a boy to the saloon?"

She bristled at the biting tone. "He's staying at Lil's with her boy, Frank."

"Good."

She gave a tight smile. "If you see Mother, will you kindly tell her that Pete has gone with me and Riley?"

"I certainly will, Miss Julia," he drawled, making her feel

as if she'd ordered him about like a field hand. "Nothin' I'd like better."

"Thank you." She gathered up her skirts and walked out, fighting frustration and a sense of regret. She and Marsh had agreed to leave things unexplored between them, but even so, pain still gnawed at her.

She intended to do more than play the piano tonight; she wanted to dance until she didn't have the energy or the inclination to think about Marsh Granger.

The strains of "Aura Lee" swelled in the room. Julia rhythmically pressed the foot pedal, watching the dancers whirl by in a muted palette of lavender, red, gold, and blue. She refused to think about Marsh.

Several men waited out the dance at the bar, and glass chinked under the rhythmic melody. The scent of toilet water mingled with the aromas of hair oil and lye soap.

Next to her, Riley shrugged out of his coat and draped it over the back of a chair. His white shirt molded to his well-formed torso and the gray trousers emphasized his long legs. He was handsome, fun, and a decent man. So why didn't her palms sweat or her heartbeat race erratically? Why hadn't she ever begged Riley to kiss her, like she had Marsh?

She slipped easily into a smooth melody by Chopin, her fingers moving flawlessly over the keys. Music resonated from the tall ceiling and seemed to flow with the light.

The notes were energized yet somehow haunted. Riley danced past with Dorothy Webster, and Julia again wondered about her mother. She had thought India might have arrived before she and Riley, but her mother was nowhere to be seen.

Two hours later, Riley walked up with a lemon punch. "Tully says he'll play for a while if you'd like to dance."

"Oh, yes. I'd like to very much." She savored the tart sweetness of her drink.

He smiled warmly. "Good. I've been wanting to dance with you all night."

She smiled, wishing she could respond in kind. Tully's selection began with a crescendo, leveling off into a haunting melody. Couples glided around the room. Diamond-white light winked from the chandelier and spilled over the swinging doors into the street. A sweet-scented warmth filled the air.

Tully played long, soulful notes that stirred her soul, stroked her body like a caress. Riley placed her punch on a nearby chair and drew her into his arms, pulling her closer than he usually did. He folded one of her hands in his and placed it on his chest.

Surprised at this unusual show of affection, she smiled up at him. His eyes sharpened with desire, and Julia's breath caught in shock.

Oh, my goodness. She realized for the first time that Riley wanted her. She had known all along that he was interested in courting her, but seeing desire on his face and feeling it in the tense lines of his body slammed the insight home.

Feeling suddenly conspicuous, Julia glanced away. Why didn't she feel this unease with Marsh? When he looked at her this way, she ached to get closer to him, as she had in the barn.

Julia's skin tingled at the memory of Marsh's eyes burning like tempered silver. His gaze had branded her with hunger and possession, lingering on her breasts until she ached for him to touch her. Excitement clenched low in her belly and a shiver jumped up her spine.

"What?" Her attention jerked to Riley. "I'm sorry. I didn't hear you."

"I just asked if you were cold."

Stop thinking about Marsh, you ninny. "Don't be silly. It's the end of summer."

"Good." He guided her around the floor as Tully began another waltz.

". . . that hired hand of yours around lately."

"I'm sorry, what?" Julia mentally shook herself. What was wrong with her?

Speculation flitted through Riley's eyes. "You all right?"

"Of course!"

"Not too hot?"

"No." She teasingly patted his shoulder. "Don't fret. I'm not about to miss the first chance I've had to dance in ages. Now, what were you saying?"

"I haven't seen Marsh Tipton around much. How's he doing out at your place?"

"Er, he's been busy." Why did Riley want to talk about Marsh? A blush heated her cheeks, and she hoped her partner would think it was due to exertion. "He's been clearing that upper twenty acres and we've got enough firewood for three winters. I'd be glad to donate some for a needy family."

"I'll keep that in mind. He must be a hard worker. I noticed your fence had been newly whitewashed."

Her gaze flew to his. He couldn't possibly know what had happened at that fence. "Yes, he seems to work all the time."

"I'm glad your mother hired him. The farm needed some repairs. I know you were wary when he approached you, but you seem fine now."

"Yes, I am." Or at least she would be if she could rid herself of this fascination for Marsh.

Riley's gaze rested thoughtfully on her features, and she shifted against a surge of disquiet. "What is it? You're looking at me as if I had two heads."

"Hardly." His gaze, gentle and warm, roved over her. "You look exceptionally pretty tonight. Did I tell you that?"

"Yes, three times."

"So you *were* listening to some of the things I said."

She wrinkled her nose at him, feeling a surge of affection. Why, oh, why, was that all she felt? Riley was a good man, decent and strong, who would never run off and leave her.

But instead of appealing, the notion chafed like wet wool in the summer. She loved Riley Carmichael as a dear friend, not in the way a wife should.

Abruptly, he pulled her out of the circle of dancers.

"What's wrong?"

"It's late. Are you ready to go?"

"No," she replied spiritedly.

Before he could mask it, she spied the pain of rejection in his eyes. "I've been talking to you for nigh on five minutes, Julia."

Shame and frustration writhed through her. Because of these silly dreams she harbored about Marsh Tipton, she had hurt one of her dearest friends. "I don't blame you if you're ready to leave, Riley."

"I can take you home. It's all right."

"But I—"

"I don't think your mind is on the dancing, Julia." His tone, while firm, didn't condemn, which only made her feel worse.

"You're right. I'm sorry." She searched his eyes, desperately hoping she wouldn't see the hurt she knew she had caused. "I do have other things on my mind."

"I thought so." He smiled, the same old friendly smile she'd always known. "Let me take you home."

Relieved, she smiled too. "All right."

"The party's breaking up anyway." He cupped her elbow and turned her toward the piano. "Go tell Tully and I'll get the buggy."

As Riley threaded his way through the crowd of people jostling their way out of the saloon, Tully bade her good night. She met Riley outside, and they picked up a sleeping Pete at Lil's. After Riley arranged a pallet in the back of the buggy, she lay her son carefully on the narrow seat.

Riley touched the whip smartly to the horse's rump and his gray mare started off at a smooth trot. The wagon wheels clattered over the footbridge, the sound harsh in the still of the night.

A translucent moon glowed in an inky sky. Clouds, nearly invisible, became shadows as they passed over bright patches of light and stars played tag behind them. Off the road, a night bird cooed. A puckish breeze plucked at Julia's hair, teasing the ribbons woven into her upswept coiffure.

They rode in silence, and she snuck a glance at Riley. How did she apologize for hurting him? "It's a beautiful evening, isn't it?"

He smiled faintly, unable to completely hide his hurt. He kept his gaze fixed on the reins he held between his knees. "It's not really working, is it, Julia?"

"What?" Dread settled like a cold lump in her chest.

His voice was steady and quiet. "Your feelings aren't like mine."

"Riley—"

"It's all right." He glanced over at her, his gaze earnest. "It's no one's fault, but I'm right, aren't I?"

"Maybe in time."

"I don't think so," he said quietly.

"I'm sorry." Julia squeezed his hand, then quickly removed hers. She hated hurting him. He had become a third party in the unexpected futile dance between her and Marsh.

Riley's gaze searched hers. "Is it John?"

"No!" Caught off guard, the word exploded from her. "It's nothing like that."

He studied her for a long pause, then comprehension bloomed in his eyes. She realized that he suspected Marsh held her affections, but to his credit, he said nothing.

Once home, he saw her to the front door and said good night without even a kiss on her hand.

"Will I . . . see you?"

"Sure." His eyes were friendly, but nothing more. "In town, at church."

Sadness twisted at her. She ached at the hurt she'd caused, but she couldn't encourage him that she might someday return his feelings.

As he drove away, she realized she would never fall in love with him. He was exactly what she thought she wanted —safe, stable, loving with her son and her.

But she couldn't stop thinking about Marsh. He was a man who became whatever was necessary for a particular

job. A man who embraced danger, escorted it straight into
his life. A man she'd sworn to forget. So why couldn't she?

Marsh's plans of going into town evaporated as he watched
Julia and Riley drive away. A man could stand only so much,
and seeing them again tonight would test his control.

Resentment crowded through him. He knew she belonged
with a man like Carmichael, but he hated the thought of it.

He clenched his fists and turned on his heel. She'd looked
so damn beautiful. He'd wanted to spear his hands into her
hair, release the golden curls to cascade around her delicate
shoulders, ravage her mouth.

A groan of frustration escaped him. He couldn't sit
around thinking about her all night or he'd go crazy. Fervently hoping he'd soon hear from Allan or Brill, Marsh retrieved his leather pouch and pulled out John Touchstone's
papers, easing down onto the cot. How close were the
Thompsons?

They'd raided and robbed all over the state but had stayed
well away from Spinner. A quick scan of the newspaper release revealed no more than it had before, nor did it tie Tully
to anything. Restlessness chafed Marsh. He *knew* Tully was
into something shady.

He shifted the newspaper release and stared at John's
handwritten message. It was only then that Marsh realized
he didn't have the map. Grabbing the pouch, he thrust his
fingers inside, knowing even as he did it that the paper wasn't
there.

Where was it? He slid off the cot and dropped to one
knee, peering underneath the thin mattress. Cigarette butts
littered the floor, and there was no sign of the map. Gyp
moved up next to him.

Marsh moved systematically around the bed, running his
hands between the stuffed mattress and the flimsy iron
frame. The dog shadowed his every move, his wagging tail
brushing against Marsh's face.

He found nothing and concern changed to alarm. *Where was it?*

He dropped the mattress and reached for his bedroll, finding only the clothes he used as a disguise. He searched his saddle bags and under the band of his hat. At the bottom of his holster he found the decoded message he'd received from Brill.

Had Pete been playing out here, found the map, and taken it? Marsh didn't think the boy would take something without asking. Then who?

India. The realization jolted him.

Julia hadn't been able to find her. Marsh himself hadn't seen her since early that morning. Had India taken the map and gone to search for the cave? She'd said she might be able to find it.

He knew with a sickening thud in his gut that India *had* taken the map. He had to find her. If anything happened to her, Julia would never forgive him.

He'd never forgive himself. He would not be responsible for putting this family in danger.

Three hours later, Marsh reached the end of the roan's tracks. He had followed India's horse easily from the house, although he had run into trouble when she moved into a creek and stayed in the water for almost a mile.

As darkness fell, the soft Missouri dirt gave way to hard ground and finally rock as Marsh climbed the sharp hills that leveled out into a clearing. Shadows drifted over the land like sooty powder.

His gaze scanned the indefinable landscape as he waited through the torturous minutes between sundown and moonrise. Frustration burned across his shoulders.

In front of Sarge, Gyp zigzagged a line, sniffing the ground, then raising his nose high in the air. His ears pricked for the slightest sound.

Marsh reined the gelding to a stop, impatient for the slowly growing finger of moonlight to spread over the land.

Gradually inky shadow faded to pearl gray, then the pale milk of moonlight. Hills and grass turned black in the darkness. A hawk carved a figure eight against the sky.

The air was sultry and heavy with the scent of animals and grass and flowers. A hundred yards in front of him rose another sharp line of hills. To his left stood a heavy copse of oak and hickory trees. Between the hills and the forest was a stack of boulders, clumped tightly together, as if they had all once been part of the same rock. The odd-shaped boulder resembled the one on the missing map.

Gyp darted toward the rocks, then stopped, turning in a half circle. The ruff of hair on his neck bristled, then he abruptly tore into the night, disappearing between the boulders and the hills.

The hair on Marsh's neck prickled. He clucked softly to Sarge and the horse moved toward the same spot. The sickle-shaped yellow moon emitted a hazy glow, and stars scattered over the gunmetal canvas like silver dust.

He reined Sarge up beside the rocks and dismounted, proceeding on foot. The horse remained behind as Marsh moved through the grass, searching for Gyp. He spotted the dog pacing in front of a tree, his snout raised high.

"You better not be treein' a squirrel, you mutt," Marsh muttered. His gaze swung from the trees to the back side of the hills he'd passed.

Gyp circled the tree, then trotted off, nose to the ground. Marsh halted at the tree Gyp had just investigated. Spying a branch with several broken twigs, he skimmed a finger across the exposed inner flesh of the twig and felt moisture that indicated the breaks were recent.

Apprehension prickled up his spine. Gyp nudged his thigh and he touched the dog's head to quiet him. "Okay, boy. I hear you."

Caution tautened the muscles across Marsh's shoulders and down his back. Keeping a careful eye on the surrounding area, he crept through the trees toward a lone boulder that rested at a forty-five-degree angle from his position.

Behind him, Gyp traced the same path on silent feet. Together they rounded the boulder and Marsh's eyes widened in surprise.

Thick ankle-high grass fluttered in the breeze. Wild hydrangea and yellow lady's-slipper grew in clumps every few feet. Moonlight dappled the ground, and his gaze followed the wedge of light to a pocket of blackness. He blinked. It was the opening of a cave.

The cave on the map. Now that he stood there, he could discern the landmarks of the drawing. On paper this appeared to be a scramble of trees and rocks with a cave drawn conspicuously in the middle. What he had thought an obvious landmark was now revealed to be the back side of John's drawing.

Touchstone had drawn the map as the landscape would look if one approached from the direction Marsh had. Unable to distinguish the dimensions of distance or depth, he hadn't been able to tell that until that moment. Brilliant.

Pressed as he was against the boulder, his dark clothes melded into the shadows. Gyp sat quietly beside him, his fur standing on end.

He smelled no lingering odor of a fire or doused candle, and no smoke curled from the opening. Still, someone could be hidden deep within. Silently he slipped from the side of the boulder into a pocket of shadow, inching closer.

Gyp growled and Marsh froze, reflexively sliding his gun from his holster. A faint vibration rolled beneath his feet, and he stilled, anticipating it again. The vibration came, stronger this time. Then heard a shout, the distant rustle of underbrush, the thunder of horses. At least three, he decided, spinning toward the sound.

It came from beyond the trees to his left. Moonlight filtered between lush leaves, cloaking everything in thick, distorted shadows. The sound veered in another direction. He tilted his head to the left, listening intently to the rush of hooves on the ground.

He heard the low hum of voices, then a shout, and

sprinted toward the closest tree, taking cover. His gaze cleaved through shadow, past trees and brush, but he saw no one.

Rocks clattered and groaned. Steel struck stone as the horses skidded to a stop. A sharp scream pierced the air. A woman's scream.

India! Marsh's skin prickled. He froze, searching for direction. Dread curled through him and pushed him toward the sound. Gyp raced ahead, scenting the trail through thick patches of grass, then a tangle of brush which Marsh skirted.

He crashed through thickets and underbrush, unable to hear anything now. His heartbeat drummed wildly. Bush and brush and vines clustered in abundance, tangled around his legs. The sound of hoofbeats rumbled through the air, and he slowed, angling his body slightly toward the sound.

"Somebody's comin'!" hollered a masculine voice.

The noise was closer, more distinctive. Then horseshoes clattered on rock, scrambled, and the rhythmic cadence of cantering animals faded. They were leaving, whoever *they* were.

Gyp turned in an agitated circle and Marsh strode over to him. The dog sniffed the ground, whined softly, and dashed through the underbrush. It *was* India, Marsh realized with a sinking heart. But where? Drawing his gun, he followed the dog over a stump tangled with Virginia creeper and wild honeysuckle. Was she all right? What had happened? Who else had been there only moments earlier?

Gyp stopped abruptly, rocking forward before steadying himself with broad paws. Marsh jogged to a stop beside the dog, throwing out his arms to balance himself.

They stood on the edge of a cliff. Shadows and moonlight fused together to form a deceptive curtain so that Marsh couldn't judge the distance, but he could see a definite drop and jutting pieces of limestone and spidery branches. Fear plowed through him and he gulped in a deep breath. Had India fallen? Where was she?

Gyp whimpered and Marsh called in a low voice, "India?"

"Marsh?"

"Yes." Relief swept through him in a powerful wave, and his chest hurt. "Where are you?"

"Down here. Uh, in the brush." Her voice was strained and shaky. "Are they gone?"

"Yeah." Following the sound of her voice, he spied a spindly bramble quite a distance down. He holstered his gun and scanned the ground below, unable to pick out anything definite besides the bush.

Gyp sought a foothold and eased over the edge, starting down the steep incline. Marsh made out packed dirt, then rock and faint indentions in the face of the cliff for a hand-hold.

"Keep talking so Gyp can find you." He felt for a secure place with his foot and levered his way over the side. "How'd you get down there anyway?"

"They heard me and chased me to the edge of this cliff. It was either go over the side or face them. Ouch!"

"India?" he called sharply.

"I think . . . I hurt . . ." Her voice was faint. "My ankle."

"Can you move it?" Marsh slipped, and rocks crashed down the hill. He grabbed the nearest handhold, scraping his palm but managing to keep his balance.

Gyp jumped the last few feet to the ground and disappeared behind the brush.

"Hello, puppy."

A bubble of relief swelled his chest. India sounded like she'd be fine.

Her voice floated up to him. "I can wiggle my toes, but it hurts like blue blazes to do anything else."

"With luck, it's only a sprain." Breathing hard, he worked his way down the treacherous path by sheer feel and instinct.

He slipped again, catching himself on a sharp piece of rock that gouged his hand. On level ground at last, he walked around the end of the brush. He knelt beside Gyp and saw the pale oval of India's face, her eyes huge and dark with fright.

She grinned, and her white teeth flashed in the darkness

as she reached out a hand to him. "I've never been so glad to see anybody in my life."

"Are you hurt anywhere else?" He pushed up her skirts a fraction and felt her right ankle. It seemed fine.

"Fresh," she teased.

He grinned and reached for her other ankle, probing gently. "Behave yourself."

He touched the swollen joint and she sucked in a breath. "That's the one."

"It's pretty bad." He moved his fingers around her ankle, then over her foot. "It seems to be only a sprain. You sure you're okay?"

"Yes. Just get me out of here."

He balanced himself on his heels and glanced around. "I've been trying to figure out how to do that."

"There's a path that leads back up."

"Then why did you come down the hard way?" he teased, but the guilt returned. She'd come here to help him, and ended up like this.

"I didn't intend to come down at all." She winced as she took his hand and rose, placing weight on her uninjured foot. Latching on to his arm, she hopped out of the bush, grumbling, "I'm sure this dress is ruined."

Gyp licked her hand, whimpering, and she stroked behind his ears. "Thank you, Gyp."

He moved out of the way, enabling Marsh to place an arm around her waist. "Put your arm around my neck. If it's too painful, I'll carry you."

"And have your back go out? Then I'll never get out of here."

Marsh chuckled. "India, you're something else."

"Aren't I just?" she said dryly.

With one arm anchored around her waist, he guided her around a thicket of wild honeysuckle and to a stand of trees. "This way?"

"I think so." She peered around him. "Yes, over there. See? There's barely a break in the grass."

He spotted it, and together they limped toward the makeshift path while Gyp trotted ahead.

They established a rhythm, *step, hop, step, hop.* India was panting, as was Marsh, but she seemed to be faring okay. "What the hell happened, India?"

"I'm glad you found me."

"Me too. What were you doing out here?"

"I told you I could find this place. It only took me a little while to get my bearings. John must've drawn that map—"

"From the back side. Yeah, I know." Marsh lifted her over a protruding tree root, and they continued. Sweat slicked his back and neck. Guilt threaded through him, but he pushed it away. Answers first.

"I went inside the cave. Someone's been there, but I don't know when."

"And?"

"I heard voices, so I hid behind the boulder in front of the cave."

"Yeah?" He kept one eye on the trail. The incline grew steeper, and he slowed his steps, giving her a moment to catch her breath. Impatience rushed through him. He wanted to know if she had discovered anything before he reprimanded her. "Tell me the rest, India."

"I couldn't see their faces. It was dark and they all wore hats."

They reached the top of the incline and Sarge snorted a welcome to Gyp. Breathing hard, Marsh guided India toward the horse.

"Did you hear anything they said?"

She nodded, regarding him somberly. "They were talking about robbing a train in St. Louis. It might have been the Thompsons."

"Might not have," he countered, but it was. The information checked with what Brill had told him.

When they reached Sarge, Marsh released India and grabbed a kerchief from his saddle bag, kneeling to bind her ankle.

"Marsh?"

"Hmmm?" He pulled the makeshift bandage tight and knotted it.

"I recognized one of the voices."

He rose, alarm kicking at him. "Yeah?"

Silence.

He struggled to temper his impatience. "India?"

She reluctantly met Marsh's gaze. "It was Tully."

"Damn." Even his suspicions didn't diminish his shock and regret. He'd wanted Julia to be right about Tully.

"I almost called out for him to help me," she said shakily.

"Good thing you didn't."

"Like you said, it might not have been the Thompsons," she said hopefully.

"Yeah." Marsh agreed so as not to alarm her, but knew it had been they. He needed to hear from Brill, but already a plan was forming, a surefire way to get Thompson's attention. A way Marsh could control.

As soon as he spoke with Allan, he would set it up. Right now he had to get India home. He didn't relish the prospect of facing Julia. From the apprehensive look on India's face, she wasn't eager to see her daughter either.

After settling her on the horse, he mounted in front of her. He was grateful that she hadn't been more severely injured. She shouldn't have been there at all, but because of him she was. Guilt twinged again.

"There's no way Julia will overlook this, huh?" India asked morosely.

"Probably not."

"Fiddle. Are you going to tell her about Tully?"

"Yes. She can't stay at the saloon."

"Don't order her to quit, Marsh. She won't do it."

"She can't stay!" He craned his neck and looked at India.

"I agree, but you should let her make the decision."

"She'll listen to reason. I'll explain—what!" he exploded as India vehemently shook her head.

"I know how Julia is. If you push her, she'll go just to be stubborn. Why, she would move in there!"

He didn't answer. He'd promised no harm would come to Julia or her family, and India had very nearly tangled with the Thompson gang.

Guilt pricked like a needle and hardened his resolve. He wasn't sure he could allow Julia to make up her own mind.

CHAPTER FOURTEEN

Marsh had deposited India on the divan and ordered her to "tell Julia." Julia had followed him out, worried and anxious, but he wouldn't answer her questions, telling her instead to talk to her mother.

Julia's heart squeezed. "You've been helping Marsh from the beginning?"

"Well, since that time I followed him to see where they'd found young Gordon."

Fear pricked at her. "Mother, what were you thinking?"

"I thought I was helping," India said in exasperation.

"You might've been killed."

"Thanks to Marsh, I wasn't," she said soberly.

Julia sank onto the divan, hugging her mother.

"He blames himself, you know?"

"How can he?" she cried. "If it weren't for him, you might not be here."

"I don't understand it either." India settled into a more comfortable position, wincing as she did so. "Strange as it sounds, I think he feels responsible."

"But you involved yourself."

"Yes. And it's not as if he encouraged my help. In fact, he didn't like it one whit, even though he indulged me somewhat. I shouldn't have taken the map," she admitted in a subdued voice. "But he wouldn't share a scrap of information."

Because he hadn't wanted to involve her family, Julia realized. How many times had he sworn that to her? And what had *she* done? She'd accused him of putting her family in harm's way.

Was that why he blamed himself? Pain ripped through her. Despite her resentment of him, he'd gone heedlessly after Pete the time Gyp had knocked him into the water. He'd gone after India tonight and most likely saved her life.

Julia surged from the divan. "It wasn't his fault."

"I agree."

"I've said horrible things to him."

India sat up straighter. "What are you going to do?"

"Talk to him." She started for the door, then turned. "What about you?"

"It's just a sprain. I'll be fine. Go, go."

She crossed back to kiss her mother. "I'm glad you're okay."

"Me too."

Her nerves raw with anticipation and uncertainty, Julia hurried to the barn. She had to see him, tell him she'd been wrong. But he wasn't there.

Disappointment wrenched until she realized where he had to be.

She moved quietly out of the trees and through the clearing. As she'd hoped, Marsh stood looking out over the creek, hands clasped behind his back. Broad shoulders sagged with weariness, and for the first time since she'd known him, he appeared fallible.

He didn't turn as she walked up. Tension sketched his jaw, and he asked hoarsely, "Is she all right?"

Her heart squeezed. He *was* blaming himself. "She's fine."

"Good. I was getting ready to come look for you." He cleared his throat and looked at her, his eyes bleak with regret. "I'm sorry, Julia."

"It wasn't your fault."

He weighed her for a moment, then turned away. "Your mother recognized one of the men's voices tonight."

Julia frowned. "She didn't mention that."

"I didn't think she would." His gaze swerved to hers, measuring. "It was Tully."

"I don't understand." Alarm knocked at her.

"It's possible—likely—that he's involved with the Thompsons."

"But Mother said she didn't see anyone. How can you be certain Tully was with *them*?"

"I can't, but whoever she saw hightailed it outta there when they heard me and Gyp."

"Just because Mother heard Tully doesn't mean he's part of that gang," Julia denied hotly.

Marsh sighed and rubbed his neck. "Look, Julia. I know he's your friend, but there are some things that don't add up about him."

"What things?"

"It's better that you don't know, but you're not going back to that saloon," he decreed fiercely. "In fact, you should quit."

"I will not!"

"Well, then stay away." He took a deep breath, gentling his voice. "At least for a while?"

"Tully would never hurt me!"

Regret and sadness slipped over his features. "Sometimes men have to do things they don't want."

"I suppose so." She sensed that he was referring to himself as much as to Tully. He was wrong about the saloon owner, but she knew she wouldn't be able to convince him. "I didn't come here to talk about this."

"Oh?" His voice was rusty with fatigue. He glanced out over the water, one hand kneading the muscles of his neck.

She wanted to soothe his tense muscles, ease the worries he wouldn't share. "I came to thank you."

"Thank me? For what?"

"For saving Mother, of course."

"She could've been killed, Julia." He spat the words as though they stung his tongue.

"Thanks to you, she wasn't."

"She took that map, searched for that cave, and fell into that ravine because of me, because of this case." He bit off each word, brittle silver eyes spearing her.

"Oh, forevermore! You couldn't have stopped her from going. No one could've."

"She should never have had access to that map, Julia." His harsh voice was completely at odds with the tenderness on his face. "If it weren't for me, she wouldn't be involved at all."

"Marsh—"

"I swore to you that your family would be safe. Hell, I looked you right in the eye and promised to protect you." He closed his eyes briefly, agony twisting his features. "You said I'd put your family at risk, and I did."

"No!" she cried. "I was frightened and suspicious. I never should've said those things to you."

"She never should've gone, Julia," he said tiredly.

She wanted to erase the haunted look in his eyes, to reassure him that she would be forever grateful for what he had done that night. "Once you realized what had happened, you went after her. Where's the fault in that?"

"Don't paint me as a hero. That's not how it is." Anger and recrimination tightened his features.

She reached out and laid her hand gently on his arm. "Marsh, I accused you of endangering my family, and you've done nothing but save them since you arrived."

"No, Julia." Denial fired his eyes and he shook his head. "You're wrong."

"When Gyp knocked Pete into the water, you went straight in after him."

"Anybody would've—"

"*You* were there for me when he jumped from that tree into the creek." She gave a small laugh. "Tonight you were there for Mother."

Astonishment stole through his eyes, then disappeared. "Stop."

"I can't." Her gaze caressed his strong features. "I'm seeing you as I should've from the beginning, a good, decent man who cares about people, who believes in honor, who loves—"

"Get out of here, Julia." His voice broke. "Go back to your preacher. He'll keep you safe."

Julia knew then why she had really come to him. It was more than the need to reassure him. She had searched him out to answer this keening call of the spirit that drew them together. "I can't, Marsh. I want—" She broke off, uncertain and a trifle embarrassed. "I want you."

"Don't do this, sugar." Desire merged with protest ravaged his eyes. "Don't."

His voice drifted over her like sweet, silky heat. Even though she was willing to give him up for Pete's sake, she needed Marsh now and knew that he needed her. Tonight would be all they had of tomorrows. "I've never done this before."

"You shouldn't be doing it now." His voice was strained with pain and want.

The same want burned through her. She wanted one night where they could give to each other without the burden of danger or family or guilt. "I want to stay with you."

"Julia." His eyes closed, his features creasing in the struggle against surrender.

Yield, Marsh. To me. For me. The words emboldened her. "I want you to kiss me."

A breath shuddered out of him and he turned away. "Have you forgotten what I am? Why I'm here?"

"I know what you are, Marsh."

"Do you?" he demanded roughly. "You don't want me, Julia. You need somebody safe, somebody who'll stay home and help you raise Pete. You need Riley."

"No. I need *you*. I want *you*."

"Hell, I'm no different than John." A muscle rippled along his jaw, and leashed power vibrated through his body.

"Think about those long days and longer nights when he was gone, the resentment, the anger, the abandonment. Remember, Julia?"

"Yes, I felt all those things."

"It would be the same with me, and you know it."

"Just tonight. No promises, no regrets. One night to last the rest of our lives." Did he waver? She moved closer, her silk skirt rasping on the ground. Frustration and pent-up longing marked her agonized whisper. "Marsh."

Heat flared in his eyes. "It *was* you," he breathed.

She was only vaguely aware of his words. His gaze seared where it touched her face, her bared shoulders, the swell of her breasts.

"It was you that night." His eyes fastened on her face. "I heard you call out to me. Maybe I dreamed it, but it sounded so real."

He had dreamed of her? She moved closer, wanting to feel his breath on her lips. The memory of her own dream rushed back, and she recalled whispering his name, burning to feel him inside her, but he couldn't possibly have heard her. Could he? "I want to be with you, Marsh."

"Julia—"

"If it will salve your conscience, don't look at me. Or think of me as someone else, but take me. I want you to take me." She was astonished at the wanton plea, but her need was greater. "Please."

"We can't do this." The struggle to yield was plain in his eyes. "You'll regret it, resent me. No. No."

The only thing she would regret was leaving him. She pressed forward until his arousal nudged at her. "Marsh, I know you want me."

"Obviously I can't deny that," he said hoarsely. "But this is not a good idea. It's damn stupid. There's too much at stake."

Though she was charting new territory with him, she harbored no adolescent uncertainties. She knew what she wanted from this man. "Just for tonight, Marsh. Only tonight."

"Julia, do you have any idea how difficult you're making this?" On the edge of surrender, his voice shook. His muscles tightened against her. "You should go."

She touched the deep lines that bracketed his mouth and leaned full into him. His silver eyes were turbulent with the battle between desire and conscience.

Air crowded her lungs, and she felt as if she wouldn't be able to draw a full breath until he touched her. "Kiss me." Her breath skimmed his lips. "Please. I'm asking you ever so nicely."

"Julia," he groaned. "Stop."

"Like you can't get enough of me." In a whisper, she repeated his words from the first time they'd kissed. "Like you could just eat me up."

Restraint snapped and his lips covered hers with desperate hunger. He thrust his hands into her hair, forcing out the ribbons and gold pins and releasing her chignon in a cascade of silk that brushed her bare shoulders.

A sob of relief worked through her chest. She gripped his arms, memorizing the oak-hard feel of his muscles, the heat pulsing from his body. Her fingers whispered over his neck, then his jaw. She caressed the scratchy silk of his beard, keeping his mouth locked to hers. With deep plunging thrusts his tongue stroked the deep midnight velvet of her mouth, and a wanton wetness bloomed between her legs.

She craved his heat, his bare skin on hers, and pressed closer. Her hands moved between them, and she fumbled at the buttons on his shirt. He changed the angle of the kiss, capturing her lips with ruthless demand. Triumph and heat and love slid through her.

He pressed kisses on her jaw and cheek and eyes. He nuzzled her ear and heat showered through her. She moved restlessly against him and he lifted her, his arms snug around her waist. She latched on to him and dragged in a deep gulp of air, feeling light-headed and on fire.

She had no sense of moving, but suddenly she slid down his body, felt the scratch of a hickory tree against her bare shoulders, the catch of bark on her Parma silk. Marsh held her arms above her head just as he had in her dream, and she moaned in anticipation. Tension coiled between her legs, and her control slipped.

He dipped his head, nibbling at her neck until she said breathlessly, "You're tickling me."

"You tickle me every time you move, sugar," he rasped.

Her heart swelled and she wiggled against his hold, wanting to touch him. He released her arms, trailing his tongue from her collarbone to the swell of her breast above her neckline. She skimmed her hands up his nape, enthralled at his hard strength. Her fingers delved into the silk of his hair and stroked the warmth of his scalp.

He nipped at her flesh, wetting the silk of her gown. Her nipple pearled, and a shock of pleasure jolted her nerve endings. His hand moved over her back and the bodice loosened.

Impatient to be free of her clothes, she shrugged. The bodice dipped low and Marsh's mouth followed, burning through her linen chemise.

He fumbled with the tiny buttons down the front until the thin material sagged down her arms, baring her breasts. She moaned and pressed his head to her, silently begging for more.

He raised his head, eyes burning like the fired point of a sword, and his lips poised achingly close to her nipple. "This, sugar?"

"Yes," she moaned. "Yes."

He took her fully into his mouth, tonguing her nipple into rigid awareness. An invisible wire snapped taut between her legs. His arousal throbbed against her, echoing the desperate rhythm of her own body, and she strained toward him.

She shoved her dress and chemise down her hips and ripped at the tapes on her drawers, then leaned into him, naked save for her pale stockings and kid slippers. Her nipples teased the hair on his sculpted chest.

He dragged his hands over her hips and waist, then

cupped her breasts, looking at her. "You're the most beautiful thing I've ever seen, Julia."

"Kiss me."

He did, his tongue moving in her mouth with the same slow stroke as his hands, stinging every sense to razor sharpness. His swollen length throbbed insistently against her, and tree bark grazed her bare bottom. The knot inside her coiled tighter.

The coarse bark accented the smooth doeskin feel of arms, his shoulders. He cupped her bottom and pulled her into him. She opened her legs wider, riding a crest of sensation. His hands slipped over the curve of her bottom, then delved into the moist heat between her legs.

Her inner muscles clenched and she buried her head against his shoulder, aching. "Marsh, I can't wait for you."

"It's okay, sugar," he panted. "There's time for me later." With one finger he pushed inside her and she moaned. His tongue played in her mouth, matching rhythm to the movement of his finger, coaxing her complete surrender. Warmth exploded through her and slicked his finger. Still, she ached to feel him inside her.

She reached for his gun belt, pulling at the buckle while he untied the leather thong at his thigh. Yanking at the buttons of his Levis, she pushed them with his drawers to the ground. Her hand, cool and trembling, closed around his heated velvet shaft.

He bucked against her, and she loved that she had evoked the same wildness in him that he did in her. Tension corded his muscles as he allowed her to explore him.

Wonder shifted through her. Huge and heavy, he pulsed in her hand, urging her to meet an inner rhythm. She stroked his hot length, leading him to her center.

With trembling arms he lifted her, then lowered her slowly onto him. His gaze locked on hers, beckoning, urging, loving. Tree bark grazed her skin, heightening the sensation of his probing fullness.

As he slid inside, desperation clawed through her. She tightened her legs around his hips and pushed down, drawing him deeper. A groan escaped through his clenched teeth. She threw her head back, struggling to slow the frantic racing of her blood, resist the temptation to move against him. She wanted release, but not yet.

He bowed his head, his breath hot against her sensitive breasts. Sweat slicked his back, her neck, the cleft where their bodies met. His muscles quivered with control.

Sensation exploded through her and reason slipped away. "Marsh, Marsh," she called.

One broad hand moved up her back and gently shielded her shoulders from the bite of the tree. He wrapped his other hand around her waist and steadied her hips, thrusting slow and deep.

Light and warmth charged through her, fused in a sudden explosion of sensation. Her inner muscles clenched, and tension unraveled. She clutched at him, fighting the urge to move against him. "Marsh, I want to wait for you."

"I'm . . . with you, sugar. Right *here*."

She arched, intoxicated by the dark scent of him mingling with her scent of wildflowers. He thrust and withdrew, penetrating, claiming, until she cried out his name. Light exploded behind her eyes, and she clutched at him for support.

He threw back his head and his release pulsed inside her like a stream of fire. In a voice raw with longing, he cried, "Julia!"

Tears slid down her cheeks at the love in his face. She had felt his gentle worship of her body and known the moment their hearts joined.

Gently he lifted her from his body and carried her to the creek. Using his shirt, he cleaned her inner thighs, then himself. At that moment her heart surrendered totally to him, and she felt the soul-deep loneliness she would carry from then on.

He rinsed the shirt and tenderly cleansed her breasts and back. Though his gaze caressed her with love, an invisible wall rose between them. He was saying good-bye.

Hand in hand, they walked silently to the house. Guilt lashed him. Not for what he'd just shared with Julia—he would never condemn that—but for what he had come here to do, for the danger he'd brought to her doorstep.

Like the oft-unnoticed change from winter to spring, he had retreated from the precipice of disillusion and darkness, the reckless disregard for his own life. Making love with Julia had shown him how bleak his existence had been.

And would be again. Her strength and light filled the dark corners inside him. He wanted to hold her, protect her, stand beside her forever.

For the first time, he wanted to try a new life, give up his days of roaming and investigating and putting first the care of other people. He wanted to selfishly take the chance for a life of love and dedication and trust that Julia had offered him.

Spending time with Julia and Pete had infused Marsh with a burning urge to try life again, to give more than he took. He had fallen in love with her, and because of that he wouldn't permit his job to threaten the security she craved.

"This can't happen again, Julia."

"I know." She halted beside the corral. But instead of releasing his hand, she gripped it tighter. "Can't we wait a little while before we—"

"No, sugar. We can't." Agony pinched his insides. "It won't get any easier."

He fought the urge to kiss her one last time, knowing he would find love there and reassurance, but never absolution. He couldn't ask Julia to sacrifice the stability she had worked so hard for. He couldn't disregard her life the way he had Beth's.

He ran a hand over his face, frustrated and sick about what he had to tell her. "I want you to know what happened to my wife, Julia. It won't make a difference with us or what I have to do, but I want you to know."

"Marsh, you don't have to tell me anything. Remember, no promises."

"I want to tell you." He wanted to pretend he'd never been the man who had married Beth Catlin. He wanted to be, for always, the man who had just made love to Julia. But he was both. "My wife is dead because of my job."

Denial flared in her green eyes, but she watched him quietly. "Tell me."

Her sweet warmth floated around him and somehow gave him the strength to turn away. He hooked one arm around a corral post. "I was a detective when we married. She knew that about me, but she couldn't abide the uncertainty, never knowing if I was coming home. You went through the same thing with John."

Julia looked as if she wanted to deny it, but finally she nodded. "Yes."

"She left me. And she had every right."

"Oh, Marsh." Julia eased closer, not touching him but close enough to show him that she offered comfort. "Was there someone else?"

"At least one."

"I'm sorry." Her voice ached with sadness.

"That was because of the job too," he said bitterly. "She was going away with him, so desperate to escape me that she couldn't wait for the steamer she'd booked. She—they—hired a man to row them out to a boat that had just left the dock, but a sudden storm came up—" His voice broke and the memory surfaced of Beth's blackened, unrecognizable features. "They were struck by lightning."

"That wasn't your fault!" Julia cried.

"Promise you'll stay away from me, Julia. I can be only so strong. Promise me," he urged savagely. "Promise."

"Marsh—"

"Go to Riley."

Hurt flared in her eyes. "I don't want Riley."

"It would kill me if something happened to you or your family because of me." He touched her cheek, tucked a stray strand of hair behind her ear. "It would kill me."

Tears glistened in her eyes. "I can't promise, but I'll try."

He expected relief, but there was only a gnawing emptiness.

A lone tear trickled down her cheek. She reached out and gripped his hand as if garnering strength from him.

His heart ached and he wrapped his hand around her smaller one, wishing he could stay, make a family with her and Pete. *I love you, Julia.*

The words remained unspoken. As she'd asked, he would make no promises.

"Weren't you the one telling me not to be so overprotective?" She smiled through her tears in a valiant attempt to tease him. But her welfare and that of her son weighed too heavily on him.

He raised her hand to his lips, brushing a kiss across her knuckles. "This is different."

Her hand tightened on his and she moved into his arms. He gathered her close, inhaling the sweet perfume of her hair and the tantalizing scent of him on her skin. They stood by the corral, thinking words they couldn't say, pledging silent vows they couldn't honor.

They would never again share what they had a few moments before, and the realization drilled into him like a dull blade, causing his resolve to waver.

Remember Beth.

Reaching for a strength spawned by guilt, Marsh eased away from her. "Sugar, you're gonna have to—" His voice cracked and he steeled himself, not wanting her to see the effort this cost him. "You're gonna have to go in."

Her eyes glimmered like wet emeralds. "Now?"

"Now," he choked. His willpower was as flimsy as gossamer. If she didn't leave, he wouldn't be able to release her. "Please."

With trembling fingers she tenderly traced his lips. Her eyes, tortured and wounded, held his as she moved away.

He gripped the fence rail and forced himself to remain there until she was gone.

Marsh bowed his head against the rough wood of the
fence, pain screaming through his body as though he'd been
horse-whipped. He'd done the right thing, but the knowledge didn't soothe the racking pain.

CHAPTER FIFTEEN

Julia had never agreed to steer clear of Tully. Irritation chafed and Marsh tried to focus on that rather than on the memories of last night. Damn, he was ready for the whole thing to be finished.

He'd heard from Allan, who'd slipped up unexpectedly while he worked in the pasture. They had arranged to meet that night at an abandoned cabin close to the cave where he had found India.

At dark he saddled Sarge and rode out. When Gyp followed, Marsh sent him back. "Stay with Pete."

Leaving the dog behind, he kneed Sarge into a canter, disappearing into the trees. Staying hidden as much as possible, he took an indirect route to the cabin.

He stayed within cover of the trees until he reached the mesa. Slowing the horse, he rode across the flat, unprotected expanse of land toward the hills that rose in the distance. His thoughts seesawed between Julia and the upcoming meeting. How was he supposed to forget her, when he could still taste her honeyed fire, hear her ragged moans?

He pulled his thoughts from her and focused on the surrounding landscape. Scant moonlight sketched shifting patterns on the dark earth. The scents of grass and heated animal flesh flirted on the breeze as he neared the hills. Clear and distinct, they seemed sculpted from the ebony sky, and moonlight drifted over the peaks like a silver-blue mist.

Despite his efforts, he couldn't dismiss the images of last night. Julia, a wild golden flame in his arms, had melted his caution and peeled away the old scars and guilt to reveal his need for her.

He'd never wanted Beth the way he wanted Julia. Maybe because he and Beth had grown up together and been expected to marry since their childhood. Whether or not it was the familiarity of lifetime friendship, he had never been consumed with this raw, aching need. Until last night.

He hadn't been able to resist the temptation of making love with Julia in the dark, sheltered by trees and rocks and midnight. Had she realized how closely that paralleled his life? The act had been covert and shadowed and more precious because of it.

While he had savored every glorious second, he wanted to make love to her in freedom, court her in plain view of everyone, declare openly that he wanted her.

There was no chance he could do that now, but what about when this job was finished? Not for the first time, he wished he could stay, make a life with Julia and Pete.

Could he settle in one place and remain there all his life? He hadn't been able to commit before, nor had he been able to give Beth what she needed in terms of love or trust. How could he with Julia?

He'd never considered doing anything other than detective work, but the last few weeks of physical labor had spawned a different kind of pride. He was building something, clearing the way for a future, and he felt proud of that, but for how long?

His job with the agency was the one thing he could depend on, the one thing that had given him a reason to live after Beth. With the job, he knew what was expected and what he was capable of giving.

He passed the clump of boulders he'd discovered the night before and guided Sarge into the thick forest that ringed the hills. Anxiety crawled over his skin.

Up ahead a light glimmered. Allan? The light flashed again, the blink of a lantern outlining a man's bulky form. By the signal, Marsh knew it was Allan who waited for him. Nor did he worry that Allan would mistake him for anyone else. Pinkerton had probably been watching Marsh since he'd passed the boulders.

Allan's blocky form took shape, and that of the rickety cabin behind him. Marsh dismounted and walked toward his boss. "Glad you got here so fast."

Allan motioned Marsh to silence and strode past him. "You were followed."

"Impossible!" He whirled, his gaze scanning the trees and bushes that were distinguishable only by the pale light that filtered through the leaves. "I was careful."

"Since the clearing," Allan whispered. "Stay here."

He disappeared without a sound, and Marsh shook his head, stunned. Wouldn't he have known if someone were following him? From long years of practice his senses were honed to detect any threat, audible or otherwise.

A loud *thump* sounded, then the snort of a horse. He eased his Colt out of his holster and sidled alongside Sarge.

As though emerging from a blank canvas, a horse and rider suddenly formed out of the shadows. Allan materialized at the horse's right shoulder. At that instant Marsh recognized the interloper.

"Julia!" Irritation spiraled into anger, and he strode to her, hauling her down from her horse. "What are you doing?"

"I need to talk to you. If I'd known you were meeting Allan, I would've waited."

"*You* followed me? How far?"

"From the house."

He started. "From the—no. I would've heard you at some point."

"You obviously didn't." She pulled away from him.

"She's got you there." Allan chuckled and patted Julia's shoulder. "It's good to see you, dear. Though I would've preferred an invitation for some of your mother's peach pie."

"You know you're always welcome, Allan." Her teeth flashed white in the darkness.

The two of them carried on as if they were at a damn social! "Allan, I apologize," Marsh said stiffly. "This has never happened to me before."

"It's all right. Obviously you don't perceive Julia as a threat, or you would've been aware of her."

Marsh blinked, uncomfortable with that explanation. Angry at himself for leading Julia into this situation, he growled, "What's so important that it couldn't wait?"

"How was I supposed to know if you were coming back?" she hissed, then said more calmly, "It's about the saloon."

"The saloon? What about it?" Suspicion stabbed at him. "You didn't go to work today?"

"Well, yes. Before church. I wanted to tell you—"

"Julia, you can't do that!"

"I already did," she informed him coolly. "And I've decided to help."

Help? He stared at her for a full minute.

She sighed. "If I don't go in to work, Tully will think something's wrong. Besides, this way I can tell you if I notice anything odd."

"I thought we already decided you weren't going."

"No. Actually we didn't discuss it because we—" Her gaze shot to Allan, then back to Marsh, and she finished lamely, "We were busy."

She was talking about their lovemaking. Even though he couldn't distinguish in the dark, Marsh knew she was blushing. Heat stirred low in his belly, but he refused to be put off. He took her arm. "It's not a good idea. You can't do it."

"You're not forbidding me?" She tensed, and in the murky light her steady green eyes appeared black.

He realized then that he had no claim on her, no right to forbid her to do anything. With a jab of regret he released her. "I wouldn't *forbid* you, but consider what you're doing. If Tully's involved with the Thompsons, it could get ugly."

"If I'm there, you'll be able to find out if he's involved. I can look around his office if you'd like."

"Julia, explain this to me." Marsh folded his arms and regarded her dubiously. "You've wanted nothing to do with this case since I arrived. Less than nothing. And now this?"

"I don't understand it completely myself, but I just know I have to try. I have to do something."

She sounded more like her mother than the Julia he knew. At the realization, India's words scrolled through his mind. *Let her decide, Marsh. For herself.*

Fear niggled at him. What if something happened to her? "You said you'd keep a distance."

"From you, not this."

He felt Allan's steady gaze and looked over at his boss, who studied them both with open curiosity.

"Excuse us." Marsh pulled Julia farther away and lowered his voice. "I can't let you do this. If you won't consider the danger to yourself, at least think about Pete."

"Don't you think I have?" Fear and uncertainty sharpened her features. "In a way, this is for him too."

"This makes no sense, especially coming from you."

Her eyes glittered in the darkness and he felt the pain go through her. "I've been talking about putting the past behind me for a year, but I haven't done it."

"This isn't the way."

"What better way to finally say good-bye to John?" She gripped his arm. "Don't you see?"

Panic shoved through him, but he reined it in, finally giving voice to the fear that tore through his heart. "What if it's your *final* good-bye, Julia?"

Her eyes softened and she moved closer to him as if seeking comfort. Or giving it. "You're taking the same risk."

"It's *my* job, dammit!" His chest tightened until he thought the pressure would tear him apart.

"It's more than that now," she said quietly. "You proved that last night."

Unable to deny it, he held her gaze. No matter how fleeting, he had made a commitment by making love with her last night. He'd sworn not to involve her. Now, despite her gallant efforts to the contrary, she was involving herself. He wanted to shake her, force her to see reason.

Compassion and understanding flitted through her eyes. "I want you to agree, but I'll do it even if you don't."

He gave her a flat stare, knowing refusal would only make her more stubborn. "I don't like it, but I appreciate your willingness to help."

"You'll be there to protect me." Her gentle smile made the nerves in his stomach dance. "If I'm not worried, why are you?"

"Because you shouldn't be doing this." The thought of taking responsibility for her made him skittish. All he could remember was how he'd failed Beth. "You can't depend on me, Julia."

"Yes. I can." Her eyes shone with faith and trust.

Marsh's gut twisted. He had meant that she shouldn't depend on him to the point of becoming complacent about her safety, but it didn't matter. He would die before he let anything happen to her.

"You'll ride home with me," he said pointedly as they rejoined Allan.

As she passed him, protest screamed through his body. He didn't want her involved in this, but at least with her at the saloon, he could step in to protect her if necessary.

"Everything okay?" Allan asked.

Marsh gave a sharp nod, his gaze scouring the trees beyond. "You and I need to talk." Noting Julia's interest, he jabbed a thumb behind him. "Over there."

They stopped at the corner of the cabin, far enough so that she wouldn't be able to hear but where Marsh could keep an eye on her.

Allan stood with his back to the cabin. "Brill said you had a hunch."

"Have you heard from him?"

"Not yet."

"He's checking on someone for me." Marsh recounted what he had discovered in Tully's office.

"You think Tully's tapping the wire?"

"I don't think he has to. My hunch is that he's interpreting the code as messages are sent or received. And he can do that from his office." Marsh kept his gaze locked on Julia, alternately wanting to kiss her and tie her up to keep her out of this mess. "You can hear the machine through the wall as clearly as if you're standing next to it. No one would ever know Tully was listening."

"Damn, that would certainly explain how two of our agents were killed. What about the others?"

"I don't know. Careless, maybe, or just downright unlucky. We'll probably never know."

"I'll come into town with the money," Allan said slowly. "You and I will meet behind the bank. There will also be some stagecoach security."

"Julia works at the saloon. Someone needs to keep an eye on her."

"We'll get somebody, but not you. It wouldn't do for Tully to suddenly get wise." Allan paused for a moment. "Hodgkins, I think. Brill may not make it in time."

"Good. I may have someone who can help us inside the bank."

"Who?"

"The sheriff."

Allan's eyes widened. "*You* trust him?"

Marsh considered how long ago Kisling had voiced his suspicions, yet he had never threatened or interfered with the investigation. "Yes."

"Okay, talk to him. We'll set it up for Friday."

"Five days isn't much time. Brill said Thompson just robbed a train outside of St. Louis."

"Two days ago they hit a stage at Gallatin."

"What if they don't hear about the money coming through Spinner?"

"They will. I'll make sure of it," Allan said firmly. "We're not going to lose them this time, Marsh. Especially now that Julia's involved."

"Do you think they can make it to Spinner by Friday?"

"If there's enough money, they'll make it."

"Listen, Allan." Marsh didn't want to give away the extent of his involvement with Julia, but he wouldn't leave anything to chance either. "I want guaranteed protection for Julia and her family."

"Besides Hodgkins?"

"Everyone you can spare."

"What's going on, Marsh?"

"I promised."

"They should be well assured." Allan slapped him on the shoulder. "Your word is better than most—"

"They can't depend on me, Allan." His voice was raw with desperation. "I can't protect them, not the way they need. Promise me you will."

"I will." Pinkerton frowned, his gaze shrewd with understanding. "Nothing will be left to chance. You have my word."

He sighed in relief. "Thanks."

After a long pause, Allan asked, "How long have you been involved with her?"

Too long. Not long enough. He pinched the bridge of his nose. "Don't worry. It's not . . . I won't jeopardize the operation."

"Never thought you would."

Marsh wished he felt as certain. He had no objectivity where Julia was concerned and didn't know how he would react if she were threatened in front of him. He didn't want to find out.

He and Julia rode out ahead of Allan. Tension quivered across Marsh's shoulders and lashed the air between them.

He hated everything about her involvement, but knew she wouldn't change her mind.

Only when they dismounted in the barn did she speak. "You think I'll ruin your case?"

The hurt in her voice tugged at him. "It's not that. You make me forget myself, things I should do, precautions I should take," he said roughly. "I don't need that kind of distraction."

"I find I don't want you to be angry at me," she said with a self-deprecating laugh.

He deposited Sarge's saddle on a stall gate and turned. "I'm not angry." *I'm scared out of my wits.*

She lifted the reins over her horse's head, fingering the ends. "Honest?"

"Honest," he said around a tight lump in his throat.

Her green eyes were vivid with relief and tenderness. "I'm glad."

He wanted to go to her, but if he touched her, he wouldn't let go. Clenching his fists against his sides, he walked over to her mare and removed the saddle. "I'll finish this."

"I can do it."

"Hey, I'm the hired hand." He spoke lightly even though his gut squeezed with her nearness.

She studied him for a moment, but he didn't trust himself to look at her.

Finally she walked over and hung the bridle on the wall. "Good night."

"Good night."

"If anybody asks why I'm driving you to work, just tell them your horse is lame."

"All right."

The next morning, as they drove the wagon into Spinner, Marsh tamped down his frustration. He *hated* that she was doing this and his latest attempt to change her mind had been futile. It grated like rock on steel, but he'd been instructing her since they'd left the house.

There were things she needed to know, though he talked mainly so he wouldn't think about what he really wanted to say and *do* to her.

"How am I supposed to stay away from you when you ride with me everywhere?"

"You're not going to town alone." Trying for physical distance in the wagon, he perched like a skittish bird on the narrow seat edge.

She looked prim in a red-checked daydress with tiny jet buttons down the front. Her skin glowed like dewy velvet in the new morning light, and he helplessly recalled that her skin was like that all over. From the corner of his eye, Marsh could see the sun winking off the onyx fasteners.

Perturbing shards of light bounced off the buttons. Her fresh scent teased him. Her hair shone like spun gold, and the dress turned her eyes to smoky jade.

The buttons winked incessantly at him, daring him to reach between the placket, pop off those black bastards, and spread her bodice. The effort to restrain himself caused his muscles to cord.

After what seemed a torturously long ride, they reached the saloon. For the benefit of any listeners, Marsh kept his tone neutral and polite. "What time would you like me to fetch you, Mrs. Touchstone?"

"About eleven, please."

He helped her down, ignoring the fire that stroked along his belly. He squeezed her fingers and said under his breath, "Be careful."

"Thank you." She walked through the swinging doors without a backward glance.

Not for the first time, he was amazed at her. She abhorred the risk and entire lifestyle his job encompassed, and yet she was downright cool about her involvement. He hoped nothing happened to shake her calm demeanor.

Marsh had once thought her delicate, but he knew now that her daintiness veiled a fierce courage. Julia Touchstone had more heart than many men he'd known, a valiant spirit that had enabled her to survive after her husband's sudden death, nurse her son back to health, and work to improve their future.

She still didn't completely believe his suspicions about Tully, but he knew she had doubts about the saloon owner.

He left the wagon at the livery with a request to check the chestnut's shoes, then walked over to see the sheriff. By the time he left Kisling's office three hours later, he and Allan had a more-than-willing partner.

Julia was waiting when he pulled up to the saloon. He helped her into the wagon and kept a wary eye on the street, eager to get her out of town. He slapped the reins against the horse's rump, and they lurched down the street.

They passed several people, and she spoke to them, her voice warm and open. As they left Spinner behind, the strain on Marsh's neck eased.

A gentle breeze plucked at Julia's skirts. The air was warm and light with the end of summer, and the soft blue sky was dotted with pale, spongy clouds. She seemed tranquil, and Marsh wanted to claim a little of that peace, but concern and desire tapped at him with every rolling *swoosh* of the wheels.

Had everything gone all right at the saloon? Would she tell him if it hadn't?

"Nothing strange happened at the saloon. Tully was there all morning."

"Good." Marsh wanted to forbid her participation, but instead he asked, "Did you see anyone unfamiliar?"

"No. I didn't realize you needed to know that, but it makes sense. I didn't have a chance to look in his office."

"Don't," he commanded flatly.

Her spine stiffened. "I'm not going to ruin anything for you."

"I know that." He met her defiant gaze and softened his tone. "I've already been in his office."

"Oh." Her gaze drifted to his lips, then she glanced away. "You'll never guess who did come in today."

"Who?" Awareness fingered through him, tempting him to scoot closer.

She smiled, and her eyes glowed like heated emeralds. "Hazel and her new husband."

"Hazel? Her new what?" His gaze swung to her.

She laughed. "Hazel ran off and married Bill Young."

"Do I know him?"

"I don't think so. He's a cowhand out at the Websters' place." She said quietly, "They're going to have a baby. Isn't that romantic?"

"I bet Tully didn't see it that way," he said dryly.

Julia giggled, and the sound floated over him like a light caress. "His expression was priceless. He was stomping around as if Hazel were his wife and she had been caught with another man."

"He didn't hurt anyone?" Marsh asked sharply.

She waved her hand in dismissal. "No, no. He was just angry, though I think that was more due to surprise. By the time Hazel and Bill left, he'd given them twenty-five dollars. He said it was for back pay, but Hazel argued that. Anyway, they're going to live in one of the Websters' bunkhouses until Bill finishes their house."

"That's nice." Marsh stared, taken by the way the smile lit up Julia's entire face. He was going to miss her smile.

Under his steady regard she flushed and folded her hands in her lap. "If Tully was as bad as you say, he wouldn't have given them that money. Don't you think?"

"Julia—"

"He did more than just give me a job, you know," she rushed on. "He paid for John's burial. And a marker."

"I'm sorry, Julia," he said gently. "I know he's been a friend to you, but I can't ignore what I've found."

"I know." The light in her eyes dimmed. "I just hope you're wrong."

"So do I." He meant it, even though being wrong meant this case would drag on.

"If Tully isn't involved, you'll be staying, won't you? To investigate further?"

"Someone will. Maybe me."

"Would Allan take you off the case after all the work you've done?"

His hands gripped the reins and the leather bit into the fresh calluses on his palms. "No."

"Oh," she said quietly. "You would leave because you wanted to."

Not because I wanted to. "I might be needed somewhere else."

"Couldn't you stay?" She looked out over the rolling landscape. "Just until you've cleared the pasture?"

Marsh glanced at her and frowned. "You're gonna want me to leave, Julia."

"I don't think so."

An ache sprouted in his chest. Damn! His job was starting to shackle him like a set of leg irons.

Stilted silence sprang up between them and set the tone for the next three days. He drove Julia into town and back home. Not once did she report that Tully had left the saloon or done anything remotely suspicious.

She was keeping something from him, but he knew it concerned him rather than the case.

As Friday neared, want drove through Marsh like a spike. Duty tangled with desire, and he admitted that Julia had become more important than this case.

How could he walk away from her when it was finished? How could he stay and risk alienating her the way he had done Beth?

CHAPTER SIXTEEN

By Thursday night Marsh's gut knotted with anxiety. Tomorrow, if all went according to plan, Scotty Thompson and his gang would be in custody.

Allan had made sure that a wire had been sent to Sheriff Kisling informing him of the arrival of a twelve-thousand-dollar mine payroll. A request had been made for Spinner's bank to keep the money in their vault overnight.

In case Tully had missed the message that had come over the wire, two agents posing as stagecoach officials arrived that afternoon to check out the bank and wait for the armored stage to arrive the next day. By nightfall the entire town was buzzing about the money.

By the following night Marsh could be on his way back to Kansas City. As he gathered his belongings, a sense of heaviness pressed in on him, penetrating his nervous anticipation.

He sat down on the army cot to remove his boots and stockings. He would miss Pete's infectious laugh and bold spirit, India's peach pie and wide-open embrace of life, but mostly he would miss Julia, as much as if he were leaving part of himself behind.

For an instant, only one, he closed his eyes and allowed his mind to conjure up her smile, the soft scent of wildflowers that traced her steps, the aching need in her voice when she whispered his name.

But it served no purpose except to torture him, so he walked out to the corral and grabbed a wooden washtub that sat in the nearby corner. After pumping it full of water, he whistled to Gyp.

"Come on, boy. It'll take just a minute."

Gyp peered around the barn, then slunk toward Marsh with his tail tucked between his legs.

Marsh grinned, rolling back the cuffs of his white linsey shirt. "Big sissy."

The shepherd climbed gingerly into the tub and settled on his haunches, splashing water over the edge. The horses wandered over to stare curiously, and Ginger nudged Marsh's shoulder.

He pushed the mare away. "Get on back, Ginger."

He dipped in both hands and sluiced cool water over Gyp. Once his coat was soaked, Marsh took a square of lye soap and scrubbed it over Gyp's back, scratching as he went.

Uneven footsteps sounded, and Marsh looked up.

"Hiya, Marsh."

"Hi, yourself." An unfamiliar warmth spread through him at the sight of Pete.

Gyp's tail thumped against the side of the washtub, shooting water over Marsh.

"Hey!" He laughed and tweaked Gyp behind the ear. The dog's tail wagged beneath the water, but he sat quietly.

Pete bent and eased between the two bottom fence rails. "You givin' Gyp a bath?"

"Yep."

In the moonlight the boy's hair glistened the same shade of gold as Julia's. Suspenders dangled from his waist, and his light-colored shirt was wrinkled and untucked. "Can I help?"

"Gyp would probably like it better if you did."

Pete knelt opposite Marsh and reached in to dip water onto the dog's back. Gyp whined in greeting, then swiped at Pete's chin with his tongue.

Marsh passed the soap to Pete. "Lather up that side real good."

"Okay." The boy diligently worked up a lather in his hands, then reached for the dog. "I'll hurry, Gyp. I hate baths. At least you don't have to take one every Saturday night like I do. Ma says God likes clean boys, but I'm pretty sure he likes those who ain't so clean too."

Marsh hid a smile and reached around to scrub Gyp's chest. The shepherd rested his head against the tub and stared up at Pete with adoring eyes.

The boy's tongue poked out the left side of his mouth as he concentrated on washing around Gyp's ears. "You like to fish?"

"Sure do. Have you ever caught any in that creek down yonder?"

"Yeah, a couple of catfish. One of 'em weighed about three pounds."

"You're joshin' me!" Marsh thought he sounded suitably impressed.

"No, I'm not. I swear."

"That right?" Contentment inched through him, a mixture of belonging and kinship that he'd never felt with anyone besides his family. He wished tonight weren't his last night there. He would like to go fishing with Pete.

Cooler air swirled through the corral. The scents of horses and wet dog were cut by the gentle perfume of wisteria. Lantern light filtered from the barn and melded with the moonlight that flooded the corral and spilled over to the yard and the house.

The subtle click of oak and hickory leaves floated on the breeze. Water, turned to liquid silver by the moon, sloshed rhythmically against the side of the tub, keeping pace with the wash and rinse of the animal. An owl called into the night.

He dashed one last fistful of water on Gyp's chest, then shook off his hands. "I never thanked you for the soap."

Pete kept his gaze fixed on Gyp as he rinsed the dog. "Did you like it?"

"Yep. It's been a long time since anybody gave me a gift."

"Mrs. Henner said ladies like it when men smell good."

"Is that right?" Marsh knew Pete had Julia in mind when he referred to "ladies," and he bit back a smile. He shifted, resting his elbow on one knee.

Pete slanted a glance at him. "You like it here, don't you, Marsh?"

"Sure, it's real pretty. It sounds like there are a lot of big fish too."

"I meant . . . do you like Spinner and my house?" The words rushed together as if he were afraid to ask.

Suspicion nudged him. What was going on in Pete's quick little mind? "Yeah."

"Maybe you can move in." Pete stared intently at Gyp's nose. "To the house, I mean."

"Might be a little crowded, don't you think?" Regret and sadness pinched. How could he tell Pete that he would be moving, not into the house, but out of his life?

"There, Gyp." Pete wiped his hands on his trousers and stepped back. The dog leapt out of the tub, spraying water over both Pete and Marsh.

Pete moved over next to Marsh. "Every fall we go to the St. Clair County Fair. They have sack races and the kind where two people tie their legs to each other, and even the kind where one person pushes the other person like a wheelbarrow." He glanced up, gauging Marsh's reaction. "You could be my partner this year. We'd lick everybody, even Frankie and his pa."

Marsh's heart squeezed and he said gently, "I don't think I'll be here then, Pete."

"But . . ." The boy's alarmed gaze shot to him. "Don't you want to stay?"

"It's really not a matter of wanting to." He wished Julia were there to fend off the questions. "Your grandmother might not need me anymore."

"What about me?" Pete's small body bowed with tension. "I need you."

The boy's voice trembled, and Marsh felt a surge of fierce

protectiveness. Pete was more attached to him than he had realized, despite his efforts to keep a distance. "You've got your ma. The two of you do pretty well."

"Yeah." Pete paused for a moment, then he said, "Well, I need a pa and I want you."

Marsh's chest ached as if the wind had just been knocked out of him. He answered carefully, feeling as if he were trying to avoid a battery of minié balls. "Son, you can't just pick out somebody to be your pa like you would choose a stick of candy from Henner's."

"Why not?"

Hell. Why was the kid asking *him* these questions? *Where* was Julia? He glanced toward the house, hoping to see her or even India. "Where's your ma? Won't she be looking for you?"

"How come you don't want to be my pa?"

"Hey, now. I didn't say that."

"Good!" Excitement brightened Pete's eyes. "This is swell. I can't wait to tell—"

"Wait a minute. There's more involved, Pete." He tried to simplify a conversation that had suddenly taken on complicated significance. "What about your ma? Don't you think she has something to say about it?"

"She likes you." Pete sneaked a glance at Marsh. "I *know* you like her."

"Well, yes, but—" How could he explain that he had already ruined one marriage? That he couldn't bear to hurt Julia the way he had hurt Beth? "There's more to it," he finished lamely.

"Like what?"

"Like . . . love."

"What if she needs you?"

Marsh nearly laughed. Julia was one of the most self-sufficient women he'd ever known. "She has you to take care of her, remember?"

"I know you could love her," Pete insisted. "I saw you

kissin' her hand the other night and huggin' her. Right here by the corral. Doesn't that mean you want to stay with her?"

He sagged back, his breath whooshing out in surprise. *Oh, man. Oh, man.*

"Then you could get married, right? That way you could stay with us forever."

Marsh had no idea how to answer. He rose and dragged the washtub over to empty it at the far side of the corral. "Where did Gyp get to?"

"What about being my pa?"

He gritted his teeth and hoped he handled this correctly. "We're good friends, aren't we?"

The boy didn't answer.

Marsh turned. "Pete?"

"Yeah," he mumbled, his chin tucked into his chest. "That's why I thought it would be so great if you were my pa."

An ache bloomed in his chest and his grip tightened on the washtub handle. "I can't stay, Pete. Once my work is finished, I'll have to move on, but we'll still be friends."

The boy's chin quivered. "How can we be friends if you leave?"

"You can write me." There was no harm in that limited contact, was there?

The boy brightened and limped to the side door of the barn. "And you can visit!"

Marsh cursed both himself and his damn job. How could he expect Pete to understand that he couldn't keep such close ties because of the life he led and the men he sought?

"I can't promise you that, son."

Bitter disappointment etched Pete's face, and Marsh felt it like a knife in his chest. The boy ducked his head and gripped the door until his knuckles poked sharply through his skin. "Is it because of my leg?"

"What does your leg have to do with it?" He set the tub next to the door.

"Some people don't like me because I'm different from them."

"No!" Marsh dropped to one knee and squeezed Pete's shoulder. "Absolutely not."

The boy's gaze searched his, then skittered away.

"Don't ever think that, certainly not about me. Maybe some people are uncomfortable around people who are different, but that's because of something inside them, not because of anything you are."

"Really?"

At the desperate hope in the boy's eyes, Marsh's heart turned over in his chest. "Really. In fact, the most special people I've known have been people who are different, like you are."

"Messed up like me?"

"You're not messed up," he said firmly. "You had an accident and it left you with a bum leg. Everybody has some kind of flaw, but most people hide theirs on the inside. Do you understand what I mean?"

"I think so. Is it kinda like what Gran said about invisible scars?"

"Kinda." Marsh eased back on his heels and shifted so that they were eye to eye. "You know what's different about you, Pete?"

"It's not my leg?"

He shook his head. "You don't hide from anything, and that's something most people can't claim. That takes a special sort of courage, and I'm honored to call you my friend. Never, *never* think that I can't stay because of you. That's not the reason."

"Then why?"

The anguish in the boy's eyes tore at Marsh. "I wish I could explain, partner, but right now I'll have to ask you to trust me."

"Is it a secret?"

"Sort of."

Pete silently studied Marsh, his eyes huge with an attempt to understand. "Okay."

"Thanks." He smiled and levered himself up.

Unexpectedly, Pete threw himself against Marsh, burying his head in Marsh's belly. "I love you, Marsh."

"I love you too." He patted Pete's back awkwardly, pain and regret pushing through him. The boy's arms tightened around his waist, and he leaned down to pick him up, hugging him tight against his chest.

Marsh wished he *could* stay, but he couldn't make promises when he didn't know if he would see the next sunset.

Despite common sense, he was deeply involved with Julia and her family, rendering them all too vulnerable for his peace of mind. He thought he knew how to avoid that kind of vulnerability, but Pete proffered a different kind of trap, a soft velvet net of belonging and family and the tempting promise of a home.

Julia stood unnoticed in the shadows of the corral, tears streaming down her face. Upon seeing Pete and Marsh bathing the dog, she had come outside to join them, to spend some time with Marsh in a situation where he wouldn't feel the need to send her away.

It was their last night together. He hadn't said as much, had told her only that Pinkerton would arrive tomorrow with the money, and they expected the Thompson gang. But she knew that he planned to leave. She refused to believe that he could actually walk away from her and the feelings that had developed between them

Oh, he'd never said he loved her or even hinted at it, but she knew that too. She could see it in his eyes when he looked at her, hear it when he said her name, feel it in the frustration and protectiveness that he exhibited every day on the drive to and from town.

Nor had she confessed her feelings to him. She had given her word the night they made love—no promises, no regrets.

Now he held her son, talking to him, *loving* him just as she did. *Stay, Marsh. Tell Pete you will.* But he didn't, just as she knew he wouldn't.

She wiped her eyes and stepped out of the shadows. He caught her movement and his gaze moved to her over Pete's shoulder.

Their eyes locked. In his she read pain and regret and a raw agony that caused her eyes to burn. Refusing Pete had hurt Marsh as much as it hurt her son.

Determined not to make it any more difficult for him, Julia said brightly, "There you are, young man. It's bedtime for you."

"We were just talkin'." Pete wriggled out of Marsh's arms and gave him a warning look, as though telling him not to worry her with what they had discussed. "And we gave Gyp a bath."

"Aren't you glad it's not Saturday night?" she teased as he limped toward her.

He gave her a tremulous smile, but in the hazy veil of moonlight and shadow she saw his strained features. She battled the urge to sweep him up and sob for him, with him.

Marsh took a few steps after Pete, then stopped. Longing twisted his features, and Julia's heart swelled until her chest ached. Pete climbed through the fence and joined her.

"Good night, Marsh." Her voice cracked, and she turned quickly away, her arm curving around Pete's slender shoulders.

Her son glanced back at the man who stood barefoot in a pocket of lantern light. "Good night, Marsh. See ya tomorrow?"

"You bet." Marsh's voice was hoarse and rusty. Even in the dim light Julia saw his shoulders sag.

She and Pete walked slowly into the house. She ached for the hurt she knew Pete harbored, but she didn't press him to talk. As usual, he was trying to protect her.

Marsh believed that leaving would keep her and Pete safe. She believed the only way to do that was to join forces, form

a family. She wanted Marsh to believe that too, and somehow she would convince him.

Marsh wanted to go to her. He started after her three times
and forced himself to stop each time. Until finally she and
Pete disappeared into the house.

I want you to be my pa. Marsh alternated between wondering how he could ever be a parent and thinking he might
be a pretty good one.

Frustration ripped through him. Denying the lure of par-
enthood was easier than denying the lure of Julia. He wanted
her with a savage need that shocked him. Was it only because he knew this was his last night there?

No, he admitted. He had fallen in love with her. Courage,
hidden vulnerability, and her sacrificial love for Pete all
comprised the woman who had redefined Marsh's own self-
perception and reshaped a part of him that had been marred.

She had survived one husband with a job such as his.
How could he risk that she might not survive another?

He would have chosen to spare Julia the startling conversation he'd had with Pete a few moments before. He hoped
the boy had understood and accepted Marsh's explanation.

While Pete's request had torn at him, it also drove home
the dangers of *any* involvement with the searing power of a
newly fired brand.

He couldn't risk Pete or Julia. He wouldn't. So he tried to
forget the plea that had shadowed her eyes, the answering
loneliness in her lovely features. Tried to forget the heart-
breaking disappointment on Pete's face when he had explained he would be moving on.

Her scent lingered. Before he realized where he was
going, he found himself in front of Julia's bedroom window.

Through the white curtain he could see the fuzzy outline
of her bed, the blurred form of a vanity, the black gleam of
mirrored glass. Soft golden light fanned under the closed
door and revealed that the room was empty.

What was he doing? He shouldn't see her tonight of all

nights. Thankfully she wasn't in her room. He padded back to the barn, glad at least one of them had kept their common sense.

Nerves strung taut, Marsh rolled a cigarette and lay down. He took a deep drag on his smoke and blanked his mind.

Resentment boiled through him, and with sheer strength of will, he quelled it until he was blessedly numb. Tonight he couldn't allow himself to feel anything.

After an hour, Pete finally drifted off to sleep. He hadn't asked Julia to stay with him, but she had. Relaxed, his features reflected the innocence of his age rather than the sober responsibility that had been forced on him

I need a pa and I want you. Pete's plea to Marsh haunted her, as did anxiety about tomorrow. Would the Thompsons show up? Would she be able to convince Marsh that she wanted a chance at a life with him despite the job? She'd shied away before, unwilling to risk her stable, predictable world.

But now it seemed a greater risk to let him go. With her stomach fluttering and sweat dampening her palms, she walked to the barn. Gyp met her at the door, his tail whacking at her skirts in his excitement to see her. She patted his head and moved inside, reassured by the blue curl of smoke in the back corner.

The cot creaked and Marsh stood, a cigarette dangling from his mouth. "Julia?"

His wary tone tickled the nervousness that already tightened her stomach.

"You shouldn't let Pete catch you out here. He's already got ideas."

"Yes, I heard." She stopped at the corner of his narrow bed. "I think he's on to something."

"You can't be serious." He ground his cigarette against the wall and rounded the cot, stopping a few inches away. "You know it's unwise for me to stay."

"All I know is we want you to."

"We've been through this." Desire flitted through his eyes, but he kept his hands locked at his sides.

Her gaze roamed over his chiseled features and rested on his sensitive lips. How had she ever thought them cruel? "I know."

He shifted under her regard and stepped away. "I wish you would stay here with India and Pete tomorrow."

"What if it made Tully suspicious?"

"You shouldn't be reminding *me."* A muscle flexed in his jaw. "I don't like this, Julia. You don't have to do it. We'll be fine without you."

"Marsh, it's almost over. I want to see it through."

Protest flared in his eyes, but he nodded sharply. "Take extra precautions. And I want you to know where I am so you won't spend your energy wondering what I'm doing."

"Aren't you going to be with me?" Concern fluttered.

"No, Gyp will be. I'll be in the bank."

"Waiting for them?" she cried. "No, Marsh!"

"I'll have the element of surprise. Don't worry. And don't come into that bank for any reason. Do you understand?"

"But what if—"

"For any reason," he repeated sternly. "At the first sign of trouble, get the hell out of the saloon. I don't want you anywhere near that bank when this goes down. Promise me, or I'll truss you up and leave you here."

"Not even to warn you?"

"Promise."

She took a deep breath, aching for him to take her in his arms and let his strength close around her.

"Julia?"

Her lips flattened. "I promise."

"Good." His silver eyes softened. "Now I can concentrate on what I need to."

Kiss me, Marsh. Tell me everything will be okay. Tell me you'll stay.

What if he truly did leave tomorrow? How would she bear it? Panic seized her. Her gaze traced his straight nose, the sharp angles of his cheek and jaw, then lingered on his lips. She ached to feel them scoot over her body in wet, silky possession.

Kiss me, Marsh. Just once more. "I wish—"

"Don't say it, Julia. I can read it in your eyes. Don't say it."

She gripped his hand and turned it over to place a kiss in the center of his palm. "Can you say you haven't thought about what we did by the creek?"

"Hell, no." Savage desire ravaged his eyes, and he dragged his thumb across her lower lip, his hungry gaze riveted there. "Sugar, you should go."

"One kiss?" she whispered. "One?"

"This is insane." Yearning flared in his eyes. "Stupid. Crazy."

"Tomorrow might be the end, Marsh. For you or me or all of us." Her voice was ragged. "Please don't make me go."

"I'm a fool 'cause I can't." He hauled her up against him, and his lips claimed hers.

CHAPTER SEVENTEEN

He meant only to taste her sweet fire one last time, but reason shattered the minute their lips touched. She clung to him, her mouth fevered on his.

Desperation twisted through him, and he felt the same response echo in her body. His hands moved over the buttons of her bodice, nudged the material apart. He was vaguely aware that she wasn't wearing a corset.

She shrugged out of her sleeves and clutched his shoulders. In his mind, his tongue skimmed over the swell of her breast. Then he cupped her in his hand, closing his mouth over her nipple through the serviceable cotton of her chemise.

"Make love to me, Marsh."

Her whispered words resurrected his conscience, and he reared back, astounded at the recklessness that had ruled him. "What am I doing?"

She stood before him, her skin flushed, her pink-and-green-striped bodice shoved down to her waist. Her chemise, wet from his mouth, proved only a transparent veil for her puckered nipples.

He released her. "We shouldn't do this, Julia."

"One last time."

"Julia—"

She pulled his head down and cut off his words with her lips. Reason vanished in the wake of temptation.

Weak with the feel and scent of her, his knees buckled, taking them down onto the cot. He tugged her across his lap, and the bed creaked. One hand gently stroked her cheek. "Sugar, now's the time to stop."

"I don't want to." She turned her face into his caress, and his heart tugged.

He did love her despite his fear that she would come to resent that love. Closing his eyes, he feathered his fingers over her features, tucking away in his memory the feel of petal-smooth skin, the fine eyebrows that arched above gleaming emerald eyes, the straight line of her pert nose, the artfully defined bow of her upper lip and the soft fullness of her lower, the stubborn chin.

She trembled under his touch, and his arm tightened around her waist. His thumb pressed against her lower lip, parting her lips, and he kissed her.

She shifted, fitting her arms around his neck, opening her mouth to his coaxing tongue. He ached to run his knuckles over her breasts, but he kept his fingers at her taut waist, wanting to store away each moment as a secret dream he could remember on hellish days.

Her kisses grew more fevered, and she shifted on his lap. Her bottom brushed his growing arousal, and fire yanked at his belly. He moved his hand over her skirt, fumbling with the laces on her shoes, then palming them off.

Her hands bracketed his neck, anchoring him to her as though afraid he would vanish. His heart thundered in his chest. Her sweet scent meshed with his raw, dark one.

He pushed her skirts up to her knees, slid off her stockings. His hand trailed over the velvet of her skin, then splayed on her abdomen. Her muscles jumped beneath his touch, and a primal instinct snapped within him, drawing a frantic urgency that he fought to control.

He yanked at the tapes of her drawers and shoved them over her hips, loving the feel of her bare bottom against the roughness of his denims. His fingers danced up the insides of her thighs, and she gasped into his mouth.

Need hammered at him, urged him to rip her clothes from her and ease his throbbing body, but he refused to hurry.

She pulled away, her eyes sharp with desperate need. Her lips were a deep raspberry color, swollen from his kisses and making him ache to feel them all over his body. As though reading his mind, she pressed kisses to his jaw and cheek.

Hot, moist lips moved to his neck, then farther up, where she rimmed his ear with her tongue. Deftly, she slipped his shirt buttons free and pressed kisses on his chest, her quick tongue burning him everywhere she touched.

An ache drilled into his groin, throbbing in time to his heartbeat. Heat gathered in his veins and layered want with need. With a quick motion he tugged his shirt over his head. Cool air kissed his body.

Her eyes flared with appreciation. Almost reverently, her hands moved over the crisp hair of his chest and flexed, causing his muscles to spasm in reaction. Wanting to touch her the same way, he stood, holding her tight against him.

He slid her feet to the floor, his gaze delving deep into hers, seeking permission. In answer, her hands moved to the top button of his pants. Though his hands shook, he managed to undo the remaining buttons at the back of her dress.

The striped cotton slid to her ankles, leaving her veiled in only the chemise. She watched him, her eyes sultry, beckoning him. The want clawed through him, urging him to spread her legs and pump into her with the desperate mindlessness that reached for him, but he resisted.

He wanted to watch her while he was inside her, wanted to hear her cry out for him. Anticipation hammered at him as she reached up and unpinned her hair.

The movement stretched the thin material of her chemise, shadowing her nipples and the fullness of her breasts. Golden hair flowed past her shoulders, silk on light, and he twined his fingers in it. Satiny strands slipped sinuously against his fingers, stinging his nerves. Urgency swelled inside him like a building wind.

He needed her to fill the emptiness in his soul, soothe

away the wasted years of his past. She watched him as he looked at her, and uncertainty clouded her eyes.

She wanted to please him, he realized in astonishment. Already she had given him more than he'd expected. "Sugar," he whispered, holding her gaze. "You're perfect."

Lowering his head, he kissed her long and leisurely, probing the midnight recesses of her mouth. Reaching up, he unbuttoned her chemise, and the garment parted, sliding off one shoulder to reveal creamy, gold-brushed skin.

He wanted to taste her everywhere, and pressed his lips to her forehead, then her closed eyelids and the corner of her mouth, laved the hollow between her neck and collarbone until she shifted restlessly against him. He pulled her into him so that her breasts pressed against him and her abdomen nudged his arousal.

Fire circled in a slow arc. She rose on tiptoe and kissed his jaw, his chin, nipped at his lips. The chemise gaped wide and revealed full, pale breasts. Savage want hooked into him, playing havoc with his reason.

He pushed the undergarment from her and rested his shaking hands on her tiny waist. As he looked fully at her for the first time, his breath folded in his chest.

She was golden light and silk and cream. Her skin was as flawless as burnished moonlight, and delicate pink nipples crowned her pale breasts. Her slightly rounded stomach attested to the birth of her son.

Overcome with awe, he knelt in front of her. Her heartbeat fluttered rapidly in her chest, and she gripped his shoulders for balance. He bowed his head, brushing his cheek against her breasts, inhaling the heady sweetness of her as he struggled to calm the restlessness that charged through him.

He kissed the faint scars just above her pelvis, skimmed one hand over the dark gold curls at the apex of her thighs, then continued down to her ankles. She shivered and he dragged his hands up the back of her velvety legs.

The harsh cadence of their mingled breaths was the only

sound in the barn. Pleasure edged through him, nearly ex-
cruciating, and he smiled. Cupping her bottom, he stroked
the inside of her thighs.

Sharp nails dug into his back, and she sagged against him.
"Marsh, I think I'm going to die."

When he drew her nipple into his mouth, she cried out
and surged against him. Fire inched through his belly.

She moaned his name and reached for his denims, drawing the lust into a gut-searing knot. Her fingers worked at his
buttons, pressing into his arousal, and he throbbed harder.
He helped her shove his pants down, then he lifted her, his
kiss growing fierce with the need to claim her.

He was assaulted by a sudden fear that she might be
ripped from him, and vowed that he would make her feel
safe and cherished and loved. He lay her on the bed and followed her down, adjusting their bodies on the narrow cot so
that he rested atop her without crushing her.

Her breasts pressed against him, and her soft belly nudged
his solid one. Tiny feet teased his calves, and her thighs
opened wider in welcome.

Marsh dragged his lips from hers, staring into her eyes,
which were wild and smoky with need. Stroking his back,
she urged him to her, and he positioned himself between her
thighs.

"Now, Marsh." She clutched at him, her eyes a stormy
green. "I want you now."

He moved over her and slid inside with a long, smooth
thrust. Friction lashed his body and ricocheted to his toes. A
breath shuddered out of him and his arms quivered with the
effort to ease his way slowly.

But she couldn't wait. Gripping his buttocks, she locked
her eyes on his and urged him deeper.

Inch by tight, delicious inch, he surrendered to her snug
velvet heat and claimed her fully. She shifted her body, urging him to move, and he retreated, then drove into her
slowly. Long and slow, over and over, until his body shook
with need.

She picked up the rhythm, answering his thrusts with her own as she pulled him closer. Pleasure knotted in his belly. They moved faster, striving for a unified completion, and focused only on the rhythm and scent and feel of each other.

Marsh wanted her to know his heart, but he couldn't speak. The knot of fire twisted sharply. He was aware only of the sweat-slicked feel of her, the soft scent of her wildflowers twined with his muskiness. His heart opened, warmed, and the damaged part of himself grew whole again. He had come home.

Her inner muscles clenched around him, and she clutched at his back, crying out. His restraint snapped. Throwing back his head, he pumped into her again and again.

"I love you, Marsh," she panted against his ear. "I love you."

He looked down at her, wind rushing in his ears. Overwhelmed by her trust and the violent need of his body, he couldn't speak. With one final thrust he collapsed atop her, cradling her head against his chest.

Slowly his body calmed and satisfaction rolled through him. He shifted to look at her, feeling himself still pulse within her.

"Mmmm." She smiled, drowsy and sated, and snuggled closer.

He stroked her hair out of her eyes and pressed a kiss to her forehead. "Julia, about what you said—"

"Don't say anything. Please." She pressed her lips to his.

"I—"

"Please," she begged, a hint of fear in her eyes. "I only wanted you to know."

He wanted to tell her he felt the same, but it would change nothing between them. Finally, he nodded.

They lay together until their bodies cooled. Reluctantly, he released her and rolled to his feet, slipping into his denims. After gently helping her dress, they walked to the house.

On the front porch, regret jabbed at him. He would never

again walk into this house, eat at her table, spend time in her bed.

She stepped inside her open door. "We could make it work, Marsh. You and me and Pete, together. I know we could."

He hated himself for refusing her, but her love would turn to resentment and he wouldn't be able to live with that. "I know what you went through because of John's job. I couldn't do that to you." His tone was wry, but his heart twisted with regret. "Even though after what just happened I'm damned tempted."

"We could be different."

"I'd rather you hate me for leaving now than come to hate me for trying to live a commitment I couldn't make."

"I could change your mind if you'd let me."

"I'd end up hurting you, and I couldn't live with myself over that, Julia."

"I know." Protest burned in her eyes, then was replaced by a steely determination. She rolled up on tiptoe and kissed him. "But I won't stop loving you because of it."

With that she walked inside and closed the door. Feeling emotionally stripped and naked with a loneliness that threatened to erode his soul, Marsh padded barefoot back to the barn.

Years before, he hadn't been able to turn his back on the job and it had cost him Beth's love. Now, if he did as he was tempted, it could cost him Julia's life.

She loved Marsh and knew he felt the same. His tender possession of her body and the vulnerability revealed in his eyes last night proved that.

Damn the duty and loyalty that tied him to Allan Pinkerton. She had shared one man with the agency, had sworn never to share another. She couldn't let Marsh go, but how could she convince him to stay?

That morning they stood in the front room with her

mother, both trying to keep the secret of their desperate union between them.

Even though Marsh stood at ease, legs spread wide, Julia tapped into the restlessness churning through him. His fingers repeatedly ringed the brim of his hat. His gaze searched hers, for regret, she knew, but he wouldn't find it.

She didn't regret one joyous moment, not of last night or their first time by the creek or a single minute since he'd arrived. Well, maybe the time she'd shot at him.

The thought drew a smile from her. His gaze lit on her lips, then shifted to her mother, on the divan. India had propped her injured foot on a stool and draped one of her quilts, a wedding ring design, over her lap.

Tension threaded the room. Despite the buoyant feeling that remained from their union, danger bore down on them like a runaway stallion, wild and reckless and careless of any obstacle. What were they going to do?

"I don't like the idea of Julia going to town, but she has a point," Marsh said to her mother.

India's brow puckered. "You're sure she'll be fine? That you both will?"

"Hell, no! I'm not sure of anything."

"He's taking every precaution, Mother." Julia refused to let him feel guilty or have his attention diverted from the anticipated meeting with the Thompson gang. "Even Robin is going to help."

"Darn this ankle," India groused, gesturing impatiently at her leg. "I want to go."

"India, I really need you here."

"How so?" Her mother arched an eyebrow. "What good is a crippled old woman?"

"You can make certain that Pete stays here," he said urgently. "I can't convince Julia to stay, but at least I'll know you and Pete are safe."

"All right," she agreed quickly, as if she understood how important their safety was to him.

"Thank you." A muscle flexed in his jaw. "As soon as it's over, we'll get word to you."

India reached for his hand. "You get Scotty Thompson, Marsh. Make him pay."

He nodded and squeezed her hand.

Julia pressed a kiss to her mother's cheek and India whispered, "Don't let him go, honey. Don't let him leave us."

"I'll do my best."

"Be careful." India gripped her hands, urging strength into her. Faith and love shone in her mother's eyes, and Julia smiled.

She followed him onto the porch and down the steps. Tension corded the muscles in his neck and stiffened his spine. He kept his eyes averted, snapping his fingers for Gyp to join him and Sarge, who was tied to the back of the wagon.

The dog bounded into the wagon. After sniffing the weathered wood, he curled up in the shade of the seat.

Marsh assisted Julia into the wagon, his touch impersonal. In light of what they'd shared last night, his distance hurt.

"Why are you taking Sarge?"

"In case I need to follow." His gaze met hers, no longer than an accidental glance, but she could see the silver depths were distant and haunted.

The implications of this trip into Spinner hit her, and Julia sat stunned. She was placing herself in a dangerous situation in order to finish a nightmare that had begun last year. Willingly, she had insinuated herself to help Marsh, but mostly to help herself and Pete.

Today everything would end, one way or another, and the past would finally be put to rest.

Apprehension snaked up her spine. She hoped Tully wouldn't be able to read the fear and worry in her eyes. Thank goodness, Marsh had insisted that India remain behind with Pete. If Julia had to worry about them, Tully would easily know that something was amiss.

At that moment she understood why Marsh couldn't

allow himself to be close to her despite what they'd shared last night. Emotional connection would weaken his concentration, play havoc with his instincts.

It was then that she noticed his bedroll tied behind the saddle, the rifle hanging in the scabbard, a box of cartridges tucked in the hollow beneath the saddle horn.

Panic fluttered. Was he really leaving? She realized now that she had gone to him last night harboring the hope that he would stay.

He wouldn't.

Pain arrowed through her, cleaving past the walls he had worn away and into the part of her that she had shielded since John's death.

As though he sensed her mood, a scowl darkened Marsh's features. She remained silent on the way into town, not wanting to distract him from the Thompsons.

She refused to give up. Not yet. Not as long as he was here.

I love you, Marsh. The words sounded with the rhythm of the wagon wheels, echoed through him. His heart replied in kind, but he remained silent. They sat side by side on the narrow wagon seat, and he'd never felt more isolated and alone.

It was better this way, he knew. Better for her safety, better for his concentration. But that didn't stop the ache that gnawed at him, the push of his suppressed emotions to his throat. Her skirts fluttered against his ankle, the green-and-white-checked material a vivid contrast to the dull blue of his denims.

I love you, Julia. He'd wanted to tell her last night, and she'd prevented him from doing so. In retrospect, he was glad. Those three words carried too many responsibilities, too many possibilities, too much potential for damage.

If something happened to her today—

He refused to finish the thought. She would be fine.

Once in town, he delivered Julia to the saloon. He fiddled with the harness, listening to her shoes click hollowly on the planked porch. Abruptly the sound stopped, then moved back toward him. He glanced over his shoulder and found her at the edge of the porch.

Fatigue and concern tightened her features. Her voice was raw, as though her throat hurt. "You *are* going to tell Pete good-bye?"

The morning sun slanted onto the porch, framing her in its brilliant light so that he couldn't see her eyes. "I kinda told him last night."

She didn't reply, but agony darkened her eyes. Marsh felt an answering tug in his chest, and cursed himself. She turned away and the double doors *thwacked* as she walked inside, calling a greeting to Tully.

Her voice was a trifle high, but otherwise normal. Anxiety inched under Marsh's guard, fraying the edges of a focus that had once been as fixed as tempered steel. Why had he allowed her to get involved?

Edgy now, he motioned Gyp from the wagon and ordered him in a quiet voice to guard Julia. The dog settled on his haunches outside the doors, easily able to hear her inside yet spy trouble outside.

"You know what to do, boy." Marsh knelt and scratched behind the dog's ears. Gyp thumped his tail once to show he understood and nudged his nose into Marsh's palm, his dark eyes liquid with adoration. Marsh patted him on the shoulder and rose.

Spinner bustled with activity. Bob Henner polished the windows of his store while Jeanette followed behind for a second cleaning. Smoke twined from the chimney at Lil's, and on the air he smelled bacon and coffee. Sheriff Kisling stood in the doorway of the jail. He raised his tin cup of coffee in a subtle confirmation of the plan.

So far there had been no sign of the Thompsons. Right now, Marsh needed only to wait for Allan to arrive with the money. With one last look at the saloon, he drove to Henner's.

Leaving the wagon in front of the store, he slipped into

the alley behind and eased along the back side past the jail to the corner of the bank. Fingers skimming along the wall, he felt for the door that Kisling had told him about. His hand closed on a hidden latch and he disappeared inside.

Come on, Thompson, you bastard. Let's finish this.

"I got a message from Brill," Allan whispered. He and Marsh waited in the dark vault, unable to see each other. Kisling hid behind a desk just on the other side. "Looks like your hunch about Tully was right."

"He knows Morse code?" Marsh kept his voice low, his ears attuned to any muffled sound that might filter through the heavy steel door. The inside of the vault was cool, but sweat trickled down his spine and dampened his palms.

Allan's boot rasped across the floor as he shifted his position. "Not only knows the code, but was awarded a medal after the war for his contribution. He served all four years in the Telegraph Corps. As near as Brill could figure, Tully went in when he was about seventeen."

"And the ironworks?"

"Tully Iron is owned by his family and they're quite wealthy." The whispered words crowded the small space and boomed in Marsh's ears. "Why he gave it up is beyond me."

"How did he and Thompson meet up? The war?"

"Nope. Family connection."

"Family?" His head whipped around. "I never would've guessed that."

"Their mothers are sisters."

"Tully is Thompson's cousin? What about Jasper?" He tried to recall if there was a physical resemblance between Tully and Thompson's other cousin that Marsh had killed in Crowley. "Was he related to Tully too?"

"His brother."

Damn. Alarm tapped at him. A man would risk a lot for family if backed in a corner, even more for revenge. If Tully realized that Julia knew about him—

Sweat dappled Marsh's palms, tickled his upper lip. Gyp was with her. The dog knew what to do if there was trouble, but Marsh wanted to go to her, take her somewhere safe.

Beneath his dread he felt a twinge of regret. She would be saddened to learn that Tully *was* involved with the men who had killed John and crippled Pete.

Allan touched his arm and he tried to concentrate, listening for the click of the lock, the grinding release of the steel knob. For several moments he barely breathed, and his head throbbed as he strained to hear.

He shifted to a kneeling position and kept a reassuring hand on his revolver. Kisling would stay hidden until Marsh and Allan ambushed the gang and backed them out of the vault.

How was Julia? What was happening? Did Tully know if Thompson planned to come to Spinner today? Would he help them? Apprehension coiled across Marsh's shoulders.

He would never forgive himself if something happened to Julia. If she came out of this all right, he would leave. With a clear conscience, but a broken heart.

CHAPTER EIGHTEEN

Inside the saloon, stilted air trapped the heavy odors of alcohol, unwashed bodies, and stale cigar smoke. Julia propped open the swinging doors, allowing the occasional burst of fresh air, which relieved some of the unpleasant odor.

Expectancy hovered in the air like an eager vulture, sowing an ominous hush. It was the quiet of fear, not of peace. Dread fluttered in her stomach, and once again she prayed for a quick end to this mess.

Marsh had the advantage of surprise and he would be all right. She clung to that belief just as she did to the desperate hope that she would be able to convince him to stay.

Moving to the next table, she smeared a mixture of beeswax and lemon oil on the dull wood. She polished the scarred surface, but her gaze stayed on the doorway.

Millie and Filene slept soundly upstairs. Tully whistled tunelessly behind the bar, but his gaze strayed often to the doors. Was he involved with the Thompson gang? She fervently hoped Marsh was mistaken about that.

Tully glanced at her, then moved to the end of the bar, looking out at the street. He'd been less talkative than usual that morning, which caused her to wonder about his possible involvement with the outlaws who'd killed her husband.

All the tables received a thorough polishing. As she worked, tension fractured the air and the once-fresh scent of beeswax and lemon burned her nostrils like the stench of a decaying animal.

Her boss moved from behind the bar and stood at the doors, his gaze scanning the street. What was he looking for?

Walking behind the bar, she returned the rag and polish to its place beneath the counter, then reached for the broom. Keeping a surreptitious eye on the saloon owner, she began sweeping in front of his office door.

He realigned a row of glasses, then cleaned the mirror, watching the doors all the while. He was definitely waiting for something or someone. Was it the Thompson gang? She ran the broom along the brass footrail.

"Ma! Ma!" Thundering hoofbeats shattered the heavy silence.

Pete? Startled, Julia dropped the broom and rushed outside with Tully close behind her.

Pete reined Ginger to a skidding stop in front of the saloon. Before the mare had ceased her dancing steps, he flung himself off and clumsily hurried to Julia.

Gyp leapt up from his sentry post and bounded over to Pete, tail wagging, pink tongue swiping at the boy in greeting.

"Pete! What are you doing? Is everything all right?" Alarm tripped up her spine and she glanced down the street for India. "Where's Gran?"

"I took Ginger." He hugged the dog close, his gaze darting around frantically. "Where's Marsh?"

"Honey, what's wrong?" Unnerved at the sight of him, she fought to remain calm. She leaned down, searching his anxious eyes.

"Where's Marsh? I need to see him. His things are gone. And so was Gyp." He kept a hand on the dog as if to ensure that he wouldn't disappear. "Where is he, Ma?"

If the Thompson gang did show up, she didn't want Pete anywhere near. Aware that Tully still stood behind her, she said, "He's in town somewhere, honey. Everything's fine. Now, I want you to go back home. We'll be there soon."

"I gotta talk to Marsh," he said urgently. "I gotta. He can't leave. Don't let him leave, Ma."

Her heart clenched at Pete's desperate plea, and she drew him close, rubbing his back. "Marsh isn't going anywhere right now. You can talk to him at home."

"What if he doesn't come home?"

His fear echoed her own. In an attempt to calm them both, she gripped his shoulders firmly. "Pete, I want you to do as I said."

"I feel funny, Ma." His eyes darkened with worry. "Like somethin' bad is gonna happen."

"Oh, honey." She hugged him, then picked him up, intending to him on the horse and send him home.

From the opposite end of the street she was peripherally aware of riders coming into town, and she turned toward them. Three men reined up in front of the bank, and Julia took an involuntary step forward.

The men dismounted, and the insignificant movement seemed suddenly ominous. She'd never seen them before, but she knew who they were. An abrupt stillness webbed the town, and fear snaked through her.

"No," she whispered, her arms tightening around Pete. "No."

"Ma? Ma, what's wrong?"

Her gaze darted to the jail across the street. He would be safe there. "Listen to me," she said in a low voice. "I want you to go to the sheriff's off—"

"Julia?" Tully's voice, pitched oddly, sounded in her ear the same instant his hand closed over her upper arm.

Gyp growled and Julia glanced up at Tully, noting the anxiety in his eyes, the tight features. Apprehension scraped across her nerves.

"Come on." He tugged her toward the saloon.

She strove for a casual tone. "I'm sending Pete home."

"There's no time for that." Tully tugged her toward the saloon doors, his gaze fixed on the men in front of the bank. "You'll have to come with me."

Pete's arms tightened around her neck, and the dog growled again.

Her son, with his limp, wouldn't be able to outrun the older man. She held Pete closer, trying to reassure him. *Please, Tully, don't be involved in this. Don't help those men.*

Tully's eyes narrowed, and purpose flared in the blue depths. Julia turned to follow his gaze and saw the men, now wearing kerchiefs over the lower half of their faces, disappear inside the bank.

She lunged for the street, and Gyp bounded past. After two steps, brutal fingers bit into her arm and yanked her back. The dog spun, taking a step toward her.

"Go, Gyp! Go!"

"Go, boy!" Pete urged, shooing the dog away. "Get Marsh!"

The dog hesitated. Tully stepped toward him, but Gyp darted across the street and disappeared behind the jail.

Tully dragged her and Pete inside the saloon. Fear and anger collided. "What are you doing?"

"Don't ask me any questions, Julia." He tugged and yanked, struggling to pull her across the smooth wooden floor.

"Tell me you're not involved with them." Horror cut her breath and she choked down a sob. "Please tell me you didn't have anything to do with John's death. Please."

She didn't expect an answer. Somehow she knew he *had* been involved in John's death. Tully, who'd been their friend since he'd arrived in Spinner five years before. Tully, who'd given her a job and worked around her schedule so she could accommodate Pete. Tully, who'd paid for John's burial and kept her on so she could save money for the future.

He hauled her up to the door of his office and fumbled for his key. "I didn't know they were gonna kill him," he gritted out.

"You killed my pa?" Pete twisted in Julia's arms, trying to reach the saloon owner.

Julia caught him to her and pinned his flailing arms. Tully shoved her and Pete into his office, reaching inside the door for the extra keys that hung on the wall.

"Why, Tully? Why?"

"You dirty stinkin' skunk!" Pete struggled in her arms, angry tears streaking his face. "Killer! Killer!"

Tully winced, but pushed them farther inside.

Julia crushed her son to her, struggling to breathe past the fear that ripped through her. "Why, Tully? Why are you helping Scotty Thompson?"

He started to pull the door shut, then hesitated, remorse flitting across his face. "After the war I had nowhere to go. I couldn't go back to the ironworks. The noise, the smoke— it was just like being shot at." He shuddered, and agony twisted his features for a brief second. "Scotty helped me out. He gave me a job. He saved my life."

"He's a killer and a thief!" she cried. "You're not like him."

"In a way, I am." His lips twisted in a wry smile. "He's my cousin."

"Your—" Her breath knotted in her chest and she thought she would be sick.

Tully backed out of the office, regret darkening his eyes. "You'll be safe here."

"This town trusted you. *I* trusted you." She couldn't stop the tears that coursed down her cheeks.

"I'm not the one robbing the bank, Julia." Shamefaced, he looked away.

"What difference does that make?" she bit out, feeling betrayed. "You helped them kill John!"

"I didn't know, Julia."

He tried to shut the door, but she grabbed it. "Did you give me this job only so you could watch me? Were they going to kill me too. And Pete?"

"No!" he yelled in a quick burst of temper. "The job was

legitimate. I knew you needed the money." He paused, saying earnestly, "I would never hurt you or Pete, Julia."

Horror stripped away her anger, and numbness seeped through her. "I can't believe this."

Pete swiped at the tears on his face. "Marsh is gonna be my new pa and he'll make you sorry."

Tully's eyes narrowed. "How is Tipton involved—of course," he breathed. "He's with Pinkerton, isn't he?"

Julia leveled a flat stare on him.

He paused for a moment, then yanked the door from her grip.

She lunged after him. "Don't leave us in here!"

The door slammed and the lock clicked. Total darkness swallowed them.

She pounded on the door, rage firing her blood. "Tully!"

Pete slid to the floor and pounded alongside her. "Let us out!"

"Tully!" Panic swelled like the rushing waters of a spring flood, and she pounded on the door until her hands burned. "Tully!"

"Ma, I saw a candle on that desk over there." Pete moved away from her and she heard the hesitant sound of searching footsteps as he felt his way across the office. A thud echoed in the room. "Ouch," he said.

"Be careful, honey." Searching for matches, Julia moved her hands over the smooth wood of the door, then the slightly rough doorjamb. She slid her hands across the wall, then over the paper scattered on the waist-high worktable. Frustration and impatience routed through her.

"Here it is!" he announced excitedly.

Her breath shuddered out in relief. "Matches?"

A light flared, illuminating Pete's elfin features. He turned, and candlelight spread an amber glow over the room.

Spying the other door, they rushed over and pushed it open. Sunlight arrowed into the room and hope flared, only to die in the next instant, when the door wouldn't budge farther. Through the crack Julia saw a padlock.

Refusing to admit defeat, she returned to the other door. "We'll keep pounding. Someone's bound to hear us."

Millie's and Filene's rooms were situated in the most remote part of the saloon, but Julia hoped their beating on the door would be heard by the two women. The wooden door vibrated now, and the raucous noise swelled, roaring through the office like an approaching steam engine.

Why, Tully? Why? Where had he gone? What was happening? Was Marsh even now lying dead at the bank?

"Help! Help us!" Dread pulled at her. *Millie. Filene. Bundy.* Julia prayed someone would hear their pounding and respond before Tully returned. *If* he returned.

Marsh waited in silent darkness, unable to hear anything but his own heartbeat. Even though he and Allan had no way of knowing what was happening on the other side of the vault, the Thompson gang would be at a greater disadvantage.

Kisling had been instructed to wait for Marsh and Allan to show themselves before he made his move. That way the sheriff would know how many men they faced. After the incident in Crowley, Thompson had been left with only two men, and he could have added any number by now. With surprise on their side, Marsh, Allan, and Kisling had vital seconds to even the score if they were outgunned.

Thoughts of Julia fringed Marsh's mind, and he couldn't shake the foreboding that needled him. Right now she was in the saloon with a man who'd aided in the deaths of two detectives, possibly more. Marsh planned to take care of Tully once he'd dealt with Thompson.

At least Gyp was with Julia. At the first sign of trouble, the dog would come straight for him. And thankfully Pete was safe at the farm with India.

Tension tapped against Marsh's nerves like the building throb of a headache. He knelt in the darkness, muscles knotted, his Colt drawn and ready. The Winchester lay beside him.

Allan touched his arm in warning, and he stiffened, easing back the hammer on his revolver. Waiting. In the quietness, the click of the lock boomed like a cannon. He picked up the rifle and eased to one side of the vault, felt Allan ease to the other.

The hinges creaked, then light stabbed into the tomblike darkness. For a split second Marsh and Allan were revealed without the advantage of sight.

Using instincts honed from years of practice, Marsh aimed his revolver at the sound of voices. "Hello, gentlemen."

Now he could see three clearly defined bodies and the surprise on their faces. He and Allan rose, advancing on the outlaws.

"Drop your weapons." Marsh leveled his revolver at Thompson, gripping the rifle with his other hand. "Nice and slow."

The men backed out of the vault and Marsh noted there were only three—Thompson, Lawson, and the man he'd seen at Crowley whose name he didn't know.

Kisling joined them from his position behind a sturdy pecan desk, indicating his badge with a tap of his finger. "Welcome to my town, boys. Been waitin' on you."

Lawson and the other man looked around nervously, but Thompson halted, peering closely at Marsh. "I know you."

"Yep." He gestured with his revolver. "The guns, gentlemen."

"You killed my boys in Crowley."

"The pleasure was all mine." He sighted his gun between Thompson's eyes. "I'm not tellin' you again to drop that gun."

The outlaw's eyes glittered like green glass, and he leveled his own weapon at Marsh. "Say your prayers, lawman."

They fired at the same instant.

Thompson lunged to the side and rolled to his knees, popping off two more shots. The other two members of his gang dropped to their knees and sprayed bullets in a continuous round.

Marsh flew across a desk and dove to the floor. Kisling stumbled and fell, blood spurting from a wound in his arm. Allan was nowhere to be seen.

The acrid smoke of gunfire burned the air. Marsh's breath wheezed in his ear like the rasp of wood on wood. Gaining his feet, he fired again and reached the end of the counter just as the outlaws flung open the front doors and returned fire.

He ducked, firing around the edge of the counter. A shot cracked from Marsh's left, and the unidentified outlaw fell. Thompson and Lawson backed onto the bank's stoop.

"Go!" Kisling yelled to Marsh. "I'll cover you!"

He charged from behind the counter, emptying his Colt. Bullets whistled past his ear, drilled the floor and the wall. He dodged a round from Thompson and dropped his revolver, cocking the repeating Winchester in one fluid motion.

Allan appeared beside him and returned fire while Kisling kept a shield of bullets between them. Marsh was distantly aware of a small crowd outside. Women screamed and men yelled encouragement amid the rushing din of panicked footsteps.

A shot sounded from the street, then another. Shock widened Thompson's eyes. He and Lawson whirled.

"Dammit to hell," Lawson yelled. "They're everywhere!"

Another shot shattered a bank window. A blur of black-brown fur flew threw the air and launched itself at Lawson. Gyp!

Taking advantage of the men's brief preoccupation Marsh shoved in more bullets. Knocked off balance by the dog, Lawson went down. Gyp pinned him by the throat, teeth bared, body quivering.

"Damn," Kisling breathed behind Marsh.

"Damn!" Marsh exploded. Though glad for Gyp's help, the dog's presence could mean only that Julia was in trouble.

Fear turned to icy rage. Purposely, steadily, he advanced on Thompson.

The outlaw scrambled over the hitching post and onto his horse, kneeing the animal into motion. Marsh followed at a run, firing at the fleeing man.

Kisling rushed out of the bank behind him. "I'll take this side of the street," he yelled. "You take the other."

Marsh zigzagged across to Henner's store, still shooting. He and Kisling trapped Thompson in a net of gunfire, but the man didn't slow. Marsh's shot hit the outlaw in the thigh, and Kisling fired a steady volley, giving him time to reload.

"No!" a woman screamed.

Julia! Marsh jerked toward the sound, searching for her. Waving her arms, she ran out of the saloon straight into Thompson's path. Marsh's breath jammed in his throat, and for an instant he froze. No! No, Julia!

Instinct kicked in. His gaze sliced to Thompson and he moved toward the center of the street, trying to intercept the outlaw's line of fire. From the corner of his eye he detected a blur of motion.

Kisling closed in on the outlaw. Marsh spared a quick glance toward the pair, and his knees nearly buckled. "Pete!" he yelled. "Stay back!"

The boy jogged down the planked walk that connected the saloon and telegraph office. He alternately limped and hopped toward Marsh, pointing toward Thompson and the saloon. His mouth moved, but Marsh couldn't make out the words.

"Get back, Pete! No!"

Marsh's gaze swung to Thompson. Blood soaked the man's pants and streaked his horse's side. In a slowly unfolding horror, he saw the outlaw's lips twist in a cruel smile as he aimed at Pete.

"No!" Julia's scream keened like a wounded animal.

Marsh launched himself through the air, twisted his body, and pulled Pete under him as they both crashed to the planked porch of the restaurant.

Thompson's bullet burned past Marsh's right shoulder and buried itself with a *crack* in a porch column. Shots echoed in rapid staccato.

"You okay?" He rolled off Pete, searching for blood.

The boy nodded, his eyes wide and frightened in a chalky face.

"Stay down," Marsh ordered, pushing to his feet.

"Scotty, no!" Tully's horrified voice sliced into Marsh like whetted steel.

He turned and sprinted toward the outlaw. Julia stood transfixed in the street, staring at Pete. Thompson had her in his sights!

Brutal fear spurred him to move faster. By the eerie stillness of her body, he knew she was replaying the incident last year when she had found Pete and John. He ached for her, and rage pumped through him.

Reaching the general store, he slammed his shoulder into a post on the porch, steadying himself as he raised the Winchester.

Damn! Julia was in the way. He couldn't get a clear shot. Though several yards away, he could see her glassy eyes, the chalky pallor of her skin. "Julia, move!" *Listen to me, sugar.* "Julia!"

He couldn't shoot or he'd hit her. With sickening certainty, he knew he couldn't reach her before Thompson fired. He ran toward her anyway, desperate fear lancing his gut.

"Thompson!" Kisling boomed. He fired past Marsh in an effort to gain the outlaw's attention.

As though in a dream, Marsh saw Thompson squeeze the trigger, saw the spark and smoke when the gun fired.

"No!" he roared, moving toward the outlaw. Bloodlust charged through him. He would kill Thompson with his bare hands. "No!"

CHAPTER NINETEEN

Suddenly Julia was out of the way. Marsh squeezed off a shot and hit Thompson in the neck.

The man screamed in outraged pain and swung his gun toward Marsh. His shot ricocheted off the roof of the telegraph office.

Marsh fired again, and beside him, Kisling shot twice. Thompson jerked as the bullets slammed into him, then he tumbled from the saddle, a tattered, bloodied mass.

A startling quietness descended. Marsh ran toward Julia. Was she okay? What had happened? Someone had knocked her out of harm's way, but the image was a blur.

In front of the telegraph office she dazedly pushed herself to a sitting position. Her savior sprawled in a lifeless heap inches from her feet and she cried out, scooting over to him.

Marsh dropped to his knees beside her, searching her for signs of blood or injury. Fear chilled him and he gathered her close. "Sugar, are you all right?"

She nodded, hugging him tight then pulled away, tears filling her eyes. Gripping Marsh's hand, she leaned over the man in the street.

Marsh looked at the man who had saved Julia's life and his heart kicked painfully against his ribs. "Tully?"

The saloon owner lay on the ground, blood seeping out of him. His face, sheened with sweat, was pale and waxy.

"Tully?" she asked weakly. "Tully, can you hear me?"

The man's eyes fluttered, then opened with an effort. "Julia," he croaked.

She choked back a sob and took his hand in both of hers. "You saved my life."

Pain creased his features. His attempted smile more resembled a grimace. "Couldn't . . . let him"—his breath wheezed out—". . . hurt you."

"Shhh. Don't talk. We'll get the doctor. Marsh?"

She looked beseechingly at him, but he didn't have the heart to tell her a doctor would be futile. He simply held her tighter.

"You were right. He was involved with them. And—" She broke off, her voice rusty. "He knew about John."

"Never . . . wanted . . . that." Tully's voice faded.

Julia clutched his hand. "Tully? Tully?"

People moved around them, murmuring in disbelief that one of their own had been involved with the notorious outlaws.

Tully stared sightlessly up at Julia, and she bowed her head over his hand. Marsh's heart bled for her, and visions of Beth crashed back. Beth had forfeited her life to escape him, and today, because of him, Julia had almost bought a bullet. All along he'd sworn to protect her, and today he hadn't been able to do a damn thing.

Pete and India appeared, their faces drawn and sober.

"Ma?" Pete bent and wrapped his arms around her neck. "Ma, I love you."

She hugged him, her features fierce with love. "Are you okay?"

He nodded gravely.

Marsh wrapped his arms around both of them and held on tight. Through his blurred vision he saw India's outstretched hand, and grasped it. When he'd seen Thompson turn the gun on first Pete, then Julia, his heart had stopped. He could never go through that again.

Kisling and Bob Henner walked past carrying Thompson's body on a door borrowed from Henner's store.

"Whenever you're ready, Marsh," Kisling said. "We'll need you for a minute."

He nodded.

The sheriff paused beside Pete. "You all right, son?"

"Thanks to Marsh." The boy turned adoring eyes on him, and he shifted uncomfortably.

Kisling's gaze shifted to Tully's lifeless body. "I hate that he was involved in this."

Marsh rose and helped Julia to her feet, tucking her trembling body close to his. He wanted to feel her next to him, reassure himself that she was truly all right.

Kisling and Henner continued on to the jail. Taking Pete's hand, India guided him several feet away, affording Marsh and Julia some privacy.

Julia looked up at him, her eyes soft with love and wonder. With shaking hands she touched his face. Her touch soothed, yet, at the same time, it drove his guilt deeper.

She would blame him for putting Pete in danger, for nearly getting them both killed. But even that fear couldn't stop him from opening his arms to her.

Amazingly, she threw herself against him, a sob wrenching out of her. Relief and love and humility washed through him, and his chest tightened.

She pulled away with a hiccup and wiped her eyes. "You saved Pete." She framed his face, her hands grainy with dirt from her fall. "You saved him."

She pressed her lips to his and he pulled her close, savoring her warmth, her life-affirming breath against his.

She drew back, gazing into his eyes. "I love you, Marsh."

"I love you too." He rested his forehead against hers, realizing how close they'd come to never sharing this. "If you'd been—" He broke off, unable to complete the thought. "If something had happened to you, I would've turned the gun on myself."

"I'm fine, thanks to you."

India and Pete limped over, and India hugged her daughter for several moments.

"I'm okay, Mother." Julia managed a wan smile and leaned into Marsh. "So is Pete."

"I'm so sorry, Julia. By the time I realized what Pete had done, he'd already torn off down the road. With this blasted ankle, it took me forever to get the buggy hitched."

"It's not your fault." Julia stroked Pete's hair and gave him a mildly disapproving stare. "He knew he was supposed to stay at home."

Marsh knew that later Julia would be angry at Pete's disobedience, but right now she was glad her son was unharmed.

India grabbed Pete in a tight hug, closing her eyes in relief. "You scared the daylights out of me, young man. Don't you ever do that again."

"I just wanted to tell Marsh good-bye." He looked from his grandmother to his mother.

"You disobeyed, but we'll discuss it later." Julia's arm tightened around Marsh's waist as she smiled at her son. "I'm very glad you're all right."

"Can you believe I missed everything?" India planted her hands on her hips. "After all the time I put in on this case!"

Marsh shook his head, unable to believe India's resilience.

Allan Pinkerton walked up, herding a subdued Lawson in front of him. Gyp growled at the outlaw, fur bristling on his neck.

Lawson edged away. "Git that damn dog away from me."

Pinkerton grinned and said to Marsh, "I believe this is the first time you can claim a live one, Granger."

Julia and India both looked at Marsh curiously, and he waved them off. "Don't ask."

"Damn fine job." Allan clapped him on the back. "And that dog of yours—every time I see him, I'm more impressed. You wouldn't consider—"

"No!" Marsh and Pete said in unison.

Gyp seemed to know they were discussing him, and barked.

Everyone laughed, then Allan pulled Marsh aside. "I can see you're blaming yourself for this."

"If I hadn't—"

"Listen to me," his boss ordered. "If I thought you were at fault *in any way,* I'd be hauling you in on the other end of these wrist irons. You saved lives here today, Marsh, and that's how I'm writing it up."

He prodded his prisoner in the ribs, and they walked toward the jail.

"Amen," India said.

Maybe he hadn't directly placed them in danger, but he hadn't prevented it either.

Pete's hand grasped his. "You're not gonna leave, are you? 'Cause my ma needs you, and so does Gran."

"He's right." Julia wiped her eyes again, smiling at him. "I do need you. We all do."

He couldn't bear to see the hope, the trust in her eyes. He looked over the boy's head, unable to face either of these people he'd come to love. "My job puts people in danger, Pete."

"Is that why you can't stay?" The boy struggled to combat the tears that glistened in his eyes. "Is that the secret you were talkin' about last night?"

"Yes." His heart tilted. What he would have given for a son like Pete, a wife like Julia. But he'd had that chance and destroyed it. "I want you to know my real name, Pete. It's Marsh Granger."

"Granger," the boy repeated softly as though he'd been given a gift.

"And I'm not really a farmhand. I came to get the men who killed your pa."

"You mean you're a bounty hunter?"

"No, I'm a detective. Like your pa."

"Gosh!" Awe sketched Pete's voice, and his eyes widened. "Ma, did you hear that?"

"Yes."

Marsh could read nothing in her voice. "That's why I can't stay."

"But you can live here and catch bad men!"

"My job puts people in danger, like what happened to you and your ma a few minutes ago." Marsh knelt, meeting Pete's eyes. "I didn't like that you were in danger, son. And I wouldn't want that to happen again."

"But you saved me and Ma!" Confusion clouded his eyes. "I know you wouldn't let anything happen to us."

"I would *try* to protect you, but—" His voice cracked. "I wasn't able to help your ma today, was I?"

"Yes, you were!" Julia protested vehemently, squeezing his hand.

Trust shone in her eyes, but instead of reassuring him, her faith only made him feel naked and vulnerable, made him doubt his ability to walk away.

"I want you to stay and be my pa."

"I'm honored, son, but I don't want you to ever be threatened again because of me." He squeezed the boy's shoulder, and Pete hurled himself against Marsh.

Behind him, Julia and India sniffed. Marsh held Pete tight, memorizing the sweet scent of child sweat, the feel of silky hair beneath his cheek, the trusting arms around his waist.

Pete looked up at him. "I wish you'd change your mind."

He wished he could.

Gyp, who had been waiting patiently, now whined and butted his head against Pete's leg.

The boy reached down to scratch the dog's ears. "Ma, say something!" he urged.

Julia studied Marsh for a moment, then patted Pete's shoulder. "Go with Gran to Robin's office. We'll be there in a minute."

The two of them started toward the jail, and Pete glanced

back hopefully. Gyp padded close to the boy, who kept one hand on the dog's head.

Marsh watched them go, and his throat knotted up. When he turned, Julia faced him with blazing emerald eyes. At her anger, pain bit into him. "You'll never be able to forget or forgive this, Julia. I'm right to leave."

"Hmmph! You don't know anything! What I won't forgive is if you walk away from us." She took a few steps, then whirled, throwing out her arms in exasperation. "You'll be leaving us, just like John."

"And you would rather I stay, put you through exactly what he did?" He hardened his voice deliberately. "I won't, Julia. I've already ruined one woman's life."

"Oh, yes, I know." She moved closer, her skin flushed, arms akimbo. "No, you didn't make a commitment to your marriage. Yes, you let your job come first, but I believe people change, Marsh Granger. I believe things like what happened today—" She faltered, turning pale. "That kind of danger makes people realize what they have and admit they don't want to lose them."

"I do realize those things—"

"You couldn't control Beth's decision to leave." Her eyes burned into his. "Nor could you control the risk she took. You can't control everything."

"Regarding you, Julia, I have *no* control." He bared his soul with a rueful laugh. "That scares the hell out of me."

"Love isn't about control, Marsh." Her hand closed on his arm. "It's about give and take, sacrifice, partnership, and compromise. I'd like to do all that with you."

"It was my duty to take care of you." His body ached as if he'd been whipped, and his heart throbbed a hollow cadence. "I promised to protect you, and I didn't. I don't take that lightly."

"Neither do I." Steely determination threaded her soft voice. "But that wasn't your fault."

"You could've been killed." He grabbed her upper arms,

giving her a shake. "If that doesn't convince you that you're better off without me, think about what almost happened to Pete."

"You saved him," she cried. "As well as me. And Sheriff Kisling and Allan and—well, I'd venture to say you had a hand in saving most everybody here." Her voice grew urgent with a plea. "We're alive because of you, Marsh. Why would I want you to leave? If I blamed you for what happened today, would I be standing here? Would I want you to kiss me until I swooned?"

"You don't swoon," he growled, feeling his resolve give under the pressure of her arguments.

"Maybe you haven't tried hard enough."

Temptation tugged at him. How could she survive another marriage like the one she'd had? She hadn't asked him to quit the agency, and if she did, he wasn't sure how he'd answer. Could he walk away from something that defined him, that had saved him?

Anger flushed her features. "I can see your mind working. You're making decisions that affect me. I hate that."

"Julia, I love you, but I can't put you through that kind of life again. I know now how selfishly I acted. I know what Beth endured because of my job. You taught me that, because you'd been dealt the same hand."

"I learned something from you too. You showed me that I was stifling Pete, but more importantly you taught me that I can't miss out on the future by being afraid of the past. Isn't that what you're doing?"

"It's not the same thing," he dismissed with a snort.

Her nails dug into his arms. *"It is."*

"I don't have to spell it out for you, Julia. Long hours, prolonged absences, the uncertainty, the risk. You can't convince me you're willing to go through that."

"No," she said firmly. "I'll never go through that again."

"You shouldn't have to." Pain hooked into him. Finally she had relented. "I'm glad we agree."

"We don't, but I know a way around all of your objections. A way we can be together. That is"—she looked down, and a delicate rose blush tinted her neck—"if you want to be with us. As a family."

More than anything. But he didn't see a compromise that could work. He watched her, waiting, and tension lashed his shoulders.

Julia searched his eyes. "We'll go wherever you go."

"What?" The word exploded from him. "That's impossible!"

"Is it? We won't travel together, we won't use the same name. In public we'll pretend not to know each other. But we'll take lodging close by. And at night, or for a while during the day, you can be with us."

"Where did you get such an idea?"

"I've had a lot of time to think about it," she said quietly.

Hope nudged at him, but he was afraid to examine the idea too closely for fear he'd find a hole.

She gripped the front of his shirt. "It would work. You know it would. We'd be together, and that's all that matters."

Overwhelmed, he tried not to give in to the hope that raced through him. "What about your mother? Your friends? Pete's school?"

"Mother can visit or come with us if she wants. Pete will make new friends. We want to be with you, Marsh."

"You wanted to raise Pete in a stable environment. And what about the security of knowing where I am, what I'm doing?"

"If we do this, I'll have that to a great degree. You and I love each other," she said softly. "What more security does Pete need?"

He wanted to forget all his reservations, but it wasn't fair to Julia or Pete. "You'd have to move from town to town, maybe between states, every time I got a new case. You're willing to do that?"

"As long as we're together, I don't care where we are or how long we stay there." She curled her arms around his neck. "Say yes, Marsh," she whispered against his lips. "Say yes."

He wanted to so badly, his gut twisted. "I can't ask you to do that, Julia. It's not fair."

"You're not asking. I'm offering." Her green eyes, expectant and hopeful, held his.

Myriad feelings rushed through him—need and want and sheer exhilaration that she wanted him despite his job. He hardened in a rush and said hoarsely, "You'd really do that? For me?"

"For us." Her eyes glowed with tenderness, urging him to claim the promise of a love he'd never dreamt of finding. "Say yes." She pressed a butterfly kiss on his lips, stirring the heat low in his belly. "Say it."

He searched her features for doubt, but saw only love and desire. "It's too generous, Julia. I don't deserve—"

Her fingers pressed against his lips, and she looked up at him, her face open with surrender and yearning. "*We* deserve *this*, Marsh. I know I can convince you if you'll let me. If you *have* to think in terms of owing me something because of today, owe me this chance with you. Even if it's only for Pete's sake, I want you for the rest of our lives."

"Not for Pete's sake," he breathed against her lips. "For ours. Mine."

"Oh, Marsh!" She wrapped her arms tighter around his neck, her eyes shining with a love that made his heart ache. "You mean it?"

"Absolutely." He captured her lips with his, his hands stroking over her back.

"Ma, does this mean we're gonna get married?"

Marsh chuckled and they drew apart. Julia turned, reaching for his hand. Pete and Gyp stood in front of a group that included India, Sheriff Kisling, Bob and Jeanette Henner, and Allan Pinkerton.

"I think it does." Julia smiled blindingly, as if she were proud to be with him.

He knew at that instant he'd been blessed with the equivalent of another life, and he would cherish this one carefully. Smiling at Pete, he said, "Yep, we're gonna get married if we have your blessing."

"Yes! Yes!" Pete shouted, hopping around Gyp. "Yippee!"

Gyp leapt in the air, barking wildly. The people behind them laughed. Pete knelt, wrapping the shepherd in a hug. "You get to stay, Gyp. And Marsh is gonna be my new pa!"

The dog's long pink tongue swiped at the boy's face, and Pete giggled.

Marsh and Julia laughed. His arm tightened around her waist, and he leaned down to whisper, "You won't be sorry, sugar. I swear it."

"Neither will you. *I* swear it." She turned to him with a tremulous smile, and tears sheened her eyes.

Emotion clotted his throat. "This is really going to work, isn't it?"

"Yes."

His hands flexed on her waist and he kissed her tenderly. "I love you, Julia."

Her hands slid up his arms, clasped his shoulders. Sultry promise smoldered in her eyes. "Show me."

"Here?" Heat stirred through him and he drawled, "How would you suggest I do that, Miz Touchstone?"

Her eyes sparkled. "Try kissing me until I swoon."

He did.

EPILOGUE

Spring bloomed in the cool breeze that shifted across the rolling hills. Budding daffodils and daisies and wild roses, stingy with their faint perfume, peeked up through the carpet of emerald grass. Marsh topped the rise that led to the farmhouse outside of Farrell, where Julia and Pete were staying.

In the two days since he'd last seen his family, his life had changed drastically. As would theirs in a few moments.

With *this* change there was no uncertainty as there had been in each of their three moves in the past six months. No anxious internal questioning of his decision.

Marsh had begun to think that his wife and son were more suited to this vagabond lifestyle than he. He had been surprised at how well they adapted to their oft-changed surroundings and how frequently he resented each new adjustment.

Despite his misgivings, Julia's plan had worked beautifully. Pete and Gyp were inseparable, and the pair made friends easily. Pete had grown in stature—he was at least two inches taller than when they'd left Spinner—but also in strength. Because he was now allowed to swim often, his legs had developed wiry muscles and his limp was barely noticeable unless he was fatigued.

Julia had changed too. She no longer hovered over Pete, and the worry had disappeared completely from her eyes, leaving them the clear green of new spring leaves.

Every time Marsh returned home, she was more beautiful. Impatient to see her, he gave Sarge a swift kick and they galloped down to the house his wife and son had occupied for the past month.

At the front door he dismounted and dropped the reins, pushing open the door silently. She stood at the stove and he watched her for a moment, mesmerized, just as he had been that first time he had seen her.

Flaxen hair, darkened to a ripe honey color by the room's shadows, was piled atop her head. Loose strands trailed down her slender nape and teased the smooth line of her jaw.

His gaze skated over her figure. Though still delicate, her breasts seemed fuller, her hips more gently rounded. Hunger rasped through him, and he imagined the private welcome they would later share.

Filled with love and desire and gratitude, Marsh smiled. Even six months later, he couldn't believe his good fortune.

Julia pushed a wayward strand of hair from her face, and her bodice pulled tight across her breasts, outlining her slender frame.

His throat tightened. How could he miss her so much in two days? "Sugar?"

She whirled and dropped the spoon she'd been holding, flying across the room. "Marsh!"

He caught her to him, his lips covering hers fiercely. Her hands curled around his neck, and she opened her mouth, welcoming his tongue. She burned in his blood like alcohol. Her soft scent teased him and his hands moved down to cup her bottom.

"How long can you stay this time?" she breathed between kisses, shifting to accommodate him when he nudged his thigh between hers. He pressed against her heat and felt her quiver.

He tore his mouth from hers, wanting to see her face

when he told her. Thumbing a stray hair from her cheek, he stroked her soft skin.

She pressed a kiss to his palm. "You're probably hungry. I have some—"

"I quit."

"What?" She frowned, then froze as realization bloomed in her eyes. "You . . . quit? Allan? The agency?" Her voice was breathless with hope, her eyes guarded in case she'd misunderstood.

Joy surged from the deepest part of his soul. "Yes, ma'am."

Her jaw dropped, and for a moment she simply stared. "Why? What are you going to do?"

"Are you nagging me about a job already?" he teased, loving the play of joy and wonder and confusion on her face. He tightened his arms around her. "I've already got it worked out."

"Well, tell me!"

"We're going home, Julia. To the farm."

"To Mother's?" She gaped.

"Yep." He grinned. "What do you think?"

"I don't know." The joy faded from her eyes, replaced by uncertainty. "I don't think I like it."

"How can you not like it?" he demanded.

"I don't want you to do this for me and Pete. I never asked you to quit. I thought we were happy."

"Sugar, wait." He framed her face with gentle hands. "I'm doing this for us, that's true, but it's time. I want to come home to *our* house, work *our* land, sleep in *our* bed. I want to fish with Pete in the creek where you and I first made love."

She swatted at him. "Don't you ever let on about that to him!"

He grinned. "I've done my share, and now I want to give you and Pete the kind of commitment I should have all along."

"Marsh," she breathed, her eyes filling with tears.

He kissed her forehead. "Those are good tears, right?"

She nodded, stretching up to place a soft, lingering kiss on his lips. Fire coiled in his belly, and he pressed against her, kneading her bottom.

Footsteps clattered onto the wooden porch, penetrating Marsh's lustful thoughts. "Pa, you're home!"

Marsh moved his hands to Julia's waist, and she nipped at his lips in a promise for later.

Pete bolted straight for Marsh's arms, and he grabbed his son in a tight hug. Gyp shot through the door, bounding and bouncing with the energy of a puppy.

"Hey, boy." He chuckled, rubbing the dog's favorite spot, behind his ears. Gyp barked and turned in exuberant circles.

"How're things going, son?"

"Swell!" Pete's eyes shone. "Gyp and me—Gyp and I—found a creek. It's not far from here, and I've already caught a fish there, so I know there are some."

Marsh exchanged a questioning look with Julia, and she nodded in encouragement. "How would you like to go fishing in *your* creek?"

"At Gran's?"

"That's the one."

"How long do we get to stay? I can take that new pole we made."

"I was thinking we'd stay awhile." He gauged Pete's reaction. "For good."

The boy looked from Marsh to Julia, then back again. "Forever?"

"Yep."

"Really?"

"Really." He squeezed Pete's shoulder.

"Are you gonna work there? With Mr. Pinkerton?"

"No, son." He knelt so that they were eye to eye. "I'm not going to be a detective anymore. Your ma and I are gonna raise those cattle she's been talking about."

"You are?" Surprise widened Pete's eyes.

"What do you think?"

"This is good," the boy said slowly. "You'll be around all the time?"

"Yep."

"Can we go fishing every day?"

Marsh smiled. "Probably."

"Can we go see Grandma and Grandpa Granger again in St. Louis? All of us?"

"Yep."

Pleasure warmed the boy's eyes, but he studied Marsh solemnly. "I'm glad you're quitting. I've been—I mean, Ma has been scared that something might happen. You know, like what happened to my other pa."

"Your ma doesn't have to worry anymore." Marsh's heart squeezed, and he held the boy's gaze intently. "Okay?"

"Okay." Pete hugged Marsh, then smiled broadly. "Yippee! Come on, Gyp. We'll be ready in five minutes."

He raced into his room and Julia called after him, "Take your time, honey." Her gaze stroked hungrily over Marsh. "We're not leaving until tomorrow."

"Ma! Ma!" Pete poked his head out his door. "Gran is gonna be so excited. Now the baby can be born at her house, just like you and me."

"That's right." Julia winked at him, and he smiled happily before disappearing back into his room.

Marsh smiled, enjoying the energy and noise he'd missed during his absence. He unbuckled his gun belt and laid it on the kitchen table. *Baby? What baby?*

Feeling as though he'd been rammed by a rifle butt, he swerved to Julia. "Are we havin' a baby?"

Her lips curved in a smug smile, and she backed toward their bedroom, crooking her finger in invitation. "You figure it out, Mr. Detective."

She disappeared behind their door, and he stood rooted to the floor. Wonder and awe and disbelief shuttled through him. Julia was having his baby? *He and Julia were having a baby?* Tears prickled his eyes.

"Sugar, I'm waiting!" she sang.

Marsh shook himself and hurried to his wife. Julia's love had given him a new life. Together they had erased the guilt and the desperation, but she had replaced the darkness with light and love and promise.

She'd made him a friend, a lover, and now a father. She had made him whole.

Our Town

...where love is always right around the corner!

All Books Available in July 1996

__Take Heart__ *by Lisa Higdon*

                    0-515-11898-2/$5.50

In Wilder, Wyoming...a penniless socialite learns a lesson in frontier life — and love.

__Harbor Lights__ *by Linda Kreisel*

                    0-515-11899-0/$5.50

On Maryland's Silchester Island...the perfect summer holiday sparks a perfect summer fling.

__Humble Pie__ *by Deborah Lawrence*

                    0-515-11900-8/$5.50

In Moose Gulch, Montana...a waitress with a secret meets a stranger with a heart.